the unforgiving city

and Other Stories

Vasudhendra

Translated from the Kannada by
Mysore Nataraja

PENGUIN
VIKING
An imprint of Penguin Random House

VIKING

USA | Canada | UK | Ireland | Australia
New Zealand | India | South Africa | China

Viking is part of the Penguin Random House group of companies
whose addresses can be found at global.penguinrandomhouse.com

Published by Penguin Random House India Pvt. Ltd
4th Floor, Capital Tower 1, MG Road,
Gurugram 122 002, Haryana, India

| Penguin
Random House
India

All stories first published in Kannada by Chanda Pustaka,
Bengaluru, in different volumes, as detailed on page 257
First published in English in Viking by Penguin Random House India 2021

ISBN 9780670094240

Typeset in Bembo Std by Manipal Technologies Limited, Manipal
Printed at Replika Press Pvt. Ltd, India

www.penguin.co.in

MIX
Paper from
responsible sources
FSC® C016779

Contents

Recession

The suddenness of the question made Devika's eyes well up. As she silently looked down and nodded, a tear fell on the glass table. She quickly pulled herself together and said, 'I am sorry,' took out her handkerchief and wiped that drop of tear on the glass even before she dabbed her eyes. Then she looked straight at the two interviewers with a confident smile. Her damp eyes reflected the piercing rays of the tube light.

Kasturi, who had asked the question, looked uncomfortable. 'Excuse me, I did not want to hurt your feelings,' she said by way of apology. Vishal did not consider the question cruel or anything, although he felt it was perhaps a bit too personal.

After having interviewed scores of candidates since the morning, Vishal and Kasturi were exhausted. It was the time of recession and there were more than fifty applicants for one position. With layoffs everywhere, thousands of software engineers were sitting at home and applying for any job that came their way, even if the salary was less than what they were getting earlier, even if the jobs were not challenging enough. With a large pool of qualified candidates available, the selection processes were becoming tough. Devika had completed three rounds of interviews for this position. Now she was in her final round, facing Vishal and Kasturi.

The company needed a quality control leader for an upcoming American project. Vishal was the designated project manager. As this was the final round, Kasturi, the HR head, was part of the interview. Vishal began with a few technical questions. Once he was satisfied, he signalled to Kasturi with a wink. Taking her cue as always, Kasturi, with her usual enthusiasm to understand the personal life of the candidate, had asked the question.

That is when the incident of the unprofessional teardrop occurred.

～

Devika had spent all her life in Bihar. But, frustrated at the lack of opportunities in her state, she had moved to Bengaluru eight years ago. Initially her parents were opposed to the idea, but reality was on her side. Her younger brother had just joined college while she was sitting at home after graduating from college. Her father worked in a post office and her mother had little education, though she was doing an excellent job of taking care of the household. In spite of their keenness to get their daughter married, they did not pursue it as they were in no position to pay a decent dowry.

Bengaluru was the answer. Two of her friends worked there, and their encouraging letters and supportive phone calls gave her the confidence. She arrived in Bengaluru on a third-class train ticket, with Rs 500 in her purse and ten sets of clothes in a suitcase. The train pulled up at dawn at Bengaluru City Railway Station. Outside, the weather was nippy, but she soon found herself in the warm embrace of her friends. As the bus ambled towards their PG accommodation, she was amazed to see hundreds of vehicles, multi-storeyed buildings and wide roads. She immediately fell in love with the city. She closed her eyes and prayed, 'Oh, Bangalore, please take me into your refuge and protect me.'

But even in Bengaluru, for Devika who had only a graduate degree, finding a job proved to be difficult. After months of searching, sending out applications, facing interviews and getting rejected, she found a job in a call centre for Rs 4000 a month. On the positive side, the lunch at office was free and she had only two night shifts every month. The job required her to talk to mobile phone customers in English and Hindi. She found an accommodation close to her place of work.

Devika was very happy when she received her first salary. She called her parents and proudly announced that from then on she would be sending them money each month and there was nothing to worry about. But as the days passed, ennui and dissatisfaction slowly began to creep in. She started to get annoyed at the repetitive questions of the customers. She felt like crying when the supervisors yelled at her if she even took a short break to drink water. Now that she started getting more night shifts too, her routine went topsy-turvy; she began to lose weight and started feeling very weak. Yet she wasn't ready to return to Bihar. The only option was to find a better job, and for that she needed to learn more skills. So she started taking courses in software testing and obtained a certificate. Eventually she landed a job as a testing executive in a small software company. The job did not pay much, but it saved her the drudgery of having to talk incessantly for eight hours over the phone. In addition, she had the opportunity to learn new things.

After three years of arriving in Bengaluru, Devika's fortunes changed. She got two promotions in quick succession. She moved out of the PG into a single-bedroom house in BTM Layout. And she met Vinayak.

One day Devika was visiting a shopping mall with her friends. Those were the early days of malls in India, and on the weekends huge crowds would congregate there, giving the malls the ambience of a fair. To top it, on that day a newly established

FM Radio station had organized an impromptu dance event. Devika was crazy about dancing. The tunes of Bollywood movies always got her very excited. That day, forgetting her shopping and the movies, she wanted to dance with total abandon.

As soon as Devika saw the open dance competition, she was in. The dance was called Paper Dance, where couples were asked to dance within the boundaries of a newspaper spread out on the floor. Stepping out of the boundary led to disqualification. One pair was disqualified, the newspaper was folded in half and a new song was played. As Devika was single, someone from the crowd, which formed a semi-circle around the dance floor to enjoy the fun, stepped forward. Rather, he was pushed into it by his friends, who wanted to have some fun at his expense.

It was Vinayak Kulakarni, a Maharashtrian. He was a very reserved young person, working in a big IT company as a team leader. As they started dancing, Devika sensed her partner's hesitation. He would forget his steps the moment he touched her. His ears turned red and he refused to look into her eyes, keeping them fixed on the ceiling. His boisterous friends shouted to him from behind: 'Hey, Kulki, come on, get closer.' But, the more she boldly held his waist and drew him nearer, the more he would shrink; he held on to her gingerly, as if he were unsure of whether or not he should touch her.

This annoyed Devika. She did not want to lose the competition simply because her partner was shy. So she egged him on nonstop, eventually helping him break out of his shyness. By the time the newspaper size shrank to the size of a paper towel, they were still in the game and, finally, Devika won. That was when she whispered her mobile number in his ear.

Exactly at ten that night, she received a call from him. She was very happy. If he could remember ten digits, he must be smart.

After a few phone calls and meetings, Devika was convinced that she liked Vinayak. He never asked how much money she made and did not pry about her friends or family. He would just smile when she got angry. It did not seem important to him to fight or argue to prove his point. The fact that he readily agreed with anything she said did bother her occasionally, but his patience and calm nature outweighed her worries. She felt she was moving around with an innocent child.

In the next six months, there were no tourist destinations they did not visit. They went on his bike around Bengaluru every weekend, from morning till late evening. They browsed the internet and discovered new places and found the routes to get to them. She liked to visit new spots and he liked speeding his bike on the highway. They visited places like Shivanasamudra, Lepakshi, Somanathapur, Belur, Halebeedu and Shravanabelagola.

At Mysuru once, they had to stay overnight. They booked two rooms. At some point at night, unable to sleep, Vinayak knocked on her door. 'Let me sleep here, please,' he pleaded. She couldn't refuse the intense longing reflected in his eyes. She allowed him in. But the next morning, feeling guilty, Vinayak said, while dropping her at her place, 'I am sorry for last night.' Devika laughed. Then she took his chin in her hands and said mischievously, 'In that case, let's get married, soon.' He stared into her eyes and nodded.

Ignoring both Maharashtra and Bihar, they opted for a simple wedding in Bengaluru. A Kannadiga priest married them off in a temple. He chanted mantras for full ten minutes, made them tie the knot in front of the fire and vanished. Devika's parents and brother were present. 'You didn't even let me perform your wedding and fulfil my responsibility as a parent. I did absolutely nothing for you,' her father sobbed. Devika gave him a hug, then scolded him affectionately, 'You keep quiet now.' But her brother, with his dreamy eyes, implored her to find him a job in Bengaluru so that he too could settle there. Before leaving, her mother took Devika aside and said: 'Devi, don't discontinue sending money home as your father's income is not enough and your brother still does not have a job.'

Vinayak's mother had died when he was a baby and his father had married a second time. He had spent most of his boyhood in a residential school in Bengaluru and seldom visited home, even during the holidays. The obvious reason was that he did not get along well with his stepmother. However, they came for the wedding and behaved well. His father even got Vinayak a new suit. 'To the extent I could, I sent you to good schools and gave you a good education. Now you have a good job and a family. I hope you would not expect, now onwards, anything else from me. I cannot stand up to your mother. Be happy,' his father said to him before leaving, his eyes moist.

Bengaluru appeared more beautiful after they got married. Vinayak rented a two-bedroom apartment and also bought a Honda City on a low-interest loan. Though a little far from his workplace, their apartment was close to Devika's. So he would drop her off at work first. On her way back, though, she would take the office drop and return early. Vinayak was generally late returning from work and would be exhausted by late evening. Food would be ready by the time he returned home.

Devika was a strict vegetarian while Vinayak was used to eating non-vegetarian food, even though by tradition he too came from a vegetarian home. On Sundays he made it a habit of visiting restaurants to eat meat. Whenever she accompanied him, she would say 'thoo' with disgust, and then laugh seeing him savour his meat dishes. Smacking his lips, he would say 'aha', and laugh. She tried a couple of pieces after yielding to his attempts at enticing her to, but somehow did not like it. 'How can you relish meat so much?' she once asked him. 'Taste does not reside in your tongue but here,' he answered, touching her head with his left hand. 'Shall I make it for you at home?' she asked him. He refused the offer, but loved her all the more for it.

Devika was obsessed with maintaining her figure. She had seen how her friends would yield to temptations of the tongue and grow out of shape. So, Vinayak's comment about taste buds being in the mind hit home. This was one of the reasons she did not want to try meat, so that she would not accumulate fat. She ate only healthy food, especially food recommended by the health books she read voraciously. Her obsession with morning exercise was a part of this. She woke up at five, ran a couple of kilometres, did some brisk-walking and then worked out until she was all sweaty. She never missed her morning workouts. But Vinayak did not want to miss his sweet sleep by waking up at seven in the morning. Devika tried to get him into the habit of exercising, but to no avail. Instead, he would be ready with a cup of tea once she was back. This pleased her.

Seeing his wife sitting in the balcony, with drops of perspiration trickling down her forehead on to the newspaper, he would be amazed. Once he asked her, 'Why are you so obsessed with working out? Can't you skip it for a few days and enjoy your sleep?' She explained: 'When I came thousands of miles away from home, I was lonely and worried that if I ever fell sick there would be no one to look after me. That's how I got obsessed with good health.' 'I am here now, am I not?' he asked, eliciting no response from her.

Within two years of their marriage, Vinayak bought a nice three-bedroom apartment, which was quite convenient except for its price—Rs 76 lakh. The tenth-floor apartment had plenty of air and light. The complex had all the modern facilities, such as a common generator, a water treatment plant, a solar heater and twenty-four-hour security, besides a gym and a swimming pool that Devika cherished. The newly built complex on Sarjapur Road was close to ITPL, Vinayak's place of work, as well as to Electronic City, where Devika worked.

The cost worried Devika. Collectively, they needed to pay Rs 60,000 in equal monthly instalments to pay off the loan.

'We could have waited for some more time,' she would tell Vinayak often. Every time he would answer, 'Both of us have good jobs. Let us clear the loan in about ten years. The cost is only going up. Don't we need a roof over our heads sooner or later?'

But when Vinayak got her an expensive diamond necklace on the day of the housewarming, she got furious. 'We have a huge burden of a loan sitting on our heads. Why did you need to spend more?' He, on the other hand, put the necklace around her neck as she stood before the mirror, embraced her from behind and whispered with his chin touching her ear, 'An apartment is for living, but this necklace is for loving.'

After the housewarming party, Devika's mother, who had come over for the occasion, planted another worry in her head. 'It's already two years. Don't you feel like having a baby yet?' she said. 'A child is even more important than a house. What kind of pleasure is there in a house without a baby crawling about on the floor?' 'Come on, Amma, no need for all that now. We are quite happy as we are,' Devika responded.

It was their joint decision not to have a child soon after marriage. So Devika saw to it that Vinayak took precautions. Within a few months, however, he got so tired of the whole thing that he transferred the burden of precaution to Devika, which she followed with diligence. As time passed, she too became casual and often forgot to take her pills. But they were not thinking about this; they had other things on their plate. Now, as she dropped off her mother at the airport, she felt a sudden urge to have a child.

Vinayak was nonchalant. 'Stop thinking about it,' he said. 'If you wait for some time things will fall in place.' But, the more she resisted thinking about it the harder it became for her to shake off the thought. Commercials on TV with cute babies began to nag her, and small talk among her colleagues about their kids irritated her. She started to make inventories of the people who had got married around the same time as she had and how many children they now had, losing her sleep in the process. Whenever she was free, she would log on to websites related to babies and lost interest in the upkeep of the house. Errors crept into her work; even informal emails sent to friends were full of spelling errors. She was distracted even during sex.

Vinayak observed these changes in silence, not knowing how to reach out to her. Finally, he decided that consulting a doctor would be the right thing to do. Many doctors were consulted and numerous tests conducted for months on end. But each doctor had his own approach and his own recommendation. A year passed and nothing changed.

Vinayak took Devika on a vacation to Europe so that she could forget about the whole thing. Next, they went to the grasslands of Kenya. A lot of money was spent on these two vacations, but he was ready to do anything to make her happy. He bought a farmhouse near Madikeri so they could spend weekends there. He tried to take her there regularly, at least once in two weeks. Their monthly expenditure kept rising, but he did not mind, as her happiness was more important to him.

Devika was stuck within a peculiar logic. Was her regular workout becoming an impediment to her potential motherhood? She took to Google for answers. She found a lot of information, all of which confused her even further. Eventually she stopped her workouts. Now she would wake up early and sit in front of the computer for hours. Vinayak saw all this but did not want to muddy the waters by asking questions. However, when a month went by without her exercising, he could not keep quiet any longer. But when he broached the subject with her, she lashed out at him: 'It's the man of the house who should be working out, not me. If you slouch around like a lazy bum, how will we have children?' The cruelty of her words hurt Vinayak. They did not speak to each other for two days. Then, on the third day, Vinayak got up early and hit the gym. Even in her warped state of mind, Devika noticed the change and realized the hurt she had caused. One week later, she said, 'No need to do all this. You can go back to your morning sleep.' And she resumed working out as before.

Then, two terrible things happened.

One of the doctors they consulted prescribed a series of tablets for Devika to be taken for six months, assuring her they would increase her chances of conception. She was ready to believe anything and began to take them. After a month, unexpected results began to show up; she began to put on weight and her body began to expand. Half an hour more at the gym would not help. Colleagues at work started warning her to do something about it, some of them even began to make fun of her. Soon the couple ran to the doctor, who did not appear to be greatly bothered. 'There will always be some side effects. Why are you bothered about some extra weight? You can lose weight later, but don't stop taking the tablets,' he said. Devika followed the advice, only to put on fifteen kilos in just four months. She stopped the medicines but the excess weight didn't disappear. Though Vinayak tried to console her, even he missed her slender body. On top of it, there was no pregnancy.

The second unexpected blow came from outside. Soon after real estate bubble burst in the US, along with the collapse of major banks, heads started to roll in companies in Bengaluru. One fine morning, as Devika swiped her card to enter her office, the door made a screeching noise but did not budge. She called the supervisor, who calmly told her to wait at the reception. After half an hour, a security guard appeared with a big plastic bag, which contained her personal belongings from her desk. He also carried a special letter for her, which said the company did not need her services any longer. A cheque was attached to the letter. She signed a couple of papers the security guard gave her. He took her laptop and identity card along with signed documents.

She sat there in the air-conditioned reception area, totally lost. Then she took a long, deep breath and stepped out. Before getting into her car she gazed through the piercing sunlight at the glass building which had been her place of work for the past four years. Now it looked like a gigantic monster, and it shook her to the core.

Devika had no alternative but to find work, as the EMI amount owed to the bank was now Rs 95,000 per month. She was also sending money home. It would take them another eight years before they could clear all their loans. It worried Vinayak too, but he tried to pacify her. He called his friends and sent them her resume to circulate among prospective companies. But the recession had begun its impact and Devika did not get any calls for interviews. Even when she received calls, the employers showed no interest in her background. Devika began to wonder if, in her obsession to have a child, she had failed to pick up new skills.

Vinayak became quite exhausted, working himself to the bone to clear the loans and make ends meet. Their savings had begun to shrink. He thought of selling the apartment, but who would buy it? Everyone was feeling the heat of the recession. He resorted to asking his friends for loans. The weekend parties took a holiday and there were no more visits to five-star hotels. The honest driver who had served them for three years was sent home, and they told the cook and the maid that their services were no longer needed.

A year passed in such difficult conditions. Even her inability to conceive stopped bothering Devika. The pain of being barren was nothing compared to the pain of penury.

It was in such a situation that Kasturi had put that embarrassing question to her and, almost automatically, a tear had dropped from Devika's eyes.

≈

After the interview, Kasturi and Vishal went for coffee to the makeshift cafeteria on the terrace. They had already selected

Devika for the job, the teardrop notwithstanding. Kasturi's question dominated the conversation. Vishal worried whether it was at all ethical to ask that question. But Kasturi defended her rationale as to why it was a perfectly valid question to ask whether Devika planned to have children. 'Vishal, don't pass on the blame to me. She's been married for over four years now but has not mentioned any kids in her resume. I know many couples these days who practice DINK, "double income, no kids". Is it not important for us to know what plans she has for the future?'

'You are right in a way, but her reaction bothered me.'

'If we become soft because of her tears and take wrong decisions, who will protect us later? This is by far the most important project for our company. It is going to be in the final stages roughly in six to eight months. By then Devika would be the key individual on this project. Suppose she requests for maternity leave at that time, who will listen to your sob story?'

'If someone wants to be a mother, do we have the right to say no? Isn't it against the law?'

'We have no objection as such, but we don't want her to be a mother within this time-frame, that's all.'

'Well, let it go. Didn't she declare that she was not thinking along those lines, anyway? Why should we break our heads over it? Maybe she is one of those DINKs.'

'No, no, if she was, she would have announced it proudly; certainly, she wouldn't have cried. Looks like she could not conceive even after trying hard. Anyway, it is enough if she does not mess up this project.'

'No, no. Her attitude is good and she has the skills to be a quality manager.'

Absolving herself of any guilt, Kasturi now decided to harangue Vishal. 'She may be bright, but it looks like the boys in your team would be very disappointed. I am sure they were expecting a slim beauty. Instead, you decided to go for a fatso.'

Vishal laughed loudly. 'You should be careful, Kasturi. What you said can be considered body shaming.'

Kasturi too joined in the laughter. Then she added, 'Still, she is young. Shouldn't she be at least a bit concerned about her figure? How can a girl who can't even spend half an hour every morning in a gym retain her shape? She looks like a football.'

'Let her husband worry about it. I am just concerned about my project. You know, I haven't got any raise in three years. I cannot think of another job either until this damn recession comes to an end. I feel like a fly stuck in gluey mucus.'

Kasturi took the last sip of her coffee, looked at her watch and decided that it was time to leave. 'I have to go up to Malleshwaram, it is already five-thirty. I shudder to think of this darned Bangalore traffic. In fact, the feeling of a fly stuck in gluey mucus may not be all that bad compared to being stuck in Bangalore traffic.'

Vishal stayed there, munching the remaining chips and remembering the interview and Devika shedding a tear. He found it very strange that before wiping her eyes Devika had cleaned the glass table.

≈

In two months' time, Devika proved to be an ideal employee. Always on time, willing to work during weekends if necessary, never getting annoyed or losing her temper—it was no wonder she was liked by one and all. Vishal was particularly proud that he had made the right choice.

Even though she was a quality manager, she took on other responsibilities, including correcting correspondence in English. It was one of the things Vishal hated doing. Correcting the emails of his juniors consumed a good portion of his day. No matter how good the engineering colleges were, most of these graduates could not write proper English. Wrong spellings and grammatical errors annoyed clients outside India, particularly those in the UK and the USA. It was also hard to follow the clients' accents and even harder to communicate in a manner that was comprehensible. Devika resolved all these issues as her English was flawless and she could converse freely with the clients. Because of Devika, Vishal could now devote his time to other important matters.

One day, while eating lunch at the canteen, Vishal casually asked Devika how she had such a command over the language. She said that while in Bihar she had appeared for the Indian Administrative Service examination, which required plenty of preparation. Even though she was not selected, the preparation and training had come in handy.

Seeing satisfactory progress on the project, the American client sanctioned money for a celebratory party outside the office. 'You guys have worked day and night. You deserve to enjoy the weekend,' said the email. Under Devika's stewardship, they selected a resort on Kanakpura Road along the Cauvery River to spend a Saturday with their families. At the party Vishal met Vinayak, a handsome chap with a responsible position at a major company. Vishal wondered how such a handsome fellow found such an obese girl like Devika attractive. At the same time, he felt that Devika was the smarter of the two. Vishal introduced his wife, Shilpa, and the children, Tarun and Kiran, to Vinayak. He was touched that Vinayak played with the boys all day.

Devika pulled another surprise on her colleagues. To make the outing fun and help break the ice among the participants, several games had been organized. Outlasting others in a dancing contest was one such. Devika won that contest! The fact that her weight did not interfere with her ability to dance was a matter of admiration, especially to Vishal. She danced without missing a beat for forty-five minutes to the catchy tunes of Bollywood songs. Thunderous applause from the men energized her so much that she danced vigorously, not caring that she was sweating profusely. Vishal complimented her by calling her 'the Saroj Khan of our company'. Once again, at dinner, Vishal said 'I just cannot believe . . .' Although Devika sensed there was a touch of derision about her weight in his comment, she ignored it with a half-friendly smile. Between mouthfuls of chicken kebab, Vinayak softly quipped, 'This is how she trapped me nearly seven years ago . . . by dancing away.' Devika heard it, and with feigned anger called her husband an 'idiot' and smacked him on his back. Vinayak pretended to be hurt badly and said, 'Oh, you're killing me.' Everyone laughed, including Devika.

~

Three more months passed smoothly. Vishal felt a sort of unease. He knew, based on his professional experience, that just when everything seemed to be going right, that was exactly when waves of disruption could strike. He had now learnt to neither get overly excited nor accept a temporary calm as a permanent one. His suspicions proved right.

One day, Kasturi and he were at lunch when Devika entered the canteen. She smiled at them and stood in the queue for her turn at the counter. Vishal was busy describing Devika's mature approach towards solving problems while Kasturi was busy watching Devika fill her plate with rice, sambar and curried vegetables. She signalled to Vishal to stay quiet for a while and watch Devika. Vishal looked at Devika but did not find anything unusual about her. 'What are you looking at?' He asked. Without changing her line of sight, Kasturi muttered, 'Three months.' Vishal did not understand. Kasturi continued, 'Your tough days are just beginning.' As she continued to eat, Kasturi made it more explicit, 'She is three months pregnant.' Shocked, Vishal looked at Devika again and said rather lamely, 'I don't think so.' Kasturi smiled and said, 'That requires a woman's eye. She is obese to start with, you could never figure out.' Vishal banged the table with his fist and spat out, 'Bitch.' Kasturi gave him another I-told-you-so smile.

≈

When Devika entered the spacious meeting room, she saw three people sitting there—Kethan Desai, head of finance, flanked by Kasturi and Vishal on either side. Kasturi began.

'Devika, we have to ask you some personal questions, hope you don't mind.'

'No, not at all, please go ahead . . .'

'We guess you are expecting . . .'

'Yes.'

There was silence for a couple of moments, and Kasturi broke the silence by congratulating her. The other two followed rather meekly. Devika thanked all three with an equally subdued voice.

'Having a child is your prerogative, and as per the company rules we cannot question your personal choice. However, there is a chance that the project schedule may be affected, hence this discussion. Hope you won't misunderstand us,' Vishal explained.

Kasturi added, 'We had asked you at the time of hiring. You had assured us that you did not have any plans of having a child. That was one of the reasons for hiring you.'

Devika took time to answer. She said, 'I agree with you, but not everything in life can be planned ahead. I am sure you are aware of that.'

'That's true. But this is an extremely important project for us. You know you have an important role in this project. You also know that within the next five months we shall be reaching a critical stage when we will need you the most. If you decide to go on maternity leave for four to five months during that crucial period, the project is sure to fail,' Vishal tried to be as reasonable as he could.

'I understand the problem, but this is a question of my life. Only my husband and I know the kind of anguish we have experienced in the last four years. Now, by the grace of God, we have a sweet moment to look forward to, which is more important to me than our company or our American customers. This is a question of my life.'

The last comment enraged Vishal. 'Doesn't it mean anything to you if my professional life is ruined?' Vishal sounded furious. Kasturi whispered in his ear to calm down. Desai too patted his back, saying, 'Cool down, man.'

Devika stood up. 'I understand all of your problems, but I am not responsible for any of them in any way whatsoever. Nor will I feel guilty.'

As she left the room, Vishal threw up his hands in the air and shouted, 'Bitch, she put me in a soup!'

'Vishal, language, please. Legally, we cannot do anything about it. A war of words will only make it worse,' Kasturi explained.

Desai had the same suggestion. 'Let's not quarrel about what transpired. Instead, let's focus on how to recover from the current situation.'

'It's clear, isn't it? We will need to find another candidate. We should make sure she transfers all her knowledge of the project to the new candidate before we ask her to go. After all, these are tough times. The Americans are sitting on our heads demanding that we complete the project using half the budget.' Vishal spoke as if he had rehearsed the speech several times over.

Kasturi cautioned: 'Vishal, you cannot give a pink slip to someone just because she is pregnant. To top it, she is your best employee. Your emails to that effect are in everyone's inbox. On what grounds will you fire her?'

Vishal announced his firm decision: 'We can find some grounds—sexual harassment, information theft . . . whatever. I am not going to tolerate any loss in my project. This is a question of my survival.'

~

Usually, on reaching home every evening the first thing Vishal did was to talk to his two boys and make them laugh. That evening too the boys ran to the portico as soon as they heard his car driving in. But Vishal ignored them, entered the house and collapsed on the sofa. Shilpa noticed this and instantly knew something was wrong. She sent the boys away, served Vishal a glass of ice-cold water and sat next to him. Once he drank the water, she asked, 'What happened?'

Vishal tried to ignore the question, saying that he had just had a hectic day. But Shilpa persisted. Finally he said, 'Do you remember Devika who works in our company?'

'Who danced like crazy in the resort, the plump woman?'

'The same.'

'Poor thing, what happened to her?'

'She is pregnant.'

'That means she cannot dance any more,' Shilpa quipped. Vishal spat out a sardonic laugh and added, 'She won't dance, but is now making us dance to her tune.' He then explained the whole saga to Shilpa. She was immediately on board with her husband's argument. 'What a cheat! Didn't she know there is a time for conceiving?' she said.

At that point Vishal heard his mother walk into the living room slowly, supported by her cane. Her body was a little bent and she was wearing dark glasses as an eye had been operated upon recently.

'Vishoo, I overheard your discussion. Don't ever talk ill of a pregnant woman, my dear son. The result won't be good,' she said.

'Amma, these are official matters, you won't understand,' Shilpa argued on behalf of her husband.

'I agree I do not understand these matters. But I do understand pregnancy and childbirth. You know I gave birth to seven children and I was lucky enough to retain at least four of them.'

'Amma, this is a project for an American client. If I mess up, I will lose my job,' Vishal said.

'Whether it's America or Afghanistan, when it comes to matters of pregnancy or childbirth, it's one and the same. You never blame someone for those things. It's as sinful as blaming God. In this life, by God's grace, you are blessed with two fine boys, as good as gold. Don't become childless in your future lives because of your sins of this life.'

'You are only seeing her difficulty, not mine,' grumbled Vishal and took off his shoes.

'There is no difficulty in this world that's as hard as bearing and delivering a child. Whatever other problems there are, adjustments must be made,' the old woman said, as she slowly made her way back into her room.

As they watched her leave, Vishal sighed in exhaustion and closed his eyes. Shilpa caressed his hair and said, 'Don't worry about what she said.'

~

But worry he did, Vishal devoted much of his time the whole of the next month looking for faults in Devika's work. He searched hard for every single error she might have committed in every task she was involved in right from day one. He looked at her resume and compared it with the results of a background-check he had ordered on her. He re-examined all the emails sent by her. He did a thorough appraisal of the software tests she had conducted, and of the results and reviews she had done. He examined her behaviour with her colleagues and viewed clips from the hidden security cameras in the office. Even her 'rental receipts' collected from her for tax exemption purposes were examined.

When you start looking for faults, you are bound to find some. So he collected a handful of errors here and there. He took the list of accumulated errors to Kasturi to see if they would suffice to fire her.

Devika, meanwhile, kept to herself. She continued to perform her duties with diligence. From time to time she took time off from work for her doctor's visits. She did not bother whether Vishal approved her leave of absence or not. If in the morning she felt tired, she sent an email informing Vishal that she would be not be in the office that day. She would imagine Vishal's face burning with anger, and smile to herself.

Coincidentally at that time, two huge projects the company was working on came to an abrupt end. Not only did the clients asked for all activities to be terminated immediately, but they also postponed payments for the work already completed. The affected employees started gathering in the canteen to discuss what lay ahead for them. Rumours of an imminent layoff started circulating in all corners of the office. That month's salary was paid three days late. The employees themselves began to prepare lists of staff who were likely to be sacked. Devika's name appeared on every such list.

Being one of the few projects still alive, Vishal's project gained even more importance. Staff from the terminated projects started approaching Vishal lobbying for a position in his project. A few of them made him uncomfortable by shedding tears as they described their family situations. Vishal felt the situation was in his favour. He thought of replacing Devika by hiring one of the displaced staff members. Paying her during her maternity leave would eat up funds from his project and that would be detrimental to his professional growth.

Everybody floated their resumes freely on the internet. Head-hunters and jobseekers exchanged telephone numbers and email IDs. The Wednesday edition of the *Times of India* and its employment section gained unimaginable significance. However, because of the bad times that affected almost all companies, interview calls were few and far between. A single vacancy would fetch thousands of applications. Those who went for interviews were asked if they would accept a 50 per cent cut in salary. Even when letters were sent confirming a candidate's selection for a position, the reporting dates would be kept a mystery.

While all this was going on, Devika skipped office for one whole week. She did not pick up Vishal's calls on the first day. He made his staff call her but she did not respond to them either. This made Vishal lose it. He swore he wouldn't tolerate such indiscipline. In the late evening he received a message from Vinayak that Devika was unwell and would not come to work for another two days. When Vishal tried to call him, Vinayak did not pick up the phone either.

This was the perfect opportunity Vishal was waiting for and he decided this was reasonable grounds for Devika's termination. He rehearsed a lengthy speech for Devika. He swore to himself that he would never again hire a woman for any important position ever.

When Devika stepped into his office on Monday morning, Vishal was writing an email. Ignoring her, he continued to look at his screen. He struck the keyboard harder. The phone rang and he took his own sweet time to answer the call. He knew that she was leaning against the wall all along, but he did not look at her. After five minutes, he shut his laptop and said, with feigned affection, 'I am sorry, now tell me.'

Then he noticed her, and her deflated belly. 'Ouch . . .' he uttered involuntarily. His legs started to shake. 'What happened?' he asked in a whisper.

'Vinayak lost his job,' she said, and sat down. 'Three weeks ago they gave pink slips to 500 people in his company. He is at home now.'

She sat impassively, trying not to show her anguish.

'So, you . . .' As he struggled to find the right words to complete the sentence, she cut him short.

'We have a lot of loans. I know you are trying to get rid of me. Vinayak cannot get another job so easily and we did not see any other option. Both of us gave it a lot of thought and went to the doctor.'

'Couldn't you have waited for a couple of months?' he asked, and this time he meant it.

'You know how the times are. I have toiled for a year to get this job. If I lose it we won't have food on the table. Please help me. It is my responsibility to make this project a success . . .' She folded her hands.

Vishal was at a loss for words. He could not even begin to fathom her state of desperation.

'Please, Devika, no need for all this,' he said finally, 'You are my best employee.'

As Devika limped out of the room, his mother's words rumbled in Vishal's ears. He began to tremble with the strange fear of having committed a grave sin.

22 May 2011

When the Music Stops

Parimala was memorizing for the umpteenth time that one line which was giving her courage: 'Let us not start our relationship by hiding the truth.' At the same time, she was afraid he might not be able to face the bitter truth and end up rejecting her. The fear of losing Sumit was so strong that she was tightly clutching the metallic rod of the seat in front of her in the city bus. The veins of her hands were bulging with the pressure. By now he must be waiting near the Rangoli Kalamandir adjacent to the MG Road metro stop. It was already decided that they should meet at the Dasaprakash restaurant nearby. He had called twice but Parimala was in no mood to talk. She did not take the calls. Instead, she sent a message that she was on her way and retreated into her thoughts. He must have got the hint; he did not call again. She firmed her resolve: 'No matter what, I shall tell him today at any cost.'

~≈~

Generally, it is either the parents of the boy or the parents of the girl who oppose a 'love-marriage'. Especially if it is an inter-caste marriage, one can be nearly certain that there will be at least one parent who will not consent to the wedding. But in this case, all four were on the same page; none of them had uttered a word of dissent. Sumit's parents, who were from Uttar Pradesh, had liked Parimala immensely. Besides, how could they oppose the choice of their only boy among their four children? He was the last one after three daughters. His father, Nandakishor Shukla, had served in the army and lived in several north Indian cities. Sumit had studied mostly in Army schools, but later he graduated from Bengaluru with an engineering degree that helped him get a job in a software company there. His parents had married off all his three sisters, who were now settled in different parts of the world. They had decided to stay with their son after retirement, so Sumit had purchased a flat in a prestigious apartment complex in Indira Nagar.

Sumit had taken Parimala home some time back; that is when she had assumed he might have given a hint about his interest in her to his parents. As they were parking the car before entering their house, he had requested her to touch his parents' feet, if she did not mind. She had simply laughed. 'Do you know how?' he had asked, and she had said in a teasing tone, 'I have seen quite a few Bollywood movies.' In Bellary, however, youngsters must literally prostrate before their elders, going down on all fours and touching their forehead to their feet, in addition to touching their feet with both hands to receive their blessings. Elders always made sure that they were facing the correct direction before letting anyone prostrate before them. But these people had it easy; all they had to do was to bend a little and pretend to reach towards the elders' feet with their right hand. The unique aspect of the north Indian way was the lack of restriction; you could touch someone's feet in a mall or a railway station, or even on the road. Parimala liked that very much, a simple act that brought a bloom of happiness to the elders' faces.

That visit was a happy one. Sumit's mother, Vaishali, had interacted very enthusiastically with Parimala. Pronouncing 'Parimala' was a bit hard for her; north Indians have a tough time with 'la'— pronounced with the tongue further back—and make it sound like a simple 'la', as in Kamala. So she decided to cut short her four-syllable name into a two-syllable one, and started calling her 'Pari'. Parimala liked the shorter version as it sounded more modern. Vaishali Shukla kept feeding her one item after another, insisting affectionately: 'Pari beta, please eat this, Pari beta, please eat that . . .' There is a big difference between the north Indian menu served in restaurants and the authentic meal prepared in a north Indian home. The light curries and phulkas prepared with minimal oil and spices tasted heavenly. Sumit teased her by saying his mother had added some fish here and some mutton there; Vaishali Shukla slapped Sumit's back in mock anger and shushed him. 'Pari beta, we eat non-veg at home. Sumit loves chicken, but today, everything is veg. He had told us.' Nandakishor Shukla did not talk a lot, but happily watched the lively interaction unfold before him. When Parimala was ready to leave, both the parents had insisted that she visit them frequently. Sumit was delighted.

Sumit accompanied her till the bus stand. There was a power outage, but the full moon shone brightly, lighting up the whole city—a rare sight to behold. On that cool September evening, they held hands as they walked. They were exhilarated beyond words. Sumit finally broke the silence and asked her, 'What did you think of Mummy and Daddy?' Parimala mischievously asked him a counter question: 'Both of them are so well built. How come you are so short and slim?' He responded coolly, 'Mother says I am the "last phulka". You see, when they prepare the dough for making phulkas, they try and make equally sized balls, but the last one left may be either bigger or smaller than the earlier ones. Similarly, the last child too may be either larger or smaller in size.' Parimala was tickled by that analogy. She squeezed both his cheeks using all her ten fingers, calling them 'phulka, phulka' as she made a funny face, and ran swiftly to catch the Volvo bus that was getting ready to leave from the bus stand. She waved to him and he waved

back; he kept looking in the direction of the bus even after it had
disappeared.

∿

On her way back, Parimala became quite agitated. On the one
hand, she was worried if this shiny north Indian family would ever
accept a rigid Maadhva Brahmin family from the south, and on
the other, she was concerned about whether her own conservative
parents would welcome a pompous north Indian family. She did
not remember her father ever being smartly dressed at home. He
would wake up, bathe, wear a small angavastra and loincloth,
perform his morning puja chanting mantras, have lunch and then
change into a dhoti and an undershirt. Mother was no different;
constantly involved in cooking and praying, she wouldn't even
have her breakfast until the sun rose overhead. They spent their
days following their ritualistic routines. It had been more than eight
years since they had left Bellary and rented a place in Bengaluru,
but they had become even stauncher Maadhvas now than they
had been in Bellary. The onion would enter the Bellary kitchen,
albeit infrequently, but in Bengaluru even that had stopped. To
people like this, how should she introduce Sumit, who is so fond
of chicken, as their would-be son-in-law?

There were two more people at Parimala's home. One was
Sundrajji, her mother's mother, who also happened to be her
father's elder sister, about ten years older than him. By giving
her daughter to her younger brother, Sundrajji had strengthened
her relationship with her parental home. She was now rather
inactive physically, due to her age, but if she even so much as
opened her mouth Parimala's parents would start to shiver. She did
not hesitate to speak the truth, however unpleasant it might be.
When she started narrating the stories of her times, people gathered
around her in anticipation. Despite her physical weakness, she had

excellent eyesight. Even if a small grain of cooked rice fell on the floor, she would spot it and scold her daughter and granddaughter, 'You people still don't know how to clean up after dinner, see . . .' Nobody in that household had the courage to stand up to her. Her daughter, Sumitra Bai, had once sadly said to Parimala: 'Your grandmother was my mother and loved me like one until your grandfather died. Once he passed, she assumed more powers for herself and truly became my "mother-in-law".'

If that were all, things would have been nice and peaceful, but because of the one additional person at home, the laughter had faded away from that household. That was Raghu, Parimala's younger brother, seven years younger. When Parimala was born, people at home had expressed disappointment that it was a girl. They prayed to all sorts of gods and begged many more for a male child, and eventually had a boy who would take the family name forward. They had named him 'Raghu' so that he might also be the shining light of their lineage, just as Sri Ramachandra was to the Suryavamsha, the clan of the Sun. They had distributed sweets to the entire town to celebrate, but the sweetness had vanished rather quickly. Even at two, the child did not crawl or take baby steps; he could not say a word, which made them suspect that he was disabled in addition to being mute. Fate was much crueller than that. Raghu would not move from where he was sitting or recognize anyone. He never smiled when spoken to, even by his mother. Instead, he would scream out of fear, and it would become extremely hard for the parents to console him. He didn't know how to respond to hunger, thirst or nature's calls. Some nights would become a living hell because he would stay awake all night. Occasionally, he would be very calm and not bother anyone, and play peacefully with his wooden toys for weeks together.

This bitter truth was hard for the family to swallow. How do you cope with a five-year-old who relieves himself wherever he sits and starts playing with his own filth? How can you expect the child to be the name-bearer of the family if he cannot even say 'Amma', 'Appa', but continues to make baby sounds like 'ga-ga'? How do you accept a child who sits there laughing when the neighbourhood kids tease him, hit him and harass him even if he does no harm to anyone? Is it possible to get excited when your ten-year-old finally gets up, slowly holding the wall, and takes a couple of steps? How do you feel when you serve food in a plate to your child and he throws it upside down and starts clapping if you leave it with him for even a minute? How do you take care of a grown-up boy who throws away his clothes and stands stark naked after you have spent enormous effort just to get him into his shirt and shorts? People who have no experience with such children have no idea of the nature and extent of suffering their parents experience.

Many a time, Sumitra Bai would say, 'Maybe God has a bizarre hobby of pairing up opposites and enjoying the show.' While the entire household's efforts were concentrated on managing the boy, the girl was growing up on her own. Her growth and progress were akin to that of a coconut tree that grows and results in a sumptuous yield even if planted in a mire and ignored altogether. Her eyes and nose made her beauty stand out. She was second to none at school. A girl of few words, she was mature far beyond her years. She needed no reminders to attend to the household chores. Above all, she stood fourth in the entire state in her tenth-grade public examination. The district celebrated her success. It was no ordinary matter that a girl from a small village had achieved glory at the state level. The district education officer had organized a programme in her honour and had taken her around in a procession in a car and had also awarded her five thousand rupees in cash. When a large picture of hers appeared in the newspaper, Sumitra Bai was moved. Tearfully, she stroked Parimala's chin and said, 'I can take care of ten children like you . . . but . . .' She could not complete the sentence; she simply stuffed her sari edge into her mouth.

By afternoon, that newspaper had somehow reached Raghu's hands; he drowned it in his urine.

Parimala grew up watching all the ramifications of Raghu's arrival. Her father, Venkanna, used to have a great sense of humour; he would tease his wife and crack jokes; he would often tell interesting stories to Parimala while putting her to bed. All that changed. Her mother used to sing Dasa compositions. Starting early in the morning at the time of drawing the rangoli and continuing until the evening lamps were lit, she would sing tens of compositions in her melodious voice and could be heard by the neighbours down the street. That custom vanished without a trace. If Parimala pleaded with her to sing on any occasion, her mother would dismiss the request with, 'What singing? My life itself has become a theme for a song that all our friends are singing . . .' Little Parimala changed too; she stopped asking her parents to buy her things the way she used to before Raghu's arrival. She had grown up so much inwardly that she would not complain even if she had a fever. Parimala thought only Sundrajji was the strong one who had the right spirit. Sundrajji opined, 'God gives us hardships according to our accumulated merits and demerits from previous lives. You should not sit depressed and lose even the good moments of life. How long can you brood over the same thing? If one of the wheels wears out, you don't throw away the chariot, you simply fix it or replace it and drive on.' She seemed to be saying indirectly: 'Have another male child and stop worrying about this one.' But Sumitra Bai was obstinate about never conceiving again. In those days, and in that village atmosphere, Parimala very often wondered later, how on earth did Mother manage this? Did she keep Father away, or did she use some other techniques?

Although each and everyone in the household had suffered the impact of Raghu's condition, Parimala believed it was Amma who suffered the most. Appa was a postmaster; if he left home at eight in the morning, he would be done with work by four.

But he had made it a habit to walk four kilometres to the Gandi Narasimhaswamy temple and return home around seven thirty. He would occasionally say, 'Narasimhaswamy is our family deity and he will cure our son one day.' Parimala, who had observed her father from close quarters, thought this was an excuse he was using, perhaps unwittingly, to escape from Raghu. It was the women who bore the brunt of looking after Raghu's hygiene, bathing him, putting up with his mulishness and wickedness, and suffering the daily humiliations. While Sumitra Bai and Sundrajji undertook the main burden, Parimala too, as she grew up, had to share the chores, though to a lesser extent than them.

Unfortunately for the family, even though many doctors, sages and godmen had given them assurances that they would cure Raghu, they had failed miserably. But Sumitra Bai had not lost hope and trusted that some day, somehow, her son would become normal. She had openly expressed such a hope to Parimala. After her engineering course, having become familiar with the internet, Parimala had read several articles related to the problems her brother appeared to have. She quickly understood that her brother's brain was underdeveloped and that his was not a 'disease' that could be cured. After that it deeply saddened her whenever her parents shared their optimism that one day there would be a cure. Once, when they were all at dinner together, Sumitra Bai casually said, 'Every dog has his day, we too will have good days in the future . . .' This annoyed Parimala immensely, and she blurted out, 'Please do not nurture unnecessary hopes, Amma. Raghu will remain like this until the end. I have read a lot about such problems on the internet.' Nobody said a word after that; they ate quietly. When Parimala cleaned up the dining area and went to the backyard to throw away the used banana leaves, she found her father sitting there near the well, waiting for her. 'Appa, what are you doing here in this dark?' she asked. 'Let me tell you something, Parimala. Your mother is still alive simply because of a tiny hope that some

day Raghu might become normal. Please don't take away that
glimmer of hope from her. She might end up feeding him poison
and consuming it herself to end the misery. Please . . .' he begged
her with clasped hands. That was the last time Parimala ever said
anything like that.

But Sundrajji never stopped saying, 'There is no escape from
the accumulated sins of the past, one must face the consequences.'
Listening to her pronouncements, Raghu's parents felt utmost
guilt, that they may have done something terrible in their past lives
for which they were paying dearly now. 'God has given us such
a son as a punishment. Otherwise, why would we have such a
progeny that no one else has? What could be the reason for our
plight?' They agonized over their fate endlessly. Venkanna would
remember how he had killed a cobra by stoning it to death in a forest
when he was out on an adventure. When he shared his suspicion
with the few friends he had left, they categorically declared that he
was cursed with nothing but naga-dosha, the flaw that results from
one's evil actions against a serpent. They would ask him, 'Is there
anyone who can be happy after going against the serpent-god?'
Venkanna then performed several compensatory rituals to please
the serpent-god—but in vain; there was no change in Raghu.

Sumitra Bai too suffered from strange fears. Once as a young
girl, during her period, an Aaraadhana special worship was going
on for Teeka Rayaru. Sundramma had given her strict instructions
that even the shadow of a menstruating woman should not fall
on the kitchen during the Aaraadhana. Sumitra confined herself
to her room, busy reading a book, while her mother cooked in
the kitchen alone. That was the time when Sumitra's father was
still alive. He was busy with the worship rituals when a monkey
entered the house and created havoc. The monkey was so huge,
Sundramma was frightened and screamed instinctively: 'Hey,
Sumitra, get rid of that monkey . . .' Sumitra ran out to her rescue
and drove the monkey out using a madi-kolu bamboo staff. In the

pandemonium, Sumitra's long skirt accidentally brushed the pot in which the cooked prasaada was kept for the offering. No one had noticed it in the chaos, and Sumitra was afraid to tell anyone about it, because if she did, her mother would have to prepare the meals all over again under 'purified' conditions. She could not bear to impose an additional burden on her already burdened mother. Sumitra suffered in silence; because of her the holy prasaada prepared under 'impure' conditions was offered to Teeka Rayaru. With time, she forgot the incident. But when Raghu was born, she was convinced it was the curse of Teeka Rayaru that had brought such a calamity upon her. She felt guilty that her son was suffering because of her blunder. She could not share this with anyone, so she observed many reparative rituals for Teeka Rayaru—she fasted, circumambulated around the deities, and even made a laksha-deepa, one hundred thousand wicks for the oil lamps—but all in vain. Teeka Rayaru did not show any mercy.

Parimala, on the other hand, believed in a different truth. Sundrajji had married her own maternal uncle and had made her daughter also do the same. Parimala had by now read the opinions of experts that the possibility of children being born with genetic defects was higher when people married their close blood relatives. She shared her knowledge with the rest of the family when she went home on vacation. Sumitra Bai responded stoically, 'What can be done now? Can we undo the marriage?' But Sundrajji was upset that Parimala might be pointing fingers at her as the root cause of the problem. She said angrily, 'Don't you talk nonsense, Parimala . . . Our country is such where, for thousands of years, women have given their daughters to their own brothers in order to strengthen the ties with their parental home. How come now people have started finding fault with our system . . .? The so-called doctors of today, wretched beings they are; nothing but idiots of the highest order.' Parimala did not argue but was firm in her belief that abnormalities resulted from inbreeding.

Parimala passed engineering with distinction, securing the third rank in the university. She qualified for a job in a software company in Bengaluru while still a final-year student. Having lived in poverty all her life, she recognized the family's need for money. She went to Bengaluru and took up the job, not bothering about higher education for herself. The company had a small group of employees who were dedicated to social service. Other software companies in the city also had such groups. All these groups had formed an organization called Avismara—'Unforgettable'. The members visited places such as hospitals with cancer patients just to lend the patients an ear, a school for the blind or orphanages to help poor students with study aids, school bags and other requirements. Parimala was naturally interested in service and had joined the organization. That is where she had met Sumit Shukla.

This group visited a school by the name of Bharavase, meaning 'hope', located in Chamarajpet. This school was for children with underdeveloped brains; the teachers were trained in dealing with such children and were teaching them self-dependence. The children were taught how to use the toilet on their own, bathe, eat without help from others and, if possible, do some simple handiwork. Parimala saw a glimpse of her brother Raghu in every child in that school. She had never imagined this possibility for Raghu. Who in that little town of Bellary district could tell them about such schools, such training; who would have even seen anything like this there? Once, Sumitra Bai had admitted ten-year old Raghu to a childcare centre run by a woman related to her. But the woman brought him back within a few hours, having failed to manage him. When a child tried to snatch a toy from Raghu, he bit the boy so badly that the boy had started to bleed. 'No, Sumitramma, we can only take normal children in our centre, sorry,' the woman had said, hinting that Raghu was not 'normal'. Later, the parents of the boy whom Raghu had bitten paid a visit to Sumitra Bai and created a huge uproar. 'Keep your retarded child at home, or put him in a mental asylum where he belongs . . . see how he has bitten our child . . . who is responsible if he gets infected?' They had cursed Sumitra Bai's entire clan so loudly that they could be heard by the entire neighborhood. They did not leave until Sumitra Bai begged their forgiveness and assured them that she would not dare to send her son to the childcare centre ever again. Ever since that incident, Sumitra Bai could not dream of sending her son to school.

Parimala had managed to obtain the cell number of Hope school's principal and kept in touch with her. She had visited the school a few times to discuss her brother with them in detail. Parimala believed that much time had been lost for Raghu. But the school staff gave her some hope, assuring her that Raghu could be admitted even at that time. They told her Raghu could pick up simple chores that would be useful in his daily life. They had shown her a few of the children in the school, describing the progress they had made from the time they had joined. When she went home one weekend, she eagerly informed her parents about this possibility at Hope school and suggested that the entire household move to Bengaluru. To her surprise, both her parents agreed. Sundrajji, however, protested, 'Why are you all nursing this evil thought of taking me to a city in my final days?'

There were several reasons why Sumitra Bai and Venkanna readily took this drastic decision. Firstly, Venkanna had retired and was totally lost as he did not know what to do. Now that he stayed home most of the time, he was able to see for himself what hardship his wife had gone through all these years. He felt guilty for having escaped all the responsibilities and for immersing himself in his work and the service of Gandi-Narasimhaswamy. Now, Hope school had opened new possibilities and appeared very attractive to him. He would take the boy to the school in the morning and bring him back in the evening every day. By doing that, he felt he could pay back, in a limited way, for Sumitra Bai's years of sacrifice.

Sumitra Bai's objective was an entirely different one; she was worried about Parimala, who had already been working for two years and was still single. She could see that no one had shown interest in her daughter although she was of marriageable age; it was not hard for her to understand that the reason for it was her son, Raghu. There was yet another blot in their family history. This incident had occurred many years ago, when Sumitra Bai was still young. Venkanna had an elder sister, Lakshmi, who was two years older than him, but younger than Sundramma. Though a bit dark-skinned, she was very pretty, with attractive eyes. She took good care of Sumitra, who would accompany her to fetch water from the well or to the nearby pond for washing clothes. Sumitra and Aunt Lakshmi used to sleep next to each other. This beautiful-eyed girl fell in love with a boy named Subhani who lived not too far, in the lane across. She would write love letters to Subhani, send them through Sumitra, wait for his reply, and look for any opportunity she could get to meet him. Lakshmi had made little Sumitra swear that she would never divulge this matter to anyone in the household. Thus she carried on her love affair. Gradually, the pair got attached to each other, and soon the so-called secret became an open secret in the neighbourhood. And soon the elders in the family came to know. They beat up Lakshmi, dragged her home and shut her in a room. They tried their best to find a boy and quickly marry her off, but the lovers did not allow any such thing to happen; they simply eloped to Mumbai. The elders cursed Lakshmi and washed their hands of her, concluding there was nothing left between her and the rest of the family. Maybe it was their curse that had borne bitter fruit: within two years, one day they received the news that Lakshmi and Subhani had perished in a road accident. Since they had cut off ties with them, they did not feel obliged to take part in the cremation, but decided to simply observe the required minimum three days of mourning. But Sundramma, who had immense love for her sister, had kept an enlarged photo of hers, which she got framed and hung on the wall. Sumitra Bai prepared a garland of plastic wire for the framed photo. Every time Sumitra Bai looked at her dear aunt's beautiful eyes in that photo, she experienced unspeakable sadness.

Because of Lakshmi, their family was stuck with a bad reputation, which made it hard to get suitable offers of marriage for Sumitra Bai. Eventually, Sundramma had decided to give her daughter in marriage to her own brother Venkanna. Though this was somewhat old news, their family was still taunted for their association with someone who had eloped. Sumitra Bai was fully aware of this. The old heads of the town had passed it on to their next generation, leaving out no details. This was an additional reason, according to Sumitra Bai, that Parimala was not receiving any decent marriage proposals. 'If we move to a big city, the people there may not pay attention to such silly reasons to reject an otherwise well-qualified bride,' was her hope. 'My daughter has a good job and makes good money, she will rent a comfortable house for us to live in, let us have at least a few good years in our life,' was the rest of her logic.

Sundrajji opposed the plan vehemently. 'You both have gone crazy. Do you think you can trust a daughter and leave your town and uproot yourselves? What if she gets married and sets up a new household? After marrying someone, even if she wants to contribute towards our needs, do you expect her in-laws to consent to it? It is a big city where people with small incomes cannot make both ends meet. We will have to pack up everything and return home if things don't work out. Do we need such misadventures in our old age?' She went on and on and tried to convince her brother and daughter against the decision, but her advice fell on deaf ears. Not that they were not aware of all the issues raised by Sundrajji, but somehow, the idea of leaving behind the old place and settling in a new place sounded very attractive to both. They wanted to forget all the unpleasantness of the past and start a fresh new chapter in the final phase of their lives.

Parimala does not have any memories of travelling anywhere with her parents. Except once, which was before Raghu was born, when they had gone on a pilgrimage to Mantralayam and had prayed for a male offspring in the family. While at Mantralayam, Appa had swum in the Tungabhadra river like a champion and had tried to teach Parimala how to swim. Nearby was Amma sitting on a stone, clad in her wet sari doing Gowri pooja, smiling pleasantly now and then at the father–daughter duo. At a distance was Sundrajji trying to air-dry her wet sari, post her bath. For some reason, those scenes became indelible in Parimala's mind. Whatever said and done, that day still rings in Parimala's ears; Amma's easy smile, Appa's joyous shouts, her own screams of fear, and Sundrajji urging them: 'You all finish it soon, OK? In this mutth everything, including feeding the Lord, is done in a great hurry.'

After Raghu was born, Sumitra and Venkanna had lost interest in visiting any friends or relatives; they were left with no courage to take Raghu to weddings or thread ceremonies. When there was an obligation, Venkanna went by himself to such events. Sundrajji went with the bhajan mandalis, prayer groups, or with members of a large extended family to fulfil her obligations of pilgrimage to places like Tirupati, Mantralayam and Udupi. But Sumitra Bai, Raghu and Parimala did not get to go anywhere. Parimala got on a train for the first time in her life during the final year of engineering when the students went on an educational tour. Unwittingly, she shared this fact with someone in the group; it became a big joke among her classmates, who harassed her throughout the tour.

Once Venkanna and Sumitra Bai had invited a swamiji to their house to perform his *paada-pooje*, a ritual of washing the guru's feet and showing obeisance to him. He said before leaving that if they performed Raghu's *munji*, thread ceremony, he would become normal. This generated some optimism among them, but they knew Raghu could not face big crowds. Besides, they could not imagine Raghu sitting in a disciplined manner before the sacred fire with a half-shaven head and a pigtail or performing the Sandhyaavandana and chanting the Gayathri-mantra three times a day—a necessary ritual for a boy who has had his thread ceremony. They decided against inviting relatives and friends and subjecting themselves to unnecessary humiliation. But they both wondered: 'What is wrong if we performed his munji, and if, because of that, Raghu became totally normal?' During those days there was a mass thread ceremony organized in their town, in which any eligible boy could participate. They took Raghu and made him go through the motions. He was so frightened that he kept crying, which alarmed the parents on their way back. The very next day, Raghu threw away his sacred thread.

Perhaps due to all this, they were all excited when the household got ready for the impending move to Bengaluru. Parimala had arranged for a lorry for their luggage and a separate vehicle for them to travel to the city. She had rented a big house in Girinagar, and it was decided that the luggage would follow them after they reached Bengaluru. As they started their journey on that beautiful early morning in a fine-looking vehicle with limited luggage, a wave of happiness washed over them. After decades, Sumitra Bai started humming to herself a Dasa composition. Parimala felt as exhilarated as a dancing peacock with unfurled feathers. She closed all the windows of the car, silenced everybody and asked her mother to sing at her usual pitch. Sumitra Bai obliged: 'Naanyaake badavanu, naanyaake paradesi, Srinidhe, Hari enage, neeniruva tanaka . . .' (Why should I consider myself poor or destitute, as long as I am blessed with your grace, O Lord Hari, the repository of all wealth . . .) She sang the Dasa composition full of emotion. When the stanza 'odahuttidava neene, odalighaakuva neene . . .' (You are my sibling, you are my provider . . .) came, Parimala joined her mother, albeit in her screechy voice. Venkanna too knew this song by heart, but he had no singing voice. He sang along inwardly as he soaked in the scenery outside. It seemed Raghu too was feeling happy; he kept saying 'gaa . . . gaa' and touched his sister's hand to express his joy. By the last stanza, with the lines *'muddu siri purandara vithala ninnadimyaale biddukondiruva nanagyaatara bhayavu'* (What kind of fear is there for me who has taken refuge in your sacred feet, O Lord?), even Sundrajji gave up all her anger and raised both her hands and touched them to her forehead as a mark of devotedly prostrating before the lord.

~

Gradually, the family got used to Bengaluru.

Soon after his morning bath, Venkanna would take his son to his school in Chamarajpet. Venkanna had felt a flutter in his guts when he took his sixteen-year-old son to school for the first time. He had wondered if he was doing the right thing or was being totally foolish. But the school had made an impact on Raghu, much beyond Venkanna's expectations. Everyone in the household could see the transformation in Raghu within six months. Now he could say when he needed to use the toilet, he would not object to a bath, he was no longer scared of unknown people . . . many other such positive changes gave the family unexpected confidence. Raghu could even say a few words and phrases, '. . . mma', '. . . ppa'. With his progress, there was a new-found happiness in the family. They also felt a sense of guilt—that they might have deprived Raghu of such an education right from his childhood.

Venkanna got attached to the Ramakrishna Ashram close to where he lived; he would spend time at the Ashram after dropping Raghu off. In the afternoons, after taking Raghu back home, he would go back to the Ashram, participate in the bhajan prayer sessions and spend time there until the Mahaamangalaarati final ritual. Now that he was used to travelling by the city bus, he started

attending the *upanyasasas*, spiritual discourses, where he realized
that the topics of discussion had relevance for his day-to-day life.

After nearly sixteen years of never-ending housework, Sumitra
Bai felt a sort of emptiness, as she had very little to do once her
husband and son left home in the morning. All these days the
chores related to Raghu would exhaust her, but now there were
biting blanks until Raghu's return from school. She took advantage
of the spare time and started visiting the nearby temples with her
mother. One day she was so moved at the Rayara Mutth that she
started to sing. The musicians in the bhajana mandali recognized
her talent and asked her to join their group. Thus Sumitra Bai
started to sing again; one by one, she remembered the hundreds of
songs that lay buried in her memory.

However, the one thing Venkanna and Sumitra Bai had
hoped would happen—that it would be easy to find a match for
Parimala in a big city like Bengaluru—did not. There were no
proper proposals for their daughter after their moving to the city,
despite repeated efforts on their side. The girl was beautiful, had
a well-paying job, had been born under a divya-nakshatra, divine
star—everything was fine. But as soon as they found out about
Raghu, the groom's side would go silent. 'It would have been nice
if the girl had another brother, younger or older,' was their smart
way of rejecting her. The fear they hid behind such statements was
that after Venkanna's and Sumitra Bai's passing, the responsibility
of caring for the retarded son would be transferred to them. There
were others who did not hesitate to say it directly: 'It is fine as
long as the parents take care of their boy.' Parimala herself rejected
such families because she had decided long ago that Raghu would
be her responsibility after her parents' time. Time was flying by,
leaving Venkanna and Sumitra Bai feeling increasingly helpless.
They enrolled her name, along with her portrait and horoscope, in
marriage registries like Vidyaapeetha, and Ananya at Malleshwaram,
but all in vain. Both were quite exhausted from their efforts and

felt desperate at their lack of success in fulfilling their obligation of finding a suitable match for their only daughter.

Maybe out of total desperation, they had given their consent to the proposal from the Shukla family without unnecessary fuss. Perhaps the few years of life in the city had given them the requisite courage. They had seen for themselves and had also heard about inter-caste and inter-regional marriages. Whenever they consulted their few close friends, they were mostly encouraged, albeit with some hesitation: 'We elders should refrain from being obstacles when the youngsters want to move forward. Young people these days are smart enough to decide what is good for them and what is not. Your daughter is very intelligent and wise, she won't make a mistake.' After seeing Sumit's photograph, Sumitra Bai gave her consent with her blessings. Venkanna, however, was about to express some reservations about what might lie ahead for Raghu, but Parimala scolded him and stopped him short. She assured him she was fully mindful of her responsibility. 'All the software workers go to America and settle there, what will happen if you do the same?' he had raised his doubts. 'In that case, I will take him with me. Don't worry, they will give him much better care there than he gets here.'

But Sundrajji was not prepared to give in so easily to such a revolutionary idea. 'We have suffered enough as a result of the shame that immoral girl Lakshmi brought on our family. We got such a bad reputation that we had to leave town to erase it. You two have suffered enough as such because of her sins, now don't commit another blunder of agreeing to this mixed marriage. God will not forgive you,' she bellowed. No one paid heed to her objections. Finally, when she realized that she was not winning, she went to her corner and wept inconsolably, saying, 'Old people should not live, O Lord.'

≋

On a special Sunday, Parimala and her family got ready to welcome
Sumit and his parents. Sumitra Bai wore a nine-yard sari, decked
herself with arishina and kumkum, turmeric and vermilion
powder, on her chin and forehead, and with great enthusiasm
prepared uppittu, sajjige and snake-gourd curry. Venkanna too
dressed up in a formal-style dhoti with a kurta, sporting gopee-
chandana-mudre and angaara akshate, hallmarks of a Maadhva
Brahmin, on his forehead, and tidied up the backyard. Sundrajji
did not want any part in this sinful action and begged to be left
alone; she went to the balcony and sat with some raw cotton, milk
and lime to prepare wicks for the oil lamps. Sumitra Bai asked
Parimala if she should leave Raghu at the next-door neighbour's
for a few hours. 'No, Mother, they have already seen me,' she
reassured them, and dressed up Raghu in new clothes. She told
him affectionately, 'Some nice people are visiting us, you won't
make any trouble, right?' to which Raghu smiled in agreement
saying 'Gottu', meaning, 'I know.' He liked his new clothes and
that made him very happy.

The other day, when Parimala had told him about Raghu
when they met at Dasaprakash Hotel, Sumit had not said anything
in response. He lapsed into silence. When he recovered, as though
he had thought of a way to respond angrily, he asked her why
she had not mentioned Raghu all these days. Parimala did not
know what to say. Sumit had indeed shared everything about his
family with her. Parimala too had shared a lot about her parents
and grandmother, but had left out Raghu. Deep inside, she knew
she was terribly scared of losing Sumit, and at the same time she
was pricked by her hesitation. That was why she had divulged
every detail about Raghu that day. She emphasized her resolve to
become Raghu's caretaker after her parents. She was not worried
whether Sumit would be agreeable to this or not; all she wanted
was to feel a sense of relief within. They did not speak much after
this. They both sat sipping coffee, watching the movement of

vehicles on MG Road. Finally, Sumit got up and said, 'Let me talk to my parents.' Parimala held his hand and stopped him. She asked, 'What is your opinion?' 'You are important to me,' he declared, before taking leave of her. The very next morning he messaged: 'Mom and Dad have both agreed. "What good are we if we cannot have that much humanity?" they asked me.' Parimala was thrilled; she felt as though she had crossed a desert on foot.

Sumit's car arrived at Parimala's residence at the appointed time. Sumit's parents did not know Kannada; Parimala's parents could understand some Hindi but could not converse in that language. But none of this mattered in making the guests feel comfortable. Sumit and Parimala provided the needed translations and interpretations, and helped the conversation along. Venkanna talked about his professional life as a postmaster; Nandakishor Shukla, in return, talked about his days with the Indian Army and recalled the mailman, whom they felt was like a God-incarnate when they were in remote areas on duty. Venkanna felt elated at the status given to his profession.

The uniquely south Indian practice of serving snacks, coffee and water in stainless steel cups and plates impressed the Shuklas. They appreciated the house with its minimal decorations and simple get-up, bereft of unnecessary show and pomp. 'Take some more uppittu. Parimala, ask if they would like more buruburi,' Sumitra Bai kept serving and attending to them, speaking in Kannada, while Mrs Shukla praised her food in Hindi: '*Buruburi bahut accha hai* (buruburi is very nice).' 'Ayyo, what is so great about that?' Sumitra Bai gently brushing aside her words of praise, simultaneously expressing her pleasure too.

Sumit went to Raghu, who was sitting leaning against the wall, and Parimala followed him. Raghu got scared a bit and came close to his sister for refuge. Sumit pulled out a chocolate from his pocket and held it before Raghu. The twenty-one-year-old child was visibly happy and a big smile appeared on his face, but he hesitated to take it. He looked at his sister for approval and she told him it was okay to accept it. Raghu extended his left hand to take it and handed it to Parimala, saying, 'Togo,' meaning, 'Take it.' She in turn opened the wrapper, broke the chocolate into two pieces and handed them to Raghu; he ate them happily. Sumit caressed his hair and Raghu let him, but he was drooling heavily as he was eating the chocolate in a hurry. Parimala quickly wiped him clean. Sumitra Bai became a bit emotional watching all this and went into the kitchen to wipe her tears.

Venkanna was thinking about his sister, who was sitting all by herself angrily, so he reminded Parimala: 'Both of you go and pay your respects to her in the balcony.' Understanding her father's intent, Parimala took Sumit to meet her grandmother. As they passed the bedroom to get to the balcony, she asked Sumit, 'Do you know how to prostrate before Sundrajji?' He quickly replied, 'I have seen enough Tamil movies, don't worry,' and softly twisted her ear. Sumit thought Parimala, who had put on a blue silk sari and worn a few ornaments, looked very attractive that day.

Sundrajji, who was sitting on a plastic chair making cotton wicks, realized they were approaching her but pretended not to have noticed. 'Sundrajji, we want to touch your feet, please give us your blessings,' said Parimala. 'Ayyo, what will my blessings do, it is unnecessary knee-strain for you,' said Sundrajji in mock anger. Parimala did not take her words to heart and proceeded to touch her feet, which made Sundrajji realize she was facing north, so she asked them to wait; she moved her chair so that she was facing east. Sumit and Parimala prostrated at her feet together; Sundrajji touched their heads and blessed them, 'May you live happily for a hundred years.'

Both lifted their heads. Sundrajji looked at Sumit and observed him closely. She was shocked to see those eyes. She took his face in her hands and looked at his eyes again with increased concentration. 'Are you Lakshmi's son?' she asked him with wonder. He did not know Kannada well, so how could he make any sense of Sundrajji's question? Neither could Parimala make any sense of it. 'What are you talking about, Sundrajji?' 'Parimala, I know Lakshmi's eyes— those unique eyes, rare and exceptional. But I did not know Lakshmi had a son!'

～

No one could have predicted that the rejection would take this shape and form. Parimala, who had fallen in love with Sumit, had now declared in no uncertain terms that this relationship could not continue. 'He is your aunt's son, why would you say no?' Sumitra Bai tried her best to convince Parimala. 'One Raghu in this family is sufficient, Mother; I cannot go through what you have. We are a family of two generations marrying their maternal uncles; I will become the third to marry a close blood relative. This is not going to happen.' Parimala remained firm. Sundrajji had now changed her views entirely and expressed a totally different viewpoint about the marriage. 'Who on earth filled your brain with such horrible views? Your parents paid their dues for the accumulated sins of their past. Aren't there countless examples of women who married their aunt's son and lived happily? Besides, aren't there umpteen examples of women who married unrelated men and delivered retarded children?' She took Parimala to task with her relentless logic. Sumitra Bai took her aside and asked her: 'Will you be okay to remain single? You are already twenty-eight.' Parimala did not budge. She said her objection was towards marrying someone who was a close blood relative; she was confident she could find someone else who would meet her criteria.

In this entire drama, it was Sumit who truly suffered; he was like a flower that had fallen into fire. A hitherto well-kept secret had been uncovered suddenly, at a time when he was in his thirties, and it had dealt him a severe blow. His parents too were hurt at the way in which this intimate fact had been disclosed. Sumit had just realized that he was not the proverbial 'last phulka' as his mother had told him all these years; that, in fact, he was a phulka brought from outside. He couldn't control his tears. 'If only this girl named Parimala had never come into my life, I would have lived in peace,' he lamented. He couldn't figure whom to share his anger, frustration and sorrow with.

When she delivered her third child, the doctors had pronounced that Vaishali Shukla should not conceive again as it would be harmful to her health. As they had three daughters, they decided to adopt a male child. They did not get many details about the baby, other than the fact that the parents were from Karnataka and had died in an accident; their boy was under the care of the orphanage that facilitated the adoption. The Shuklas had brought up the child as though he was of their own blood, not discriminating against him in any way. When they came to know that their son was in love with a Kannada-speaking girl, they had welcomed it as an arrangement made by God Himself. They were now at a loss in front of the problem raised by Parimala.

Sumit tried to meet Parimala again and again to share his grief, only to find that she had hardened her position even more. 'You cannot even begin to understand the problems one faces with a childlike Raghu. Please do not force me,' she asserted. After reading up related articles on the internet, Sumit tried to offer counter-arguments: 'Now medical science has advanced so much, there are methods available to prevent the birth of such children. They say that the probability of such children being born is only around 12 per cent.' He understood that her fears were deep-rooted. He could not agree to her suggestion of never having their own children and living the life of adoptive parents. Which man would not like to father his own child? He did not believe in saying one thing before marriage and behaving differently later. Eventually, he gave up. While leaving for the final time, he yelled at her: 'You are an inhuman demoness.' The Shuklas had to work very hard to save their son from going into a spiral of disappointment and depression.

From that day on, Parimala cut off all contact with Sumit—no emails, text messages, phone calls or visits. It was not easy to break such a close relationship, and the rejection was burning her alive. It was the same for Sumit. But she could not soften her position on this matter. As the days passed, the final link of their friendship broke. A year later, Sumit Shukla's wedding invitation arrived in her inbox; she simply deleted it without reading it.

But a strange suspicion haunted her in a corner of her mind; she asked herself: 'How did I become so hard? Is it because I grew up with a brother like Raghu? Is there a parallel to Amma suddenly stopping her singing again?'

The more she reflected on this, the more bitter she became.

26 September 2015

The Red Parrot

I was the smartest kid in class. The teacher's pet, custodian of the first rank. So the day the Kannada teacher scolded me in front of all the students, 'What do you have in your brain? Cow dung?'—I was too stunned to cry.

That morning the Kannada teacher, Bandri, had come to class in no mood to teach. He asked all the students to write a one-page essay on the topic 'Our Farmland' and started to pace back and forth in the class, cane in hand. Despite owning eight acres of land, my father had never taken us there. A clerk in a private company, he had probably never set foot on his own farm. That didn't mean I was going to just sit around quietly without writing the essay. I had seen a lot of cultivated land on either side of the road while travelling by bus. But I could not settle for describing our farmland as another ordinary piece of land. I made my essay colourful by adding all kinds of details. The teacher had asked for one page of essay, but mine ran to two pages. It went like this:

We grow onions on our land. Each onion tree is as big as a mango tree. To every leaf there are ten onions, onions of different colours. Not just white and red but blue, yellow, green and black. Between the onion trees we grow lotus flowers. On our land, we don't walk on the ground, we place our feet on lotuses. From time to time, Goddess Lakshmi, Goddess Saraswathi and Lord Brahma arrive on their private plane—Pushpaka Vimaana—and relax on the lotuses. We hear Sarswathi's veena, see Lakshmi rain gold from her hand.

For the sake of his children, our father has planted trees that yield chocolates. They grow so low that we can reach them simply by raising our hands. Ginger peppermints, Parle's, and Cadburys are also grown there in plenty. Sometimes, when Lakshmi, Saraswathi and Brahma get bored of singing or meditating, they pluck chocolates; they can pluck all the chocolates at once because each of them has multiple hands. Brahma eats with all his four mouths and Saraswathi feeds chocolates even to her swan.

Right in the middle of our land is a tiny sea. We use the water from this sea to irrigate all the plants. We also swim in the sea, like fish on a picnic. Sometimes ships come sailing by and go away with whatever we grow to America, England and China.

I can't imagine any teacher not getting mad! He twisted my ears and spanked me twice. He read out my essay to the entire class. He screamed, 'Do onions grow on a tree? Is there a sea in the middle of Bellary? Have you ever set foot on cultivable land?' The kids couldn't control their laughter. The master crossed my entire paper with a big 'X' and gave me a big zero before handing it back to me. My humiliation was complete.

As soon as I reached home, I threw my backpack in a corner and started to cry. My mother sat close to me and consoled me like never before, 'Why, Raja, what happened, my dear?' I explained the turn of events and handed my essay to her. She read it and began to laugh. I was furious and began to slap her left and right with my little hands. I said, 'You too, Amma? Stop!' She stopped at once and lamented, 'What a pity that children belonging to families of farmers, who were once tilling and cultivating hundreds of acres, have become so ignorant.' She consoled me, 'Why do you cry, son? After all, you wrote what you knew.' She mixed some rice flakes with fresh curd and sprinkled some chutney pudi on top. I made small balls of this and licked my fingers as I ate.

When Appa came home, Amma reported the entire incident to him and handed him my essay. Having read it, he scolded her. 'All because of you,' he said. Amma fought back, 'What did I do?'

'You banned onions from your kitchen simply because ours is a Maadhva Brahmin household. How will the kids know about growing onions? At any given time you are constantly engaged in some pooja or the other. That is why he writes about Brahma, Lakshmi, and Saraswathi and so on. He imitates the Harikatha-man, the storyteller, and writes that "Brahma eats chocolates using four mouths". This idiot does not know that onions are grown at ground level, not on trees.' He hit me on the head, annoyed, while I sat there eating the curd-rice balls. I started crying again softly, but continued to eat. Oh, this tasted so good.

'Why do you make him cry? Just by bringing those blasted onions home you are not going to be able to teach them how they are grown. At best, you can cry while cutting it and demonstrate how to cry when someone dies. Suppose, tomorrow, that dumb teacher asks him to write an essay about "Our Chicken", what will you say? Don't try to use this boy as an excuse to bring all sorts of forbidden stuff home just because you are drooling to eat it. I know what sort of stuff you eat outside the house. From time to time, the man of the house should take his children out and show them the world. You are nailed to your office chair all day, and leave the kids to figure out everything on their own. He wrote about all those gods because of my training. At least he knows that only Brahma, Lakshmi and Saraswathi should be seated on the lotus. Tell me, did he write about Lord Ishwara sitting on a lotus?' While they continued to fight, my rice flakes had absorbed all the curds and become a sticky ball. My hunger too was satiated by then. So I made two dolls with the remaining sticky flat-rice and called one of them 'Amma' and the other 'Appa'. I used the dry chutney powder to decorate Amma with a kumkum dot on her forehead and carved her a big mouth. I pulled a hair from my head and made a moustache for Appa and increased his ear size. I made the two dolls fight with each other—*dishum-dishum*.

After nearly half an hour, Appa began to feel hungry, perhaps tempted by what I was eating. His tummy began to make rumbling sounds. So he stopped arguing and asked Amma to give him some rice flakes mixed with curds. Amma did so and demanded that he take the kids out to the farmland. Burping, he agreed, but returned to my doomed essay.

'Your holy son has imagined a big sea in the middle of our land.' He hit his head with his hand several times.

'How do you expect poor kids from Bellary to know about the ocean? I must have begged you a thousand times to take us all to see Udupi Krishna. Did you listen?' Amma shouted from the kitchen.

I saved Amma's kumkum and shaved off Appa's moustache, and quickly gulped down both of my creations.

≈

Our grandparents had hundreds of acres of land, we were told. The carts that carried the grain to our house after the harvests had to wait for their turn after forming a line half a kilometre long. When Amma joined Appa after marrying him, it seems she anointed the bags of grain with kumkum, turmeric powder and flowers. There used to be a separate storage room where all the sacks of grain were stacked. That room had the smallest door, and anyone entering had to stoop; one had to bow to the grain before taking it out for use. Even after they stopped storing grain in that room, the short entrance door remained. Many first-time visitors to the house knocked their heads against the top of the door but Appa did not bother to increase the height of the frame. Decorative carvings of flowery creepers and an image of Goddess Lakshmi with sugar cane in one hand, pouring grains out with the other, was engraved on the shutter. Apparently, little children used to play with the grain there. They would spill the grain out of a bag and sprinkle it on each other. After the game, they would collect it and refill the sack for reuse the next day.

Grandpa had six sons and four daughters. His dream was that his eldest son would become a doctor, but that son was not smart enough for it. Grandpa could not stomach the fact that his son who joined medical school showed no sign of graduating from it. To indulge his braggart son, grandpa had to sell off half his land. For the weddings of the girls he had to sell even more of it. All that was left was about eight acres of land. When Grandpa's property was being distributed, nobody showed any interest in the land as there was not much of an income from it. Since only Appa remained in his native town, the rest of the siblings forced the land on him while they grabbed the cash, silver and gold instead. That is why Amma even today taunts Appa and calls him 'Bhole-Shankar'— 'naive and innocent'.

Appa never took his land-ownership seriously. He had to work day and night at his clerical job in a private company. The boss would send for him at all kinds of untimely hours. No matter how hard he worked, his income was insignificant. Our family consoled itself that it could afford two meals a day. He was in no position to personally till the land and grow anything. Maybe he considered working on the land beneath his dignity as he had passed the tenth standard exam in his first attempt.

Appa had given his land to Eerappa, a farmer, on a contractual basis. Eerappa and his wife, Narasakka, had a son and three daughters and lived in a hut very close to our house. Both husband and wife used to come to work for us. Narasakka used to wash the dishes, whitewash the walls when needed, and pound grain or make flour. Eerappa cut wood, carried the rations purchased by Appa home, and rarely, if we decided to go to the Gandi-Narasimhaswamy temple, drove the bullock cart. In return for the use of our land, he gave us at every harvest a bag or two of the grain he grew on our land. Amma always complained nonstop and questioned him: 'Is that all you could grow?' Both husband and wife would then express helplessness at the lack of rains and how little yield they got. Amma and Appa both knew that Eerappa was not cheating. Any leftovers at our house were freely handed to them, which they happily took home. Even when Amma said, 'the soup is stale', they would not reject it. After cutting a cart-load of wood, a profusely sweating Eerappa was glad to take five rupees for it.

Narasakka would collect in her sari pallu all kinds of greens that grew on our land and dump them in front of Amma: hakkariki, moorele, anantagondi, tirukanasaali, and so on. These days you won't find those greens even if you look for them, so unique were they. If I think of the variety of curries Amma made from them, like the dry, crispy variety, the wet, sticky kind, or the sour-tasting one, I start drooling. Eerappa's son, Kumaraswamy, also a student in my school, was notoriously naughty. Though not good at studies, he was always ahead in games like kabaddi and kho-kho. We were in the same class but had little interaction. Amma would give him my used clothes to wear. My friends knew that the clothes he wore had been once worn by me. They would often point to what he was wearing and say to me, 'Your shirt, your shorts . . .' Those words made me proud, but generated helpless anger in him.

~

One morning when I woke up, I knew from the *kattak-kattak* sound that Eerappa was cutting wood. Forgetting even to brush my teeth and drink my morning glass of milk, I ran to the backyard.

Eerappa was a repository of stories; he used to narrate fantastical tales about the forest and our land. Even though I felt his stories were not real, the way he told them enthralled me, and I wanted to believe them.

'Little master, please don't sit so close, the splinters from the wood may strike you; there, go sit there,' he pointed his axe at the steps of the basement. I went there right away without questioning. Watching him cut wood was a beautiful sight. He had a dark strong body with plenty of hair all over his chest. He had a black string tied tightly around his right arm. It was so tight I felt it might cut through his muscles anytime. There was a silver talisman attached to that thread. Each time he raised his axe and struck the wood he made a peculiar sound, *'Hayik.'* Each log took at least eight to ten strokes before it split. Occasionally, if the log was so strong that it did not split even after multiple strikes, he struck more vehemently. It looked as though a duel was in progress between Eerappa and the log; the log would eventually fail. Once the log split he would continue to further split it into thinner pieces. The sound from the second round of splitting was entirely different. He would be sweating so profusely by then that the dhoti he wore would become half wet.

He would take a break from splitting the wood in order to get some rest; talking to me or sharpening his axe was merely an excuse. If he came close to me he stank so badly that I pinched my nose.

'Little master, *that* thing came back again on our land,' he started. He sounded like he was about to disclose a huge secret. My curiosity was rising, though I already knew what 'that thing' was. 'What time did it arrive?' I asked fearfully. 'By the time I was ready to quit working, it was already evening, little master. I felt like relaxing a little before returning home and was lying down on the edge of our land. I must have fallen asleep. When I woke up, I saw it was raining. The Naaga-Panchami festival was around the corner, and no wonder it was raining, I thought. But what wonder, little master? It was raining everywhere but I was not getting wet! I looked up, and, dear me, it was right above me standing upright with all its seven hoods spread wide, just like a banyan tree, little master! Those fourteen shining eyes were like stars in the sky; the sky was so close I thought I could touch it. Those fourteen tongues were flying around like kites. It was flexing its body whichever way it wanted—once to its right and once to its left. If it hissed once, *bhuss*, little master, there would be a hole in the ground driving all the mud to the other side at once. Its tummy was as big as two tree trunks. It could lift its entire body and support itself on its tail. Can you imagine, little master, how I must have felt when I saw such a monster of a serpent right above my head with its seven hoods spread open?'

I was breathing so heavily I could hear the air go in and out of me.

'Then, what happened?' My eyes were like flying saucers. Eerappa refused to continue. Raising his hands in total disinterest and opening his mouth wide in a large yawn, he said, 'My throat is dry, little master. Please go get me some coffee from inside.'

I got mad. 'Tell me the whole story first, then you can have your coffee.'

'Please don't call it a story, little master, that's what I once did,' he cautioned. Since he sat there on his haunches without resuming the story, I went and asked Amma for some coffee for him. She gave me a steaming tumbler grudgingly; 'Tell him no more coffee till afternoon!'

Slurp-slurp went Eerappa, lifting the glass all the way up, pouring the last drop of coffee into his mouth. Then he washed the tumbler with the water he drew from the well and placed it upside down in front of the brindavan—the sacred tulasi plant. Then he quietly went back to his wood-splitting, leaving me aching from an incomplete story.

I went to him and begged without pride, 'What happened after that, Eerappa?'

He placed his axe on his shoulder and said matter-of-factly, 'What else can happen, little master? "Get lost, you stupid thing!" I told him off, "Don't you ever try to step foot in my land again," I yelled loud, showing my machete. The wicked thing folded its hoods at once and slid away slowly. Then I walked back home.' He had shortened the story too much and finished it rather abruptly, I thought. I was totally disappointed after having imagined all kinds of elaborate endings. I was simply not ready for the story to be over yet.

'Didn't you get scared, Eerappa?' I asked him. He became serious suddenly and snapped back, 'Why should I be scared, little master? Have I ever cheated anyone?' I shook my head. 'Have I ever lied?' he asked. I shook my head again. 'Have I destroyed any household?' Once again I indicated a no. 'That being the case, how can a snake bite me, little master? Snake is afraid of good people; when Lord Vishnu sleeps on it, he will be asking questions. The snake is answerable, you know.' He threw a challenging glance at me. Eerappa looked exactly like Bheemasena of the Mahabharata.

'If I yell at the snake, will it go away?' I asked him.

'Little master, come with me to the farm sometime. We can check if it listens to you or not.'

His invitation sounded more like a challenge; I certainly did not have the appetite to test my ability to command the monster serpent!

'OK, Eerappa, why would a huge serpent of that size ever move around in our land?' I asked him a totally different question. Eerappa had an answer for that too. 'Not just our land, little master, it goes to everyone's land. Not just the land, you can see it crawling around in the hills, valleys and everywhere. Our village is a holy place, little master. There are buried treasures all over the place. Wherever you scratch the earth's surface here, you can find hidden gold pots. The serpent guards the treasure so that no one can steal the treasure,' he said. 'Keep watching, little master, I have already brought that serpent under my hold; within a short time I will domesticate it and completely tame it. After that, I will ride on its hood and move around our town.

'"Hey, tell me where the hidden treasure is," I will command it, and dig where it points, collect all gold, load it up on its hood and bring it home. I will become a wealthy man. The whole town will work for me. I will become the king of this country.' He twisted his moustache.

I was thrilled by all this—the secret of the hidden gold around our town guarded by the seven-hooded serpent and Eerappa riding on it!

At dinner time that night Amma reminded Appa about taking us kids out to our land. 'I am not interested,' I said right away. 'Why do you say that?' asked Amma. I narrated slowly the story of the seven-hooded serpent and the hidden treasure around our town. Amma struck her forehead many times and rued Eerappa's storytelling skills. 'People are struggling to feed their kids two meals a day, why speak of hidden treasures? We ask him to split wood and he narrates meaningless stories and wastes his time, that wretch.'

~

As we got ready to visit the farmland, we chatted excitedly, as if going to the village fair. Akka insisted on wearing her long red skirt and blue blouse along with golden hoops in her ears and a hair-parting chain to boot. Amma was upset to see her flashy attire. 'One should go in dirty used clothes while visiting a farmland, why are you are dressed up like this? You dare not get your clothes muddy or you will be punished,' she warned her, half seriously. But Akka would not listen to her. I too put on a nice shirt and a decent looking pair of shorts. I picked up a sickle, just in case, but Appa's raised eyebrow made me leave it behind. Appa, Akka and I left for the visit while Amma made some lame excuse and refused to join us. However, she gave Akka a basketful of flowers and kumkum for the pooja, and cotton wicks dipped in ghee along with a lamp for lighting. She said, 'Worship mother earth when you reach there; it has been a long time.' She also packed a flat-rice dish and chutney pudi for us.

The farm is located about five kilometres away from our town. Appa said: 'If we take the route that gets you to the palace, proceed along the Shivapura tank-bund which leads to Jaalihalli, then take the road adjacent to the water well known as Soogambhavi, we will reach the road that takes us to our land.' We took this shortcut because if we took the macadam road the distance would be a lot more. The vast expanses of the fields around, the open sky, the strong wind and bright light—much more intense than what we had experienced inside the town—made Akka and me very happy. We walked with Appa, singing and skipping along the way.

When we reached the Shivapura tank, Akka felt thirsty. All three of us stepped close to the tank and drank from it. Appa had a special affection for this tank because our water well at home was connected to this tank. Whenever this tank filled up, our well too would fill up. If the water in this tank dried up, water in our well dried up too. Appa prayed to this tank as if to a goddess providing us drinking water. Whenever it rained in town, he would ask people if the Shivapura tank had filled up.

There were plenty of fish in the tank; the water was so clear that we could see them swimming. Seeing the fish swim from one side to the other, we too moved back and forth with them along the edge of the tank. I poured a fistful of rice flakes and chutney pudi into the water. The fish reached for them swiftly and started gulping them down. Akka showed concern for the fish, 'That is spicy! What if the fish find it hot and start coughing?' I laughed.

'Ha ha, if they find it spicy, they will drink water, can't you figure that much?' Appa guffawed and Akka felt slighted. 'How dare you talk back to your elder sister? You will become a fish in your next life!'

'It's well and good if I become a fish in my next life; neither will I need to worry about brushing my teeth every morning nor will there be a need to take a shower.'

'Not just that, my dear, when you mess yourself up every morning, there will be no need for Amma to come up with a pot full of water to clean you up,' she said, and started laughing. Now I got slighted and started running after her. Appa screamed, 'Be careful, you might slip and fall!'

Funny as it might sound, Appa lost his way to the farmland. Who knows how long ago he had paid a visit. Everything had changed. Some owners had fenced off their lands to prevent people from using shortcuts. We took whatever paths were open. Appa tried to remember where the tamarind tree was; he impatiently mumbled to himself, 'There was a dried-out tree right here,' and rattled off other such irrelevant landmarks, as though he knew where his land was. After making us walk along many a wrong path and swathe, he finally decided to ask for the way.

We could see a couple walking towards us, both carrying bundles of split wood on their heads. We walked towards them at a quicker pace, though I was complaining of pain in my legs. The couple were probably exhausted carrying the loads on their heads; they placed their bundles down in the mud as they chatted with us.

Appa asked an irrelevant question, 'Do you know how to go to our fields?' The woman started laughing with her mouth wide open. The man tried to silence her by rounding his eyes at her; she covered her mouth with her sari's end. Turning back to Appa he asked, 'You own land here, sir? I didn't know. Whereabout might that be, sir?' he questioned him, instead of helping with directions. Appa, as before, started talking about the tamarind tree, the dried-up barren tree, the earthen bund, the eight-acre parcel, and so on and so forth. The man considered what Appa had said and indicated a direction he thought we should take. However, the woman argued that he was wrong and pointed in the opposite direction. The two started quarrelling while we watched helplessly. Suddenly I asked them, 'Where is Eerappa's land? His son Kumaraswamy studies with me in the same school.' The two immediately said, 'Oh, Eerappa's land? Why didn't you say so to start with, sir? It is right here,' and pointed to a location. We thanked them and helped them to pick up their bundles and set out once again. Just before reaching the place, Appa blurted out angrily, 'It's our land, and how can it be Eerappa's?' Not knowing who he was mad at, I stayed silent.

~

Eerappa and Kumaraswamy were waiting for us. They served us boiled groundnuts, freshly picked from our own farm, along with some jaggery. The entire farm was fenced. Kumaraswamy took Akka and me around for a view. Half the area was growing maize and the other half groundnuts. As it was already August the plants had grown tall. Kumaraswamy showed us the corn he had planted and offered us tender corn to eat. At the edge of the fields they had planted some green chilli and vegetables, in one corner even some onions. Appa picked up one and held it to my face. 'Onions don't spring out of trees, you get it now?' I stood stone-faced, while Kumaraswamy made a gurgling noise.

Akka and I ran between the plants playing hide and seek. When Akka went a little too far into the field to hide, the jingling of her anklets scared the parrots. They flew away with a whoosh. One particular parrot flew so close over her head that she screamed. The momentary scare aside, which was more out of shock, she was as thrilled as I was to be so close to flying parrots. Seeing our excitement, Kumaraswamy went a little further and made a loud sound, causing hundreds of parrots hiding in the trees to fly off. As the chorus of birds flew under the dark clouds, it was as though we had entered a dream. Akka and I clapped with excitement.

Eerappa doubled our pleasure by doing something else. Asking us to be silent, he quietly went near a bush, threw his towel over a parrot and captured it. He held the parrot by its toes and brought it to us. The poor bird struggled hard to escape but then gave up and sat quietly, moving its head left and right. The bird looked very attractive, with its red beak and a variety of green feathers on its body. It was looking at us like a scared baby in a cradle. Eerappa fed the bird a green chilli, which it ate happily, smacking its beak. 'It eats green chilli and that is why it is green,' was Akka's explanation. 'The chilli is spicy, that's why its beak is red,' I added.

Eerappa asked me to stroke the bird's back. Although I was afraid, I touched it on its side and quickly withdrew my hand. The parrot scratched the side I'd touched and started cleaning it with its beak. When Akka touched the other side, it started scratching that side immediately. When Kumaraswamy caressed its entire body, it started cleaning itself wherever its beak would reach. The trouble it took to keep its body clean was fascinating. Eerappa explained: 'Parrots keep their bodies very clean. They can't tolerate even a speck of dirt on their wings. The moment they suspect any dirt on their body they start using their beaks to remove it. If they don't keep their body spotless, they get very restless.'

I teased him, 'Look at you, Eerappa, you don't wash your body every day and stink when you come close.' Eerappa smiled and said, 'Little master, I toil in the fields from morning till evening and grow grain and vegetables, but this blasted bird comes and eats them up. If someone grows crops for me and feeds me, I too would gladly bathe every day.' He then said: 'You are enjoying the sight of this parrot but we get totally upset and disgusted with it. The darn bird eats up everything and ruins the crop. To make it more difficult, they are green in colour, which makes it impossible to spot them and chase them away when they are hiding in the plants.'

I said, 'Next time I visit, I will bring my colouring box. You catch those parrots one by one and I shall paint them all red so that you can easily spot them.' Everyone laughed at my silly idea, except Akka, who loved it. 'How nice that will be! Red parrots sitting on green bushes would look like someone scattered red hibiscus flowers all over the green plants,' she said, with her chin resting on both hands, as though she was in a dream world. Eerappa released the parrot, which started singing happily and flew away, merging into the infinite sky.

While Akka got busy setting up the pooja for mother earth, I took Eerappa aside and asked him in a whisper, 'Where exactly did you spot that *thing*?'

'What *thing*, little master?' he asked in a deliberately loud voice.

'The seven-hooded serpent,' I reminded him.

'Oh, *that* thing. How can I say where? It moves around anywhere and everywhere in the fields. One day it is sleeping in the middle of the bushes. Another day—look there, that gigantic tamarind tree—it will wind itself around that tree and open its hoods over the tree like a huge umbrella. Yet another day you might see it on top of that Kurimatti hillock, curled up and looking like a pot on the mound. If you think about it, there is no telling where it might show up. Maybe close to you right here.' Just then, I heard some sounds from the bushes, which scared me stiff. I held his hand firmly and stood close to him, almost sticking to him, looking towards the sound. A creature was coming towards us, the sound increasing every moment. I tried to tell myself that it could not harm this man who was bold enough to ride one of those seven-hooded serpents . . . but what about me?

Akka moved the bushes aside and appeared before us. 'Oh, it is you,' I shouted in an unenthusiastic voice. Akka smiled sweetly and said, 'Yes, it is me. Here is some offering from the pooja for both of you.' She gave us both puffed rice, pieces of dry coconut and a mixture of spicy fries. I started gobbling it all up while Eerappa asked for more. After Akka left, he asked for more offerings because the serpent liked them too. Then he laughed, and I started hitting him with my little hands, knowing he was lying to me. The more I hit him, the more he laughed.

∾

The question of our farmland came up once again when I returned after my engineering examinations at the end of the first semester. In fact, Appa had phoned me about it when I was in the middle of my exams. Since only the warden's room was equipped with a phone, Appa had called him first and requested him to get me to the phone. As I was waiting for the long-distance phone call, my heart was beating fast, not knowing what may be in store. Even if I wanted to call I couldn't, as I neither had the money to make a call nor a phone at home.

Finally the phone rang, and I blurted out as though possessed, 'Is everybody all right at home?' Appa responded with his own excitement, 'I have arranged your sister's wedding.' From his voice I could guess he had tears in his eyes. 'The groom is from Sindhanoor; he is a distant relation of Gopanna master who also accompanied me. The groom's party demanded many items as dowry, far more than what we could afford. I was reluctant, but they all ganged up and convinced me to agree to their demands. I had no choice. Now I am spending sleepless nights not knowing how I will fulfil all those demands. I can't ask you, you have also taken loans for your college education.'

'Let it be, Appa, we will manage somehow. It is enough if the groom is from a good family for Akka to be happy.'

When I returned home, Appa brought up the issue of disposing of the farmland. A political leader in our town had come forward to purchase the land. Initially, he had shown no interest, but Appa revealed his compulsions on account of Akka's wedding. The excruciating detail with which he described his financial situation generated a lot of pity, and the gentleman agreed to buy the land. But he made it abundantly clear that he would not offer a paisa more than fifty thousand rupees. Gopanna and Kaasim Saab convinced Appa to agree, saying that it was a generous offer.

'It makes me sad to dispose of the land inherited from our ancestors,' he moaned. Eventually, he held the papers before me and said, 'This property belongs to you as the prime inheritor. I was told that because you are now an adult our land cannot be sold without your signature. I have no money for your sister's wedding expenses, so please don't feel bad. Just sign the papers,' he begged. I felt terrible at his pleading for my signature; without a second thought I signed on every dotted line they had marked with an 'X.' I handed over the signed papers and held his hands. Appa was shaking a little.

The day after my return, Appa sent for Eerappa in the evening. I was the one who normally went running to get him, but they stopped me and instead sent some other young boy. Eerappa came running without knowing why he had been summoned. When he saw Gopanna master and Kaasim Saab there, he realized this must be something important and sat in a corner with his eyes wide open in anticipation. Even in the dim light that was characteristic of our house, his eyes were flashing.

Gopanna master started to speak. First, he conveyed the news of Akka's wedding. Eerappa was happy to hear the good news. Then, Gopanna came to the issue of the wedding expenses and the need for Appa to sell the land. 'You have been tilling the land all these years. No one here is base enough to snatch grain from your mouth. Here, take all this and sign these papers so that this auspicious event can go off without a hitch.' They handed him a bundle of five thousand rupees. Eerappa had never seen such a big amount in his entire life. He was afraid to even hold it in his hands, and his entire body was trembling. He was in no position to count up to five thousand. Without uttering a word, he put an imprint of his thumb wherever it was needed and wiped off the ink on his dhoti.

Kaasim Saab with his foresight said, 'Get your son Kumaraswamy too, let us get his signature also.' The boy who went to get Eerappa went again and brought Kumaraswamy. He was taller and bigger than me. Although he had joined college, he could not finish his course and had joined his father to lend a hand at the farm. He was wearing a pair of pants and a t-shirt whose buttons had fallen off. Seeing the large assembly of people, he became suspicious, and looked at me without even a friendly smile in greeting. I simply looked down.

Gopanna master explained everything a second time, and pushed the papers and the pen in front of him, told him to sign. He read everything and pushed them back at Appa and asked boldly, 'What are we to do after you sell the land, master? All these years my father has set his faith on this farmland, what is he supposed to do in the future?'

Kasim Saab brought up the matter of the five thousand rupees and Eerappa showed him the bundle of rupees. Kumaraswamy wasn't happy. He said, 'How long does five thousand last, master? You keep the money and let the land be with us.'

Eerappa did not like his son's behaviour. He was enraged at Kumaraswamy's arrogance towards the elders. He shouted, 'Shut your mouth and sign the papers. Don't you try and show off your attitude. Don't act haughty just because you've spent some time in school. They are all better read than you.' Kumaraswamy paid little attention to Eerappa and retorted, 'You won't understand all this, just sit quietly.' Furious at his son talking back to him in front of everyone, Eerappa picked up the madi-kolu, a thin, solid bamboo cane kept behind the door, broke it in half by striking it against his thigh and started caning his son relentlessly. Kumaraswamy, who never expected such an attack, broke into a run. 'Don't you dare beat that child, you son of a whore,' yelled Amma from inside the kitchen. We all watched the scene helplessly. After receiving several beatings, Kumaraswamy held Eerappa's hand tightly. No matter how much he tried, Eerappa could not release himself from his son's stronghold. Finally, Kumaraswamy snatched the stick from his hand and threw it towards the well in the backyard. Eerappa collapsed and sat down, as if he had lost all his power.

'Sir, give me the papers and tell me where I should sign,' shouted Kumaraswamy at Gopanna master. A scared Gopanna showed with shaking hands where the signatures were needed. Without any further questions, Kumaraswamy signed the papers and marched off in a huff.

There was silence for a few minutes. Gopanna master examined all the papers and showed them to Appa. Kaasim Saab tried to lighten up the mood by asking Amma to serve coffee to everyone. Amma brought the coffee cups on a plate. Eerappa was the only one not to take coffee, he just walked out after quietly paying his respects. Houseflies had started attacking the coffee cup left behind by Eerappa. It was the first time Eerappa had refused to drink coffee in our house.

That night Eerappa got drunk and came to our courtyard and started to sing and dance. When I went out to see, he said in a loud voice, 'Little master, your Appa is a rich man, he gave me five thousand rupees.' His singing and dancing went out of control and we did not know what to do. Appa shut all the doors, put out all the lights and asked everyone to go to sleep. I could not sleep for a long time. Sometime in the middle of the night, Narasakka and Kumaraswamy came and took Eerappa away.

The next afternoon, Eerappa brought a fine, slender bamboo cane, perfect for spreading out wet clothes to dry on a clothes line. 'Yesterday, in my anger, I broke your madi-kolu, madam,' he lamented.

≈

After nearly twenty years I was getting ready to visit my native town. Other than memories, there was not much else for me to call it my 'hometown'. The farmland had been sold by Appa. I had sold off the house within two years of Appa's and Amma's passing away. After I bought a house in Bengaluru, the house in my hometown seemed too insignificant as inheritance. I used to joke with friends that one cannot purchase even a bathroom in Bengaluru from the money made by selling that house.

I had a special reason for my visit this time around. I had been invited to be the chief guest at my old school's annual day. The Kannada teacher Bandri had personally called and appealed to me: 'Don't say no, this is your school, your programme, you must come. Come and teach the kids how to become a software engineer.' How could I say no to our teacher who had taught us in school with that ever-present cane in his hand? I accepted with love.

My classmate Manjunath, who was now employed in a steel factory nearby, had convinced me to stay in his house as his guest. I was more than happy to be able to spend a day with him. He was married and had a sweet baby girl. The steel factory owners had given him a furnished house to live in.

The school looked as it had before, although there were some noticeable changes. Almost all the girls wore salwar-kameez; not a single one of them could be seen wearing the traditional langa and blouse. In my speech, I narrated an incident from my student days. It was about the only north Indian girl in the school who had once come to school in a salwar-kameez and was sent back home by the headmaster after a scolding. All the students laughed when I described how she returned home crying.

I saw that the students struggled to talk about their gadgets in English at the exhibition. When I said, 'Why don't you try to explain in Kannada?' they said helplessly, 'Master says we have to speak in English.' Yet another change I observed was that they had arranged for lavish daily meals for all the students at the school canteen. When we were students we would be lucky if we received the occasional chocolate or laddu at special functions. When I asked my friend, 'Where do you get the money for all this?' he simply said, 'Mines,' in a low voice, as if he did not want to elaborate further. The owner of one of the local mines was sharing the stage with us.

After the programme, my friend took me back in his car to drop me off at the railway station. I had to catch the Hampi Express. The street was invisible because of the heavy truck traffic from the mines. The ruts formed by the truck movement were so deep that cars could easily topple over. The entire route was covered in red dust. Tamarind trees, their fruit, milestones, hedges, electric poles . . . were nothing but red. The road of my memory did not exist.

As soon as we crossed the Shivapura temple, I remembered our farmland. 'Manju, please stop the car for a moment. This is where our farmland was.'

'Really?' he said, stopping his car.

'Yes, my friend,' I said. 'My father had eight acres of land, which we sold off to meet my sister's wedding expenses.'

'*Che, che*, what did you do? If only you had retained the land it would have fetched you nearly ten million rupees an acre. This land has the same soil as the mines,' he lamented. I could see bundles of eighty million rupees circling my head. My brilliant job and my huge income seemed insignificant in comparison. I felt as though I had lost everything just that very moment. However, life had by now taught me that there were things more important than money. So I pulled myself together. 'Manju, whatever happens is our fate. Because we sold our land then, we were able to get Akka married at the right time. Now she has two sweet kids studying in the tenth grade and eighth grade. My brother-in-law too is taking good care of the family. It's a pleasure to visit them. What guarantee was there that this eighty million rupees would have brought all that pleasure?' I said matter-of-factly. Manju jokingly called me an ascetic. He parked the car under a tamarind tree and we got out. We started walking along the dust-covered path towards our farmland.

I was shocked at what I saw. There was no farm, just vast empty fields covered in red dust. In my farmland where there should have been lotus flowers, I saw blood scattered all around. There were huge pits in the ground; mining was in progress as far as the eye could see. If I had told a newcomer that this had once been a farmland, he would not have believed me. I could see no green anywhere in the vicinity. Hundreds of earthmovers were working incessantly in the open fields. Thousands of trucks were lined up, waiting to carry away the mined earth, which apparently gets transported to China. Each basket of mined earth fetches fifty rupees. All the labourers were coated in red; there was no possibility of anything else in the air they breathed except red dust.

I noticed the gigantic machines that could easily negotiate the deeply rutted uneven ground. I went to see one of them up close. The steel arm that carried the humongous bucket at its front end could reach any part within its radius of operation. If it dented the earth with its sharp teeth the entire surroundings shook and surrendered. It excavated a bucket full of red soil, lifted it up in the air and dumped it into the container of a truck. After emptying the bucket, it stood there flashing its bare teeth. A driver sitting atop operated the machine simply by pressing a few buttons. He was so high up on the earthmoving equipment that he looked like a dot. I recorded the whole operation on my camera; the lifting and dumping, particularly, were captured beautifully. When I showed it to my friend on the little screen in my camera, he exclaimed, 'Oh. Looks like a seven-hooded serpent hissing at us!'

The image dumbfounded me. I asked, 'What did you say?' The pitch of my voice was unusually high.

'Why are you screaming? I just said it looks like a seven-hooded serpent. Our mythological stories talk about such a seven-hooded serpent on which Lord Vishnu sleeps, you know. I am talking about such a serpent,' he said.

I remembered Eerappa as I looked around. Serpents had taken over our entire land and were picking up the wealth of our country bit by bit, only to be shipped abroad, and emptying our town. They were making some unknown people wealthy enough to buy our country. The rest of the people were being reduced to eating dust. What I had heard from Eerappa when I was a boy no longer seemed like a story.

I told my friend that I wanted to click a picture of the operator of that gigantic earthmover. He shouted and signalled to the operator to come down. The operator climbed down the machine effortlessly, like a monkey climbing down a tree. His entire body was covered in red dust, even his hair. I made him stand next to the teeth of the bucket and clicked a number of pictures. I then gave him a ten rupee note, thanked him and complimented him on how well he operated the machine. I respectfully asked his name.

He smiled. I saw his red teeth. 'Did you not recognize me, master?' he asked. 'I am Kumaraswamy, son of Eerappa.'

I was stunned; after he had been beaten up by his father at our house, this was the first time I was seeing him.

I asked him dryly, 'Are you doing well, Kumaraswamy?'

'Yes, master. How are you doing? Gopanna master's son told me that you are a big man in a big company.'

'It's going okay for me. How's life treating you these days?'

'Not bad, master. They've taught me how to operate this machine. They pay me three thousand rupees a month. I am married now with two kids. I have put them in an English-medium school. My wife too works in the mines.'

'How's Eerappa doing?'

'Father died nearly ten years ago, master. After we lost your farmland, he had nothing to do and started drinking too much. Didn't survive long.'

'Is Narasakka still alive?'

'Oh, yes, she is hale and healthy.' He laughed.

'Does she still work?'

'She says she wants to, but I don't let her. I've bought her a colour TV. She watches serials all day. Her eyesight is still good.'

'How about your sisters?'

'All three are married.'

Manjunath too talked to him for a while. I asked him to take a picture of Kumaraswamy with me. While posing for the picture, he stood a little apart, fearing that the dust on his body might fall on me. He took my mobile number.

As we were talking we heard a loud noise up in the sky. We looked up; a helicopter was hovering above like the mythical Pushpaka Vimana. All the people on the ground ran towards the helicopter. 'It's the owner of our mines, I've got to go. You should go too. He gets upset when he sees people coming from the city holding cameras,' said Kumaraswamy and ran towards the helicopter. The mine owner and his associates, dressed in spotless white, got down from the helicopter. They were wearing air filters to prevent dust inhalation. After talking for a few minutes with the assembled people they took off in their Pushpaka Vimana, leaving behind clouds of dust. Manju explained: 'He is a big shot who has made enough money to buy our entire state. He owns five helicopters.' I could not stand there a single minute more, so gestured to Manju that we leave.

As we walked to the car, Manju said he was surprised that Kumaraswamy still called me 'master', though we went to school

together. I did not reply. There were peculiar-looking red birds
sitting on the car and the tamarind tree. I asked Manju to stay still
and took a couple of photos. I asked him in a whisper what kind
of birds these were, and that I had never seen them when I was
young. He chuckled and said, 'They are parrots, my friend, can't
you tell? They are coated with red dust from the mines, that is all.'

I felt sick to my stomach. I looked at them carefully. Yes, they
were parrots, just that they were red. 'Isn't a parrot supposed to
be a clean bird that cleans itself as soon as it gets dirty?' I stuttered.

'How much cleaning can they do? In our town, red dust
showers like sunlight upon us. There is no water body any more
in this place to take a dip in and wash up. Even the water ponds
have now been mined. If it ever rains, the showers are red. Do you
know, it's funny even the bird poop is red these days. God knows
what they eat!'

I don't know why, but I got scared. Suddenly my beloved
hometown started looking like a living hell. I felt like running
away. I rushed like a crazy man towards the car, scaring all the birds
away. I quickly entered the car. If I were to see another red parrot
my head would undoubtedly split into two.

Manju drove the car very carefully. I did not feel like speaking
a single word. I looked at my mobile; even though the roads were
hopelessly damaged there was full signal strength for mobile phones.
I started texting. 'Akka, today I saw red parrots. Unfortunately,
they do not look like red hibiscus flowers scattered on the green
bushes. On the contrary, they look like skinned meat hanging in a
butcher's shop.' I was afraid Akka might try to call me as she might
not understand what I was talking about. I switched off my phone
and held it firmly in my hand. Even though it was off, I was scared
it might vibrate any moment.

29 August 2008

Ambrosia

Ambaabai was an extremely traditional married woman. She had not eaten anything for the past one month, not even a drop of water. But she felt no ill-effects of it on her health. A robust woman in her forties now, she felt as strong and sturdy as ever! Her husband, Hallaachaarya, was at his wits' end. In his life of fifty years he had not faced such a bizarre crisis.

Both husband and wife had grown up in utter poverty. After all, how could one expect to get rich when the man of the house was a priest in a village? They were used to going hungry at night if they had been lucky enough to get a meal during the day. Often, they fasted even on a dwaadashi, the twelfth day of the Hindu fortnightly calendar, usually marked by sumptuous meals. Dwaadashi follows ekaadashi, the eleventh day, when the devout observe a strict day-long fast. Fortunately for them, the River Tungabhadra flowed through their village and provided them ample water to keep their bellies full. Just for this, they could have been considered blessed.

Times had changed. Standards of living had improved to some extent in the area, even for the Brahmin families. Without any strong reason, householders had started observing Satyanaarayana pooja, Gurumantra, and other such rituals, for which they customarily invited the priest couple to dinner. It had become the

norm to give priests liberal remuneration for their services in both
cash and kind, including grains and such like. Because of this, the
days of going without sufficient food had nearly come to an end
for the Hallaachaarya–Ambaabai couple. Just as they were thinking,
'By God's grace good days are finally upon us,' Ambaabai had lost
her ability to eat, as though someone had cast an evil eye on them!

Hallaachaarya had long been a bit jealous of his wife's large
appetite. Whenever she sat with the banana leaf before her, she
would easily consume four holige, the sweet stuffed flat-bread.
Even the women who served her encouraged her with extra
servings of ghee and milk to go with the holige. 'Please don't
hesitate, Ambaabai,' they would say. Ambaabai took complete
advantage of their generous offer and asked for a few more servings
of paayasa, the sweet milk pudding. 'Every meal is like a blessing of
Annapoorna Devi, the goddess of food. When you sit in front
of God, would you ever hesitate? You have prepared delicious
items,' she would say, and have two rounds of each item without
any reservations. Such was her health and physique. She could
easily draw a hundred pots of water from the well and fill up all
the storage tanks and vessels in the house. She could effortlessly
cook and prepare food for a hundred people. Whenever she
took to pounding paddy to prepare avalakki, flattened rice, she
looked just like Onake Obavva, the legendary heroine who used
her long wooden pestle to decimate intruding enemies inside the
Chitradurga fort.

Hallaachaarya's physique, however, was exactly the opposite.
Walking next to Ambaabai, he looked like a bamboo stick. If he
ever ate one too many holiges, he would have to visit the riverside
at least four times to clear his bowels. Due to the acute poverty
of his family, he had not had a nutritious diet in his childhood.
Now, when God was showering him with kindness, his body had
stopped cooperating. Other than systematically worshipping God
and strictly following all the prescribed rituals on a regular basis,

he did little else. And so, the burden of all the household chores fell on Ambaabai. Most people who invited him for priestly services were aware of his physical condition and dietary limitations. They exercised utmost caution and care. 'Aachaarya-*re*, please ask what you want and eat as much or as little as you wish. We will never force you to eat too much. We are equally concerned about your health,' they would say. At the same time, they watched with admiration Ambaabai seated next to the aachaarya, eating countless holiges along with copious amounts of milk and ghee. Hallaachaarya, on the other hand, would watch her in disgust and mumble to himself: 'How nice would it have been if there were some rules in the scriptures to prevent a wife from ever eating more than her husband. But no one seems to have thought about it.'

This couple had two children. Mukunda, the elder son, was pursuing BA while the second, Jagannath, was in tenth grade. Hallaachaarya's widowed mother Raadhakka too lived with them. She was over seventy-five and could hardly do any chores, but had a loud mouth. Even as she sat in a corner of the house she wanted every activity of the household to take place according to her will. In the early years of her married life Ambaabai feared her, but not any more. She had matured enough to shut her up when she thought necessary. But she remained considerate and highly respectful towards Raadhakka, who was the senior woman of the household. She ensured there was no shortage of anything that the old woman might need.

The expenses of the entire household had to be met by the sole income of Hallaachaarya's priestly profession. Even with the growing trend in the community of observing rituals, it was barely enough to make ends meet for the family. Ambaabai had figured out several ways to save money or entirely eliminate costs. She grew vegetables in the backyard and made disposable eating plates by tacking together muttuga leaves with grass sticks. She made new notebooks for her children from the unused pages collected from

the old notebooks of her husband's clients' children. She stitched
her own blouses and her children's clothes. She used a copper pot
filled with burning charcoal as a substitute for a laundry iron, and so
on and so forth. In a nutshell, she tried her best to meet the needs
of the household without spending hard cash. She had recently
added a new activity to this list: gathering firewood from the forest.

'Never heard of such a thing before: Brahmins, of all people,
going to the forest to collect firewood! What kind of nonsense are
you getting into?' came Raadhakka's snide remark from the corner.
Ambaabai retorted, 'Then who is going to pay the tribal Lambaani
women to do this chore for us—you?' The households of priests
were not allowed to use kerosene stoves; they had no choice but
to use firewood for cooking. There was plenty of wood across
the river, but Brahmins usually did not go collecting it, as they
could easily purchase the bundles the Lambaani women carried on
their heads and brought to their doorsteps for a bargain. These days
though, the women had started demanding more and more, almost
any amount that came to their minds. That was when a shepherd
woman named Thaayakka, who lived a few lanes down, agreed to
accompany Ambaabai to the forest and help her.

Ambaabai could go to the forest only on the days when her
husband did not have any calls for service. She could easily bring
a bundle of firewood home before dusk if she left early in the
morning. Initially, she could fetch only small bundles. But as time
passed, she was able to carry bigger bundles, so large that two trips
per month into the forest would suffice.

The forest introduced Ambaabai to several interesting items,
like muttuga leaves, seethaphala, belavala and other such native
fruits, tamarind for making chutney, hakkariki leaves, three-leaves,
sometimes even a rare piece of sandalwood, eshwari flowers, and
more. It was as though the forest was a repository of collectibles.
She wondered why Brahmins never ventured into the forest.
Occasionally, if Thaayakka's husband accompanied them to the

forest, he would collect and filter honey for her from the beehives after dispersing the bees.

Ambaabai had been open to new experiences ever since she was a little girl. While friends of her age copied the tired old designs of rangoli and outmoded patterns of floor decorations taught by their female elders, she would use the same number of dots and connect them differently to create entirely new patterns. It was the same when it came to devotional songs: Ambaabai would take the much-repeated worn-out songs and replace them with new lyrics to make them sound fresh. Not that she was successful every time; there were many instances when she was criticized by the elders for taking such liberties. But whenever she did succeed and received praise, she was inspired to experiment more and more. After she got married, her compulsive desire for 'exploration' drove Hallaachaarya up the wall. In the dark of the night he would blush and blurt out, 'Stop it, you!' When Raadhakka, sleeping across in the corner of the veranda, heard her son exclaim thus, she would turn the other way, saying 'Raama-Raama' slapping her own face for atonement.

When Ambaabai started venturing into the forest, she was drawn to endless new attractions, such as flowers, creepers, edible greens, fruits, insects, soil, ponds and water—so many strange and hitherto unknown things. She wondered why people had never utilized the wealth of the forest even though it was so close to the village and full of rich resources. She was convinced that her household could benefit immensely if she visited the forest even once or twice a week. Luckily for her, no one had paid attention to her visits. 'Never heard of Brahmins going to the forest to collect stuff!' those who did pay attention would exclaim.

Thousands of varieties of greens found in the forest became the subject of Ambaabai's experimentation. She started tasting many of them, wondering if any of them was edible and what kind of sour or spicy curry could be prepared with them. 'Careful, sister,'

Thaayakka would caution her, 'There are many evil greens in the forest. Some of them could be poisonous enough to kill you!' Thaayakka's words scared her a little, but her innate curiosity made her ignore the warning. Even so, she no longer dared to eat any unfamiliar greens without first testing them on the mongrel that visited their home regularly. She would first cook a curry of the greens she wanted to test, mix it with some cooked rice and serve a little to the dog. If the dog ate it without hesitation, she would venture to try it herself. If she liked it and experienced no adverse reaction, she would then proceed to prepare some more and serve it to the family. After they had eaten, she would mention her new discovery and name it, as though to patent it! The round green leaf was named 'moon-greens,' leaves that always came in bunches of fives was called 'palm-greens,' and a particular variety of very dark greens was labelled 'collyrium'. Moon-green became everyone's favourite, and they had demanded its curry often. But her husband was worried about its origins and asked her: 'What would you do if it was the creation of sage Vishwaamitra?' This sage had created a parallel heaven and all the paraphernalia to go with it in order to rehabilitate Trishanku who had sought refuge with him. Ambaabai had a ready reply for her husband. She laughed and said, 'I would expect to give birth to Shakuntala in that case!'

One particular experiment deceived her in a way no one could have predicted. It was on a day when Thaayakka was unable to accompany her as her relatives were visiting. Ambaabai had totally run out of firewood and she also needed to fetch some muttuga leaves. She had decided to go to the forest alone. Her plan was to return from the forest by eight and assist her husband in setting up for the pooja. She found enough firewood, which she bundled up, and also enough muttuga leaves, which she packed inside her jute bag. Before returning home she decided to rest a while. After drinking some clear water from a flowing creek she sat on a stone, immersing her legs in the water. The water would eventually end up in the Tungabhadra River. When little fish tickled her feet, she felt like a child of Mother Nature and came close to experiencing blissful ecstasy. Exactly at that moment she sighted that cave—a cave that to the best of her memory she had not seen before. She was attracted by the strange green light shining from inside the cave.

≈

The entrance to the cave was so tiny that anyone entering it would have to bend their head down, but the inside of the cave appeared large. The pleasant sound of flowing water emanated from within, and crisscrossing beams of light provided a shadowy view of the cave's interior. The atmosphere suggested that someone might be present, although no one was visible. There were several parrots flying in and out. As soon as she entered the cave, the parrots seemed to welcome her with their uniquely melodious sounds. Ambaabai stepped forward quietly and saw that the walls of the cave were completely covered with a particular kind of creeper, spreading a brilliant green all around and scattering the light beams falling on it in different directions. The leaves of those creepers looked like a palm with the five fingers stretched out. The little red flowers unfurling in the centre of the leaves gave them the appearance of human palms carrying little flowers. The flowers studded the walls like sparkling red stars.

Ambaabai felt hesitant to touch the divine-looking creeper, but was drawn to its fascinating form. She stepped closer, and slowly and gently separated one leaf from its stalk and observed the milk-like liquid ooze out. She squeezed out a drop of that milky liquid on to her index finger and sniffed it. A thrill ran through her, as though she had consumed an intoxicating substance. Its effect lasted several moments before she could recover.

She plucked a few leaves and collected them into her sari end. For some reason she felt scared to pluck more; she felt she had heard vague sounds of someone's footsteps and breathing. She did not have the courage to stay there any longer and silently retraced her steps back to exit the cave.

As usual, she made a preparation with the greens, which she fed to the street dog first. It was perfectly healthy the following day, although it refused to eat when she served it some rotis and curry the next day. Two days later, Ambaabai prepared a sour curry out of the new-found leaves. It was a bit astringent, but still tasty. Its fragrance reminded her of some sweet dessert. She mixed it with rice and consumed the entire thing by herself. She decided to wait and watch for a couple of days, after which she could make more to serve the rest of the family.

Little did Ambaabai realize what would unfold.

~

The next day, Ambaabai did not feel like eating anything at all—breakfast, lunch, afternoon snack or evening dinner. She did not desire even a sip of coffee, let alone meals, even though she was used to three rounds of coffee, which she eagerly made for herself every day. She did not feel any thirst for water, and it was as though she was involuntarily observing ekaadashi, the fortnightly fast. Now she was convinced she had done a foolish thing by eating those unknown greens and started feeling very uneasy. Soon she consoled herself, 'What is wrong if I fasted one day? Tomorrow I will certainly feel hungry and I can eat all I want. I don't have an upset stomach, no feeling of nausea or the urge to relieve, certainly no serious issues.' She thus concluded that there was nothing amiss.

The second day was a repeat of the previous day. She did not have the appetite for even a drop of water. Still, she forced herself to consume a banana, which she threw up in less than two minutes. She did not try to eat or drink again.

It then occurred to her that she had not emptied her bowels for two days. Every day she would take a companion from the neighborhood to go to the riverside for the morning routine. But for the last two days she had felt no urge to relieve herself. In the evening she went by herself and strained hard, but to no avail. When there was zero input, where was the scope for any output? Forget bowel movement, she had not even passed urine for the past two days, a fact that frightened her terribly. That night she shared her predicament with Hallaachaarya. 'I have eaten nothing for two days, I have not gone to relieve myself either, and I am really worried,' she wept. Being very drowsy, Hallaachaarya was in no state to respond in any serious way. 'If you no longer feel hungry, it is a blessing in a way. You can save a lot of money. No nuisance of visiting the riverside every morning either, be happy,' he said awkwardly, and fell asleep.

Hallaachaarya could not so easily brush off the issue of his wife's lack of hunger, as he quickly realized that the very foundation of his financial survival was now under attack. The following day the Hallaachaarya couple had an invitation for lunch at a rich man's household. Poor Ambaabai sat before the banana leaf unable to consume any food. What could she eat? She had discovered the other day that she would throw up anything she forced herself to eat. So she sat quietly without touching anything, despite being urged repeatedly by the hosts. For the host, who was observing the ritual of his mother's death anniversary, it was a severe blow and a matter of great sadness to see the priest's wife not touching even a single grain of the meal.

By evening the entire village knew what had happened. Relatives, loved ones and even those who envied the couple's rising status visited them to inquire after Ambaabai's predicament. The couple got tired of explaining the sequence of events over and over again to the visitors. Some tried to feed her unique preparations made specially for her, but she touched nothing. If she did by mistake, she invariably threw up within a couple of minutes. This delicious news moved from mouth to ear to mouth to ear.

From that day on for Hallaachaarya, the invitations for his priestly services and the associated meals dried up. After all, who would want to invite a married woman who refuses to eat even a single grain of rice? People wanted to have nothing to do with Hallaachaarya any more. They went to other priests for their routine pooja services. This shocked and stunned Hallaachaarya. 'What have you done to yourself?' he yelled at his wife. But what could she do? Finally, they went to a doctor.

The doctor examined Ambaabai and found no issues with her. When he flashed light into her eyes, he saw that the blood flow was profuse, as for any healthy person. When he came to know that she routinely drew water from the well, he had to conclude that she was energetic. Then what kind of treatment could be offered? In any case, if tablets were prescribed, she would throw up soon after swallowing them. Finally, when the doctor prodded her for more details, she revealed she had consumed those strange greens from the forest. When asked if she knew its name, she wanted to come up with a suitable one. After a few moments of thinking, she said 'Ambrosia!' The doctor said he had never heard of that name. He asked her to provide him a sample of those leaves, so that he could send them to Bellary and inquire with other doctors about its qualities.

The next day, Ambaabai took Thaayakka with her to find the ambrosia leaves. On the way she described the cave, the creepers on its walls, the parrots, the light beams and the sounds of human breathing to Thaayakka. Chin in hand, Thaayakka expressed great surprise. She exclaimed dramatically, 'Ammaavre, in all these years I have never sighted that cave!'

Let alone the ambrosia leaves, they could not find even a trace of the cave, no matter how hard they looked. Nothing even remotely fit the description. 'By any chance did you dream this up, Ammaavre?' Thaayakka asked. 'Oh no, don't you believe me?

That cave was right here, its interior seemed lit by green lamps,' gabbled Ambaabai. They kept searching well into the evening but could not locate the cave and had to return home, dejected.

The problem grew more and more serious. The news of Ambaabai's peculiar condition spread rapidly and people from nearby villages too started pouring in to talk to her, much to her annoyance. She could not take it any more when people came to view her, as if she were some kind of temple idol on exhibit. She started to lose her temper and scolded them left and right.

One day a particularly painful thing happened. Ambaabai was very fond of the masaale dosé at Gururaaja Hotel, but members of a priestly family were forbidden to eat at restaurants. Ambaabai, however, had figured out a way of circumventing this problem. She would wait for a time when her husband and elder son were not home. She would give some money to the younger son, Jagannath, and send him to Gururaaja Hotel to secretly fetch some masaale dosé for her. The favourite son would dutifully run out and bring them to her. Raadhakka, sitting in her corner, would sniff the air and grumble and warn her daughter-in-law, 'Don't you dare do such sinful things, Ambaa!' But Ambaabai would not pay attention to her. She would go to the backyard and stealthily gobble up the masaale dosé. After consuming it she would burn all the paper, leaf and thread used for the packing, leaving no evidence behind, while Jagannath kept a vigil outside to make sure that no one entered the house while this was going on.

Seeing his mother in this pitiable state, the young boy's heart went out to her. He felt that no matter what food she rejected, she would not say no to the masaale dosé from Bhatta's Gururaaja Hotel. He knew that a dosé, curled and stuffed with its spicy curry of onion, potato and garlic, would be irresistible for his mother. He somehow scraped some money together and bought her a freshly made masaale dosé from the restaurant. The moment he approached the house with it, Ambaabai realized what her son had done and felt deeply grateful towards him. They both went to the backyard and sat under the neem tree. The son opened the package and took a piece of dosé along with its stuffing, smeared some spicy chutney on it and fed it to his mother. She had no appetite but could not refuse the dosé, especially as it would mean being insensitive to her son's love. She ate it, and he smiled. But alas, the pleasure did not last long. None of it—the dosé, the masaale stuffing or the chutney—remained inside her belly; she threw up the whole thing. Jagannath despaired at his mother's condition. Ambaabai too felt extremely sad and started to cry.

One day Thaayakka brought a piece of fried chicken rolled inside a banana leaf and called Ambaabai, 'Ammaavre, please come.' Both of them went looking for the mongrel that used to come to Ambaabai's house regularly looking for food but had not visited her for days. They searched and searched in many lanes but could not find the dog. Finally, they saw it lying under a tamarind tree near the Durgamma temple on the outskirts of the village. It was looking very healthy. The dog recognized them; it got up and started wagging its tail. Thaayakka caressed it with affection and offered it the piece of fried chicken. The dog sniffed the chicken, then looked at Thaayakka and then at Ambaabai with a peculiar expression of helplessness. Then it moved away without eating it and went back to sleep. Ambaabai understood the dog's predicament only too well. She wept and wept, saying 'What kind of a pathetic condition have I put this poor speechless creature in, Thaayakka! Will God ever forgive me?'

It was during these difficult days that Fish-Baba visited their village.

~≈~

Fish-Baba, who used to visit this village once in three or six months, was well known to all the residents. He would stay for fifteen or twenty days and move on to some other village.

Fish–Baba never travelled by the regular road. Instead of walking, he swam in the river to go from one village to another. Because of this he never ever visited any place that was not situated along a river. According to him, a place without a river was unfit for living. On occasion he would swim the Tungabhadra River to reach the Hagari River. At other times, he would swim northwards into the Krishna, Ghataprabha, Malaprabha, Doni, Bheema and other rivers to visit the villages along their shores. He would get emotional while declaring that it was rivers that brought people together. He would swim to a village's shore bright and early one morning and sit there. Those who came to the river for their daily ablutions or to wash clothes would quickly spread the news of his arrival in the village.

It was but natural that he was given the name 'Fish–Baba' as he could swim like a fish, but that was not all—it was also believed he had a special ability to communicate with fish. He had never claimed such powers, but people had good reason to believe so. Fish–Baba provided people medicines for all kinds of diseases, and all his medicines had something or the other to do with fish. People eagerly waited for his arrival, simply because of his unique method of curing disease.

No matter what the disease, Fish–Baba had a cure for it. On day one, the patient had to sit with him and explain all his issues and symptoms. The baba would listen with utmost attention, after which he would ask a few questions. He would then ask the patient to meditate along with him, after which he would instruct the patient to come back the next evening. He saw only one patient a day and refused to treat people who were past seventy. 'I do not have the power to challenge Yama, the God of death,' he would say.

The next morning he would enter the river before dawn. No one knew his swimming route. The currents of the river, the crocodiles or sudden drops in water level did not hinder his speed.

It was widely believed that while swimming he talked to the fish in the water and described the patient's problems to them in great detail. Apparently, the fish listened carefully and discussed the problems among themselves and finally reach a conclusion. They would then offer him a special baby fish as a gift. This baby fish would swim along with him to the shore. The baba would use a mortar or any such implement available at the ghats, wherever he landed up, which he would clean up and fill with fresh river water. Then he would fetch the fish gifted to him in his cupped hands along with some water, and place it inside the stone mortar. He would feed that fish some specially prepared food and let it swim inside the mortar until evening.

The patient would arrive as instructed, usually along with some members of his or her family. Fish-Baba would perform a pooja for about half an hour, invoking Matsya, Vishnu's fish avatar, and lift the fish from the mortar using two fingers. Although its participation in the disease-curing process was voluntary, the fish would wiggle helplessly and appear distressed as soon as it was separated from the water. He would ask the patient to open his mouth, and chanting some mantras, Fish-Baba would quickly push the live baby fish into the patient's mouth and hold his jaw shut using one hand so that the fish would not escape. The baby fish would enter the patient's belly. Fish-Baba would then make the patient lie down on the stone outcrop and start talking to him. It would seem as though he was giving all sorts of instructions and commands to the baby fish inside the patient's belly. After a while the serene looking Fish-Baba would send the patient home. Invariably the patient was cured of his illness, no matter what the nature of the illness.

If that was all, his stay in the village, no matter how long, would have posed no problem to anyone. But it was not. Fish-Baba was a glutton, and demanded two elaborate meals every day. And the villagers had to ensure he got them. His capacity to eat was unbelievable. God knows how such a slim man could consume so much. He ate like Bakaasura, the mythical giant notorious for eating large quantities of food. Fifteen holiges, half a kilo of ghee, one kilo of cooked rice, saambaar, chutney, two chickens, goat meat if available—he would list the items as if he were entitled to them. The villagers had no choice but to tolerate his extravagant demands, only because he could heal the ailing. In spite of the heavy expenses, different households took turns to feed him to his satisfaction. If on occasion there were any shortcomings, he would get furious and threaten to curse them using his special powers. Providing food for him would invariably end up being a big headache.

As long as there were sick patients to be treated, people somehow managed to supply him food. He would not see more than one patient a day because, he said, there could not be more than one fish in the stone mortar at a time. As long as there were patients waiting to consult him, he faced no trouble in getting proper food. But once there were no more patients the villagers thought he was overstaying and would begin to feel the pinch of feeding him. After all, how long could a stranger's demands for hospitality be endured?

The villagers had figured out a clever way of conveying to Fish-Baba that his time in their village was up. They would decide beforehand which day they would bid him goodbye, and prepare a special meal for him. After he had eaten to his heart's content and washed his hands, they would all rise with folded hands and offer him betel leaves, slaked lime and areca nuts along with a bunch of bananas. Fish-Baba would get the hint. He would smear the lime on the betel leaves, fold some shredded areca nut into them and push them into his mouth. Then he would consume some bananas and jump into the river and swim away to his next destination. Sometimes the 'betel-leaf-and-nut' hint would come rather unexpectedly and make him sad; so sad that he would shed tears that fell quietly on the betel leaves. Even so, without losing his composure, he would bless the villagers before diving into the water.

Joy is not a permanent state of being. It would take only a few months before someone in the village fell sick again, and the villagers would look forward to Fish-Baba's next visit.

∿

There were too many people gathered under the stone mandap by the shore that particular day. The mercurial gold-coloured fish swam incessantly inside the stone mortar.

News that Fish-Baba would be curing Ambaabai's disease had spread like a forest fire in the surrounding villages. The description of Ambaabai's disease, which could hardly be classified as a disease, had created intense curiosity. The fact that they had never heard of such symptoms also evoked a measure of sympathy and a pinch of concern towards Ambaabai, because of which so many people had gathered under the canopy.

Raadhakka left no stone unturned in trying to enforce her judgement on her daughter-in-law. 'Don't you dare subject yourself to such a treatment, this is so inappropriate for Brahmins! Don't you think a Brahmin woman swallowing a fish before so many people would be unbecoming of a priest's family? Who will ever invite my son to conduct pooja or any other priestly services? What will be his fate? If you insist on going ahead with this, I shall find another wife for my son,' she yelled from her corner. But Ambaabai would not brook any of her mother-in-law's rants. She retorted, 'When the entire world is experiencing the pleasure of eating, ingesting, digesting and excreting, how can I be the only living human being to be excluded from that pleasure? My tongue has forgotten what it is to taste and feels more like a piece of leather. What kind of cruelty is it for me to be the sole individual forced into sacrificing the pleasure of eating! I must eat again, I must eat tasty food again, and I don't care if I cease to be a Brahmin. I must relieve myself again like everybody else, I don't care for this so-called ambrosia—actually, it is no ambrosia! I made a blunder by naming it "the immortal-green", it is in fact a "poison-green". I don't want to have anything to do with this suffocating golden palace. I must exit and exit now.' She undertook the responsibility of feeding Fish-Baba for one day and even prepared a meat dish for him with Thaayakka's assistance. She offered this to the baba and sat down awaiting his counsel.

The fact that the patient sitting before him had seen many a doctor who had all thrown up their hands made Fish-Baba a little unsure, yet he did not lose confidence in himself. Matsya would never let him down. His deep sense of faith had complete control over him. The people gathered around wondered wickedly, 'Could the baba fail?' The baba had never failed so far, but they all thought with gleeful anticipation, 'Maybe this time he may not succeed after all.'

At the exact auspicious moment, he picked up the fish with two fingers. He raised his hand above his head and meditated with eyes closed. Shining under the sun's rays, the gold-coloured fish wiggled helplessly as the Baba signalled to Ambaabai to open her mouth. Praying to God, she did as she was told. Sitting at a distance, Hallaachaarya watched the entire process helplessly. He felt a great tragedy was unfolding right before his eyes. The people gathered there forgot everything and silently watched as Mother Tunga flowed, making gentle sounds. A cold wind was blowing from the direction of the distant Matanga mountain. The evening sun was ready to set, but even he appeared anxious to wait and see the end of the event.

Ambaabai swallowed the fish. Fish-Baba made her lie down on the stone, placed his hand on her smooth, fair tummy and closed his eyes. He was talking to the fish, which sounded unintelligible to everyone else. Ambaabai felt as though the fish was swimming inside her belly. The dialogue between the fish and the baba lasted almost three minutes while the onlookers held their collective breath. That was it! All of a sudden, a nauseated Ambaabai got up and vomited. The gold-coloured fish, which was still intact, lay before the baba, wiggled on the ground for a while and became still. As far as curing Ambaabai was concerned, people understood that the baba had failed. They started murmuring amongst themselves.

But Fish-Baba did not seem perturbed. He placed the gold-coloured fish on his palm. With great devotion, he closed his eyes, as if he had Lord Linga before him. Next, he pierced the sharp nail of his little finger into the body of the gold-coloured fish and tore it into two halves. From its body he removed what looked like a hardened dark-green ball. It seemed to shine with a unique brilliance. Ambaabai immediately realized that it was nothing else but the concentrated essence of the ambrosia greens.

A soft smile and a look of joy slowly spread on Fish-Baba's face as he too recognized it for what it was. The next moment, he opened his mouth and swallowed the essence of the ambrosia greens! His face reflected his sense of rapture; he looked like someone who had conquered the universe. He gazed at the people gathered around with a profound sense of victory. His gaze also fell on the meat dishes and the rest of the meal prepared for him, but with total disregard. Even as the people watched, he jumped into the river and started to swim away.

With complete disbelief, the people who had gathered to watch the show struggled to understand what they had witnessed, but seemed unable to digest the meaning of it all.

10 March 2017

Beyond Rules

By all considerations, it would have been against the rules of the company to hire Venkayya as he had scored less than 70 per cent in his engineering course. Although he had scored well in the tenth standard and pre-university exams, for some reason his performance had deteriorated during his last two years of engineering. The rules of the company allowed an exemption for certain candidates, if their skills benefited the company. Very few high-level managers were empowered to make decisions using this exemption, and they were held responsible for the consequences of their decisions. If the selected candidate failed to measure up to standards, the selecting official would have to own up and ask for forgiveness from the upper management. For this reason, I was a bit unsure of my own decision, although I had recommended the candidate for hiring only after several rounds of robust interviews. I was very proud of all my previous selections, as my decisions had hardly ever been wrong so far. That had given me a lot of confidence in selecting Venkayya.

Venkayya was from an extremely poor background; he came from a village near Rajahmundry in East Godavari district. His father was a shepherd. None of his other children had progressed in studies. The boys struggled to complete middle school, gave up and followed in the footsteps of their father. The girls were married off before they turned twelve. But the youngest child, Venkayya, was an exception, and he had somehow managed to graduate from high school and go on to study engineering and find a job.

When he came for the interview he was working in a small company, where he had been employed for four years, overworked and underpaid. The company, though, kept showing him the carrot by promising to send him abroad. Venkayya, like typical Telugu boys, was crazy about opportunities abroad. In view of the prospect of going abroad in the future, he had not only tolerated the poor working conditions but had also not tried to look for a better job. He appealed to numerous managers about his posting overseas, but alas, his dream did not come true. The company kept giving him lame excuses and postponing his travel. Disgusted, Venkayya had applied for a job with us and had attended the interview. His poor college grades had become an obstacle to his getting a job in bigger companies. After completing his technical interviews, my junior colleagues had sent him to me for the final round.

I liked the fact that he was quite confident. He answered all my questions fluently when he knew the answers and was not hesitant to say 'I don't know'. I think it takes a lot of courage to admit that one does not know all the answers. But when one realizes that everybody does not need to know everything, it is easier to say 'I don't know'. If we have the confidence that we know enough in our own field, commensurate with our experience level, we do not feel any hesitation in saying 'I don't know'. That is how people who have this attitude are able to explain with precision what they do know. Their body language and the variation in the pitch of their voice when they speak, rather than their vocabulary or presentation skills, can give us an idea of their level of knowledge in any particular subject. I was impressed by the way Venkayya answered my questions despite his poor grip of the English language. Yet I held back and raised my concern over his poor grades so that I could negotiate a lower salary for him.

I asked him, 'Mister Venkayya, according to our rules, anyone working for our company must have scored a minimum of 70 per cent in the college exams. You know you are no way close, what do you think I should do?' I looked at his face for a reaction.

'Sir, I am not in a position to advise you. Education is simply a scorecard of a college exam, am I right, sir? Sir, please consider the fact that during my four years of job experience, I have gained enough knowledge to earn three additional college degrees,' he said with clarity.

'I agree with you, but can I disregard the rules?'

'If breaking rules results in something good, why not, sir? Private companies do have such flexibility and provisions, sir.'

I liked what I heard. After all, rules should not be allowed to become obstacles to progress. Occasionally, some rules must be broken for the good, but we should make sure that ethical limits are respected.

I still had a lingering hesitation about his selection, so I sat on the fence and told him, 'We will let you know the results by tomorrow,' and walked him to the reception area. Like a stroke of destiny, an incident occurred in the reception hall—an incident so impactful that it reinforced my decision to hire him.

～

It was already eight in the evening by then, and all the staff, including the receptionist, had left the office building. But Ranganna, one of our very senior employees, was sitting alone in the middle of the reception area with some curved metallic pieces spread all around him. He seemed rather worried and deeply engrossed in some serious problem. Ranganna, who is fifty-some years old, takes care of all non-computer-related tasks for the company. He knew how to deal with government officials and how to obtain the necessary permits, making his services almost indispensable in the initial days of the company. However, after two or three years, the company didn't need any favours from the government, making him less indispensable. Nevertheless, the management was not ready to give up a valuable resource like Ranganna. So he was retained and assigned some routine chores. Whether the managers wanted a good cup of fresh coffee or a five-star hotel for a company event, Ranganna was the go-to person, a role he had happily accepted and gotten used to.

'Hello, Ranganna-*avare*, what are you doing with these funny-looking metallic pieces?' I asked him. 'Looks like you are playing with toys,'

'Ayyo, sir, what are you saying! They are Kannada letters, sir, not metallic pieces,' said Ranganna in a sad tone. That was when it became clear to me what those pieces were.

During the previous Kannada Rajyotsava-day celebrations, a group of pro-Kannada agitators had created a ruckus as the signboard at our office was not in Kannada. The agitators had thrown stones and damaged the glass panels, in addition to smearing bitumen on the English name plate. After having to spend a lot on repairs, the company had decided to put up Kannada name plates and signboards well before this year's Rajyotsava-day.

As most people in the company knew that I was a Kannada author of sorts, I was the company's 'Kannada resource'. Usually, I was approached for help in translating or drafting letters to the government in Kannada or for selecting appropriate Kannada names for the company projects. Now I had been asked to fix this issue of signboards.

Our original signboards and name plates had been made by a company in Mumbai. The English letters were carved neatly on a flashy metallic surface. The cost of making them in Mumbai was much less than in Bengaluru. They had neatly packed the individual letters in a bag and shipped them, which we had then fastened on the outer wall of our building. The managers had praised

Ranganna for locating this company on the internet. Now, our company CEO, sitting in London, had asked us to get the Kannada name plate done by the same Mumbai company. Although that had disappointed me at first, I found that the Mumbai company was very interested in the project. 'All you need to do is to supply the fonts and the Kannada text. Our machines do not discriminate between languages, we can do it,' their person assured us. He added, however, that we would have to take care of fastening them on to the wall, as sending men for that from Mumbai would be too expensive. Fastening Kannada letters to the wall should not be a big deal, we all thought, and had agreed to the proposal. I had typed up the name of the company, our motto, address and other such details in Kannada, and sent it to Mumbai, using which they had made the metal letters for the name plate.

A problem had arisen, something unforeseen by any of us. The Kannada alphabet is not like the English alphabet. The letters are not always whole; they can be split, with attachments that go below or in front of the previous letter. Some such attachments are for turning a soft-sounding syllable into a hard-sounding one, and some attachments may combine a vowel and a consonant into a single symbol. Some attachments may be oriented differently to yield different results. The Mumbai company did not bother about all this; they had just produced all the necessary parts, put them in a bag and shipped them to us. Machines cannot distinguish between languages, only humans can.

'Please do something, sir, I can't make head or tail of these parts,' pleaded Ranganna. I looked at the metal pieces shining under the bright lights of the reception area. I was used to seeing complete letters; I was shaken on seeing those disjointed pieces, which looked like different parts of a body scattered on the street after an accident. It made me sick to the stomach. My concern and love for the language had made me believe that Kannada letters were very much alive. I began to shiver with sadness when

I touched one of those mutilated letters. I blurted out, 'I just can't do this, get those company folks to come here and fasten the name plate.'

'If a Kannada writer like you gives up so easily, how can we resolve this, sir? Pro-Kannada agitators have called for a Bengaluru bandh on Monday and the city will be shut down as a result. If we do not have the Kannada boards up, they will surely create trouble. We must fix this tonight or at the latest, tomorrow,' said Ranganna, expressing grave concern.

Venkayya, who was listening to our exchange, asked me if he could help. At first I had my doubts if this Telugu boy could help us with Kannada text, but I was wise enough not to turn down an offer of help. Life had taught me at least that. 'Try, let's see,' I said. He placed his folder on the receptionist's desk and sat comfortably cross-legged on the ground. He borrowed the original printed Kannada text from Ranganna and started assembling the pieces together one by one. He was not in the least bit conscious of the fact that we were keenly watching every move he made. Most calmly, he assembled the entire text in about fifteen minutes.

I immediately decided to hire him for the job.

Untying a tangled knot is not an easy task; it requires immense enthusiasm, skill and patience. I had learnt from experience that people with such abilities are known to become efficient programmers. For that reason, it is normal practice to ask prospective candidates to solve puzzles during interviews. As far as Venkayya was concerned, he had made a practical demonstration of his ability to solve a complex puzzle. His demonstration had reinforced my decision to hire him; I was convinced that this was a perfect example-case for demonstrating when a rule might be broken.

I recalled a childhood incident; it was customary for all members of our family to have a red-coloured thread tied on our right wrists on the religious festival of Lord Ananthapadmanabha. We used to have at least fifty people over for lunch, including friends and family on the day of the festival. The threads for all the guests were normally kept rolled up in a plastic container. The threads, most of the time, would become entangled, but none had the time or patience to untangle them. Kashavva, a destitute young widow, lived with us as our household help. For some reason she took great interest in untangling the Anantha-threads. She would sit under the jasmine canopy in our courtyard and meticulously untangle the threads while singing 'Dasara-padagaLu'—Kannada devotional songs composed by the saints. I discovered that I had a natural skill for this activity and would join her in the task. I too would separate the threads one by one from the bunch. The two of us together would easily separate fifty or more Anantha-threads in an hour's time. If you separate a few threads initially, the rest become easy. All the relatives would come to us, one after the other, to get the thread tied around their wrists. After everybody was done, Kashavva would tie a thread around my wrist. Being a widow, she did not get to tie one around hers, but after tying mine she would caress my hair and bless me, 'You are so skilled in untangling knots, you will rise high in your career. Remember what I am saying, do not avoid solving complex puzzles.' My eyes become moist even today when I think of Kashavva. I firmly believe that with proper training she could have been a good programmer. It was a pity that she spent a miserable and lowly hand-to-mouth life until her last day. Bad luck gobbles up people's skills, I guess.

~

We walked out of the building after telling Ranganna to fasten the name plate. Usually, I bid adieu to candidates at the door after the interview, but I walked with Venkayya all the way to where he had parked his bike. I guess I was still in a good mood. I had been thinking how this Telugu boy had assembled the Kannada letters with such ease. I had started to like him very much.

'How do you know the Kannada alphabet, Venkayya?' I asked him with some curiosity. The night was cool, and the full moon was casting its glow on earth. Venkayya smiled with mild embarrassment. The dark-skinned, lean and tall Venkayya was an attractive man.

'I watch a lot of movies, sir, it has been my habit since childhood to read any wall poster I come across. I see a lot of Kannada movie posters in Bengaluru and try to read them all. There is not much of a difference between the Telugu and Kannada scripts. Only the symbols for emphasis, and for stretching and combining vowels with consonants, seem to vary a little. My mind had started reading any and all the Kannada letters that fell in my line of sight, and that's how I have learnt, sir,' he said.

After he sat on his bike, I casually asked him a question. 'You are such a smart man and still you ended up with bad grades in engineering exams. How come?' While asking this rather sensitive question, I had smiled and tried not to sound insulting. But the question had embarrassed him, nevertheless.

After a slight pause, he went on. 'Sir, when I was in the third year of engineering, I fell in love with a girl and lost interest in studies entirely. I felt, "I don't need or want anything except her company." When her parents came to know, they locked her up and started looking for another potential match for her. Finally, they found a groom and arranged for her wedding. Having realized that it was all going to be over and I was going to lose her, I recruited my friends and helped her escape from the room where her family had kept her under guard. We decided to get married at the Simhaachalam Narasimhaswamy temple, with friends as witnesses, and scheduled the date for the wedding. All our friends joined us at Visakhapatnam, which is very close to Simhaachalam. My friends were trying to rush us through the rituals when they got to know that the girl's parents had hired rowdies to kill us both. But the girl changed her mind as soon as we reached the temple.

She was crying non-stop. She said, "I cannot marry like a coward, I can't do this without the blessings of my parents." How could one marry a girl who was crying like that? So we cancelled the wedding and went back. But, sir, within a few days she agreed to marry the boy selected by her parents and totally forgot me. She cheated me. Those were difficult days.' His eyes welled up as he spoke.

After listening to his story patiently, I said with a wink, 'Mr Venkayya, I think you watch too many Telugu movies.' I shook his hands and walked back to the office building. I decided to offer him a handsome starting salary. My mind was settling into a kind of jolly mood.

～

Venkayya, a young man who had almost convinced a girl to marry him and had almost succeeded in eloping with her while in college, was soon able to attract the attention of his colleagues at work with his characteristic enthusiasm. People nicknamed him 'Venks'. Everyone came to know him within a couple of days of his joining our company. Colleagues went to chat with him now and then, as though they had known him for a long time. Young women from the ground floor visited his fifth-floor office in the guise of sharing their new, tasty food items with him. There was no dearth of cackling, giggling and loud howls of laughter around him.

He was good at his work and remarkably quick at finishing his assignments. It was really hard to figure when he really did his job. He also helped his colleagues when they needed assistance. Because he had studied in Telugu medium, his proficiency in English was not so good, but he acted as if it didn't matter in a software company. He was able to communicate with others in Kannada, Tamil, Malayalam and broken Hindi; he spoke with them in their respective mother tongues. Thus far, only Bollywood songs were allowed during the Friday-evening antaakshari event—that popular

Indian game played during social gatherings, where the next player picks up a song that begins with the ending syllable of the previous song. He fought and changed that practice and made sure that songs from all Indian languages were allowed. Popular Kannada songs like '*joke . . . naanu balliya minchu*' and songs in Manipuri and Marwari were now being sung and heard.

We had a practice of celebrating 'ethnic day' once or twice a year, during which the girls usually dressed up in silk saris, south Indian men came in dhotis and north Indian men in kurta-pyjamas. The staff would receive email instructions asking them to showcase dresses that depicted their regional culture. At the end of the event, there would be a poll to select the prize-winning costume. This was a long-standing practice in the company, and the winner would get a cash prize. But at the very first ethnic day after Venkayya's joining the company, strange events unfolded: and there was no doubt that it was Venkayya's costume that made it truly bizarre.

≈

I received a panicked call from the security folk that morning. 'Sir, it is urgent, please come over quickly,' one of them begged. 'What exactly is the matter?' I asked. 'Venkayya has brought three sheep with him, sir. He is demanding that we allow the sheep into the building, sir,' he explained. I was puzzled, wondering why Venkayya might have brought sheep to the workplace. With a lot of curiosity, I made my way to the office premises. I was dressed in a kacche-panche, a stylized dhoti, and a red shalya-top. I had applied the naama-mudre religious mark—the hallmark of a Maadhva Brahmin—rather conspicuously on my face for our ethnic-day event. I was imagining the grand presence of Appa in myself that day. Although that was Appa's routine attire, I could never get used to it. So I was walking very carefully, scared that if

I walked fast my dhoti would slip away. I was also very conscious of my bare chest under the silky smooth shalya, and was constantly adjusting and readjusting its position on my shoulder. A couple of boys had doubled my pleasure by asking, 'Bhattare, revered priest sir, please give us teertha, the holy water.'

It took me a while to recognize Venkayya, who was clad in a dirty dhoti tied up as a kacche-panche. The tough calf muscle of one of his legs sported a thick silver kadaga bracelet, a torn old rug covered his hairy chest, and he held an axe with a wooden handle on one shoulder. There was a tiger-nail necklace woven with a black kashi thread around his neck, a silver talisman tied very tightly around his right arm with a red thread, and a bamboo flute tucked into his dhoti. More interesting than anything else, he held in his other hand three ropes, the ends of which were tied to the necks of three sheep. A unique costume indeed! The sheep were yelling *'bya-bya'* at the unfamiliar master. God alone knows where he got those poor sheep from. Many passers-by and several of the company staff had assembled around him.

'What is this new avatar of yours?' I asked in bewilderment.

'My father was a shepherd, sir; this is how he dressed when he went shepherding,' he said, with no hesitation.

'Don't you think it is a bit much for the ethnic day event?' I babbled.

'You have dressed like your father and I have dressed like mine,' he said, offering me no concession. My mouth was starting to dry up.

In the meantime, the security person again asked me if he should allow Venkayya inside the office building or not.

'Leave your sheep outside and you get in,' I suggested.

He flashed his sharp axe as he replied: 'How will a shepherd go in without his sheep, sir? What if some wolf attacked my sheep?'

'Stop being impertinent, Venkayya! How can we allow sheep into the building? That is against the rules of the company.'

'If naama-mudre can enter the building, sheep can too . . . sir.'
As he looked around, many of onlookers said 'yes . . . yes . . .' in
his support.

'That is against the rules of the company.'

'Aren't the rules there to be broken, sir?'

Now I was getting angry. I did not see any need to get into an
argument with this man, but at the same time I had to respond with
caution. I suggested that the sheep be allowed inside the compound
where they could graze. There were plenty of greens grown by
the company and they could content themselves eating some of
the plants. Everyone seemed to agree when I recommended that
Venkayya alone should enter the main building.

The security guard asked, 'Sir, this man has a weapon in his
hand . . . what should we do?' Venkayya was not at all pleased. He
scolded the security guard, 'Don't you call it a weapon, my father
would be insulted.' I had to relax the rules a bit and asked the guard
to let Venkayya go through holding his axe.

As soon as he entered the reception area, Venkayya shook
his torn rug so hard that a cloud of dust spread all around. The
countless dust particles he had launched flashed happily under the
bright lights in the atrium.

No one worked that entire day. Sitting next to his axe,
Venkayya played on his flute and smoked beedis. Women folk
wearing fancy saris came to him again and again and complimented
him, 'How cute, Venks,' 'Venks, you are so smart,' 'I love it,' and
so on. Many of them even felt proud for the opportunity to have
a picture taken with him. The entire office turned into a one big
happy hangout.

Venkayya was the unchallenged winner by a margin of 90
percentage points; he made it a point to come to the stage to
receive his award along with his flute, the axe, and of course the
sheep! In addition, he declared that he would use the prize money
to throw a party for all his colleagues. Not just any party, he would

get the three sheep slaughtered and throw a 'non-veg' dinner for the meat-eaters. His friends yelled back 'Super!' and agreed to the plan. Their yelling became so loud that the sheep got scared and cried *'bya . . .'*

I had had enough of this so-called ethnic day and started repenting my decision. I thought it was time to revise the rules of the company.

~

Like most other Telugu boys, Venkayya too had an intense desire to go abroad. Such a desire seems to have spread among the people of Telugu culture like a contagion. The logic behind this desire seems to be the amount of dowry that a man could receive on returning from abroad. But some people, at least superficially, offer the explanation that working outside India is a sign of prestige among the community. Even Telugu girls wish to get foreign assignments, mainly for an opportunity to earn their dowries and relieve their parents from the burden of providing all of it.

I oversaw the company's UK projects and had the final say on who got to go to the UK, which was why many staff members often flocked around me. They praised me without reason, brought me gifts and showed keen interest in my projects to stay connected and visible. Venkayya was no exception. He had received my rebuke when he had blurted out, 'Sir, send me abroad somehow. I will give you 5 per cent of the dowry I collect.'

Venkayya was technically very sharp; he completed all his assignments flawlessly. But his English was awful, especially his writing. He struggled to write even a simple email. When I recommended remedial English courses, he showed no interest. 'Well, the manager of any project I am likely to be assigned to would, in all probability, be either a Telugu or a Kannada man, and I can converse with them in their respective languages and let them handle the communication with the clients. Why do you worry, sir,' he would say.

Finally, I did select him for a project and sent him to the UK. 'Thank you, boss. I want to treat you to a party but I am not sure how I can please you. You don't drink, you don't eat meat,' he said, making fun of my so-called virtues, before leaving.

As expected, Venkayya was hugely successful in the UK, so successful that the clients said they were very pleased with his organized approach at work. Although I had expected that conversing in English would give him trouble, he seemed to have also done a decent job of communicating with the clients. I started getting reports that the clients were taking turns to take him out to parties and picnics. I got another email saying he was getting too friendly with a local girl, which made a lot of his friends uncomfortable. As I knew he was after acquiring a big dowry from rich Telugu in-laws, I was sure he would not commit the blunder of falling in love. I did not take that email seriously. The man who had gone on a six-month assignment received an extension for two years, based on the recommendation of our clients.

But Venkayya lost interest in the UK quickly. He started calling me repeatedly and pressuring me: 'This is a small country, I am bored here, please send me to America.' He added that the men returning from America received a higher amount in dowry than those returning from the UK. I ignored his pleas. Our company was UK-based, and we had very few clients in the US. Even if we did get any work from clients in the US, the company could still do with fewer staff transfers. Besides, the current UK clients were very satisfied with Venkayya and had given him an extension for two years. Under these circumstances, it would have been utterly selfish for our employee to accept an assignment in some other country. Although we are all involved in business, how would the company look if we don't abide by minimum ethical standards? I told Venkayya teasingly, 'Anyway, you are supposed to give me

5 per cent of your dowry amount; I am willing to waive my share and that should make it even for you.'

At this juncture there was an unfortunate development. Venkayya's father fell seriously ill—the family thought he might not make it. Venkayya's family members called him and pressured him to return at once. He started calling me repeatedly, asking for leave so that he could return to India and attend to his father. It was a difficult decision for me. If I let him come back, the expense for the company would be nearly a lakh of rupees in airfare alone—those were still the golden days when the companies bore such travel expenses. In addition, we would lose up to four hundred pounds per day, which we would otherwise get from the UK project for his services. How would we make up for this sudden loss? At last, I said, 'OK, come home for three weeks, we will see what happens,' and gave my permission for his leave.

That was it. I never got to speak to him again.

∾

Venkayya went missing. His phone was switched off. All messages sent by courier to his residential address went unanswered. His friends had no clue either. A thought occurred to me to send someone from my staff to his village to look for him in person, but I decided against it as it could look like a private investigation. I suspected he might have joined some other company without our knowledge. I inquired with some known personnel managers but did not get any useful information. In any case, I knew no major company would employ him without a letter from us relieving him of his duties with our company.

Our clients started inquiring about Venkayya; they would ask about his father's health as a formality, but their main interest was to find out when he might return to work. Although we tried to stall it, eventually we had no choice but to convey the facts as we knew them. They were not willing to believe my words as they too wondered how someone could vanish so suddenly into thin air. Because Venkayya was deeply involved in all their projects, his absence was conspicuous. After waiting for a month, I had to replace him with another employee and remove his name from the employee directory.

≈

After nearly three months, Srinivasulu, one of my employees who was also a Telugu man from Venkayya's home district, hinted that he wanted to talk to me in private. He said he needed to share some insights about Venkayya's disappearance. I called him into my office right away. Srinivasulu came in with a worn Telugu newspaper in his hand and asked me to read a small announcement on the fifth page after spreading the paper on my desk. Being from Bellary, I could easily read Telugu.

The news item was written by a reporter from Chennai. It was about an incident describing the story of some hopelessly ambitious Telugu software professionals wanting to go to the US to seek employment there. The story was about an incident that occurred when they appeared for interviews at the consulate. Having received advance information about some Telugu applicants producing fake degree certificates and score cards, the consulate officials had called the universities directly to verify the authenticity of all the documents. When they found that some records were fake, the consulate informed the police. As a result, the police had suddenly raided and caught fifteen such applicants, who were eventually sent to the central jail in Coimbatore. The young men who had visited the consulate with the great ambition of obtaining an American visa were now behind bars. Before being sent to jail, they were all lined up and photographed. The report appeared along with the photo of the arrested candidates, neatly dressed in ties and suits.

The picture, however, was not very clear. The pictures that appeared in that cheap newspaper were never ever clear. And this photo was rather small. And yet Srinivasulu pointed to one person among the fifteen in the photo and said, 'Sir, I have no doubt this is Venkayya.' I was shocked beyond words. It took a while for the news to sink in. I looked again at the picture and I too started to feel it was Venkayya. For some reason it hurt me too much to look again.

≈

I could not figure out the exact sequence of events that may have led Venkayya to jail. But for someone like me, with years of experience working in the software industry, it was not hard to imagine what might have transpired. According to Venkayya, he had got entangled in a love affair with a girl and had got totally distracted from his studies. It resulted in his receiving poor grades in his final year at college. Despite that handicap, he had somehow managed to land a job. Slowly but surely, he must have escaped the clutches of the love that had intoxicated him and devoted himself to his profession. He must have progressed steadily on his career path. Gradually, with each subsequent success, he must have experienced a boost of self-confidence and an enhanced belief in his own abilities.

He must have started exploring alternative ways to reach the US, once he realized that his dream would never be realized through our company. He was also convinced that his grade report from his final year would come in the way of acquiring a job in America. This conviction must have forced him to resort to some crooked approach to obtain a fake certificate with inflated grades from some sham online 'university'. After several attempts, he must have succeeded in landing a job with a well-known company that agreed to send him to America. The company must have asked him to apply for an H-1 visa with the US consulate. Because Indians could not receive an H-1 visa from the UK, he had to find a way to return to India for the purpose. So he came up with this fake excuse that his father was ill, hoping that he could quickly get the visa in India and fly immediately to the US. His intention must have been to simply send me an email stating that he was resigning from his job. But unfortunately for him, he became a victim of an unexpected sting operation conducted by the US consulate in Chennai, which sent him straight to the central jail in Coimbatore. He was probably too embarrassed to contact me.

Several times I felt the urge to go to Coimbatore, meet him in jail and speak to him. His picture amidst the fifteen Indians dressed in sharp executive suits haunted me for quite some time. Having had the opportunity to observe him closely and gauge his enormous potential—a unique combination of smartness, enthusiasm and an adventurous spirit—I experienced a deep sadness that somehow, something was wrong in our system. When someone can do a job, why do we value meaningless grades given by some stupid university? Why does our society give all this so much importance? Without changing some outdated rules and forging a way towards new systems, can there be any progress?

3 March 2017

The Cracked Tumbler

Ramabai wakes up even before the rooster starts crowing at dawn. She talks and talks nonstop the entire day. First, she pulls the blanket off her son Gururaja and screams at him, 'Get up you lazy bum, the entire world is up, and you are still in bed.' She then turns her attention to the sleeping Hulikunti, her husband. 'Get up, my dear, it is morning. I need to touch your feet,' she pleads, sarcastically. He, in turn, rubs his eyes, raises his hand as though he is blessing her, and goes back to sleep, pulling the blanket over his head.

Next, she sweeps the front yard with a broom making all sorts of *flish-flash* noises, splashes water on the courtyard, and turns towards the sky—she doesn't spare even the sun. She throws a potful of water at the sky and, yelling at the sleepy sun, takes him to task: 'You, useless bum, why don't you wake up?' Scared of her endless ranting, the sun gathers courage bit by bit and attempts to rise higher and higher. Next, when she starts decorating the floor with the traditional rangoli, the loud call of the muezzin streams in from the nearby mosque. Listening to the muezzin's groggy voice, she agonizes over why the Mullah has got no relief from his cold even after a week. Completing the rangoli, Ramabai comes in and starts washing the previous day's dirty utensils. Unable to sleep due to the jangling noise of the utensils, Hulikunti gets up and squats outside on the elevated step, smoking his usual Ganesh beedi.

Ramabai shines the dirty dishes so sparkly clean that even the sun squints at their brightness. She then sets water on the stove for the morning tea; she drinks a cup and offers one to her husband sitting outside. She starts with her usual complaint, 'You will soon make me a widow by this constant beedi smoking.' He takes one sip and simply smiles through his moustache, which is getting wet with the hot tea. She returns inside to find her son still sleeping. Now she resorts to force; she drags him out of bed, folds the sheets and rolls up his mattress. Gururaja asks in a pleading voice, 'Tea for me . . .?' 'Do you want to drink tea with a stale mouth, like your father? Go . . . at least rinse your mouth and come.' Gururaja runs to the bathroom obediently.

Paddakka from the Rayara Mutth sends some fresh jasmine flowers in the evening regularly, which Ramabai saves in a wet cloth; in the morning she takes out the flowers and laces them into a garland. When her hands get a bit tired of lacing them, she does not even spare the saint, Sri Raghavendraswamy. She asks him, 'What kind of a strange desire is it for a male saint to sport fresh flowers?' By this time, Gururaja finishes finger-brushing his teeth with salt and splashing the bathroom with several mugs of water; he comes and shows his teeth to his mother—'eeee'—and Ramabai examines his mouth to see if all his teeth are in their respective places.

This is how the morning starts in this two-room windowless house on Kalamma Road, equipped only with small holes that serve as vents for smoke—and all this for just a rent of Rs 30.

≈

Ramabai was somewhat agitated and overly anxious that day. A fifteen-paise postcard had arrived the previous day from her brother Varadanna, who lived in the distant city of Visakhapatnam. The summary of what he had written in the card—which was adorned with the auspicious red kumkum on all four corners and also right in the centre between two lines—was the happy news of his daughter's wedding. The wedding was next week, and Varadanna had fixed the alliance with an Andhra family.

Ramabai had been brought up by Varadanna as their mother had passed away when she was still very young. Neither had any memory of their father. They had enough income from the wetlands on the banks of the Tungabhadra river inherited from their ancestors, which took care of their livelihood, food and clothing. Varadanna, nearly ten years older than Ramabai, had taken good care of her, showering her with a lot of affection. Even today, during times of distress, she thinks of Varadanna, not her mother. When she cries, she does not say 'Amma,' rather, she says 'Anna.'

Varadanna had married a woman from Andhra—one Mr Subrahmanyagaru, who had come on some business to Bellary, had not only helped Varadanna find a government job but had also made him commit to marry his daughter. Although Varadanna had stayed back in Bellary after the wedding for a couple of years, his wife had insisted that he ask for a transfer to the Andhra circle. Until Ramabai married Hulikunti, Ramabai accompanied her brother and her vainy, her sister-in-law, wherever they went. Varadanna had worked and lived in places like Kurnool, Anantapur and Adoni.

To find a suitable match for Ramabai was not easy; she was dark-complexioned and had protruding upper teeth. Nobody had shown any interest in her as she was also lanky, like a cane. Varadanna had made several trips to Bellary in search of a suitable boy; however, vainy didn't care to take part in this matchmaking. She would state, with a show of 'Andhra-arrogance': 'No one from our side in Andhra would ever agree to marry her.' After several rejections, Varadanna too had started accepting the fact that his sister wasn't the best-looking girl around. This broke his heart.

It was during one of those days when Varadanna had gone to see the village fair and also to pay a visit to the family deity, Gandi-Narasimhaswamy, that someone suggested Hulikunti as a prospective groom for her. Once upon a time, it seems, the Hulikunti family was very well-to-do in the region. However, Hulikunti's father resorted to the 'company of women' from the infamous town of Kudligi and lost all his riches to them. Eventually he had contracted 'secret' diseases, to which he succumbed. The remaining assets were confiscated by the loan-sharks, leaving Hulikunti literally on the street. Some well-wishers had helped him get a job in a printing press; he had to say goodbye to school and become a permanent employee of Kommanna's Sreevenkateshwara Printing Press.

Hulikunti was lean and dark, and shorter than Ramabai. Knowing his own limitations, Hulikunti had readily agreed to marry Ramabai. Vainy had started acting as if the world would end if the wedding didn't happen on its proposed date. She kept asking, 'Do you agree? Do you agree?' Ramabai felt compelled to say 'yes' to end the constant nagging. Varadanna was not at all comfortable about this alliance, but he was worried that they would have to return to a future of rejections if this didn't go through. One day, when Ramabai was watering the jasmine plants, he went to her and expressed his concern: 'He is shorter than you . . .' She emptied the pot over the plant and said, 'He is a man, isn't he? Anna, that is more than enough for me. I shall think of him as the Lord's avatar—Vaamana the dwarf—who has come to save me.' She was emotionless when she uttered those words. Seeing Varadanna looking downcast, she said, 'At least, he doesn't have buckteeth like me, right?' and laughed. Varadanna too smiled.

The wedding bells rang under the auspices of Gandi-Narasimhaswamy. Varadanna and vainy took on the parental role of handing over Ramabai in the *kanyaadaana* ritual. But they did not have their counterparts sitting across them alongside Hulikunti for the ceremonies. Although Kommanna, his employer, had brought two pairs of dhotis and a shirt for the groom, and a sari for the bride, he was not allowed to be a part of the Vedic rituals as he belonged to a 'different' caste. 'How can we proceed without a couple on the groom's side to welcome the bride into the family and be a part of the rituals?' the priest said, in a harassing tone. Helpless Hulikunti requested some of the invited couples to take his parents' place, but they all refused as they felt it was not appropriate to take on the role of parents for a total stranger. They said they had come just to sprinkle the coloured rice, mantraakshate, on the couple at the end, bless them and partake of the feast. They would do nothing beyond that. Finally, the priest Venkannachary of the Rayara Mutth and his wife Paddakka agreed to play the role of the groom's parents. Paddakka said, 'We are the priest-couple for our town and we don't discriminate, every child is our child,' and resolved the issue. Varadanna's daughter, Rohini, got to be the bearer of the sacred kalasha pot for both the bride and the groom.

Ramabai and Hulikunti started their family with love and blended together like ragi-cake and honey. For an orphan like Hulikunti, who had no one to share his love or happiness with, a loving wife like Ramabai made a world of a difference, and he surrendered himself completely to her. Ramabai too became like a bird that had just flown its cage. After living under vainy's restrictive shadow, the sudden freedom she now had in Hulikunti's household allowed her to slowly show her true colours. She started to yell at the maid who supplied the milk, 'If you keep adding water to milk like this, I will add water to the money I owe you.' From then on, Gowrakka supplied only unadulterated milk. Ramabai took control of the entire household. Huge rangolis started appearing in the courtyard. Hulikunti, who was used to wearing simple white pyjama and kurta, had to wear shirts in various colours tailored by her. She made sure he wore them to work, even though Hulikunti said 'I feel odd wearing coloured shirts.'

Once they got married, they slowly loosened their ties with Varadanna's family as her brother's work took him farther and farther away, to towns like Bezwada, Guntur and Rajahmundry. When he was in Rajahmundry, his father-in-law helped him buy a transport bus; the bus started plying between Rajahmundry and Visakhapatnam twice a week. The goddess of wealth Lakshmi opened her eyes for him and his fortunes doubled. Before the year ended he was able to purchase another bus. Eventually, Varadanna quit his government job. Now Varadanna owns ten buses. His father-in-law has passed away, leaving all his assets to him. He has become so prosperous that he is now addressed as 'Varada Rao-gaaru' among his kith and kin. He is so busy now he does not have the time even to 'scratch his butt', so to speak. So, obviously, he has not found the time to visit his sister in Bellary. In a courtesy letter to Ramabai, he wrote: 'Whenever you feel like seeing me, just come over,' and washed his hands of his brotherly duties. But Ramabai did not feel any strong urge to visit him either. Even when Gururaja was born, she did not go to his place for post-natal care or for rest and recuperation. She simply took some help from her local friends for around ten days and got back on her feet to resume the tough daily routines.

When Rohini got her first period, Varadanna wrote to Ramabai and insisted that she attend the ceremony; the three visited him at the time. Although she had some inkling of Varadanna's finances, she had no clue as to how much he really made. They spent those few days in unfamiliar luxury; all they did was eat, drink, sleep and while away their time. There were servants for every little task. Hulikunti had no knowledge of Telugu; he sat like a mute person watching people's faces. When he squatted in the backyard smoking a beedi, some relative of Varadanna's offered him a cigarette out of pity.

Something happened one morning that made them leave for Bellary immediately, even though Varadanna had insisted that they stay a couple more days. Ramabai had brought a dhoti from Bellary for Varadanna and a sari for vainy as gifts. Vainy had opened the boxes out of courtesy and put the garments aside for a wash, along with the rest of the laundry. The red sari had bled colour and transferred its pigments to the rest of the laundry of the guests. Everyone was talking about this, which embarrassed Ramabai. When she went to the backyard, she saw all the laundry hung on the ropes to dry; the clothes were tinged with the red dye from the cheap sari she had given as a gift to vainy. She felt extremely humiliated and ashamed. She decided to pack up and leave that very moment. Varadanna too did not stop her.

Now, it is Rohini's wedding. If the event was in some other random town, she probably wouldn't have cared to go, but the wedding was going to take place in Tirupati. They wouldn't have ventured on a Tirupati trip on their own, but now there was a compelling reason. A great opportunity had presented itself for the pilgrimage to the holy town—they had to go.

～

Hulikunti leaves home at nine in the morning after breakfast and does not return until nine at night. He gets a break for lunch at around the same time when hit movie songs are broadcast from the Dharwad radio station. He takes a nap after lunch and returns to work, around the same time that Radio Sri Lanka station broadcasts Telugu songs by Ponnadore. Because of the nature of his work, he must stand all day, while assembling metallic letters or pedalling the printing machine. He has developed constant pain in his legs from this activity. As soon as he comes home, he squats in the courtyard and smokes beedis. He doesn't volunteer to do even a small chore at home. He doesn't mind the constant bickering and cursing from Ramabai, which he has learnt to ignore. In fact, he goes looking for her if the bickering stops.

Ramabai had given him a major task that day of asking his boss, Kommanna, for three days' leave to attend the wedding and some money for travel expenses. Kommanna is a man who makes him work even on Yugaadi—New Year's Day; Hulikunti didn't know how to approach him for three days' leave. How do you ask for extra money from a man who doesn't even pay the monthly salary on time?

On his way to work, Hulikunti routinely picks up some fresh flowers, a coconut, a few lemons and incense sticks from a store near the bus stand. He starts his daily ritual of worshipping the printing machines as soon as he reaches his workplace: he removes the dried-out flowers and stale lemon halves and cleans the machines thoroughly. Then he cuts the lemons into halves, places one half on each side of the press, lights an incense stick, breaks open the coconut and offers it to God. He takes a small piece and offers it to Kommanna as prasaada and later to the two boys who work with him.

Soon after the pooja that morning, Hulikunti approached his boss, 'Kommanna, I need to go for a wedding . . .'

'Whose wedding?'

'Wife's brother's daughter's. She thinks very highly of her brother . . .'

'How many days?'

'Three days . . . also, need some advance for miscellaneous expenses . . .'

Kommanna said nothing. Hulikunti continued with his work, not knowing what else to do.

In some time, when he went to review the draft of a wedding invitation, Kommanna found a typo in the name of the groom—the name was 'Manjunata' instead of 'Manjunatha'. The soft consonant would change the meaning terribly. Kommanna gave Hulikunti a good scolding.

Hulikunti hesitantly tried to remind his boss again before lunch about his leave. 'If it is her brother's daughter's wedding, let her go and attend, we have weddings here too, don't we? Who will print those wedding invitations?' He flatly rejected Hulikunti's request. In the evening, Hulikunti got ready to go home with a sad face.

'Which town is the wedding going to be?' Kommanna asked. 'Tirupati,' said Hulikunti. As soon as he heard the name of the town, Kommanna stood up and brought his hands together with great reverence and said Edukondalavada, Lord of the Seven Hills. 'Why didn't you say that first? You made me say no to a person going to Tirupati! Lord Venkataramana, please forgive me, forgive me.' He slapped his own cheeks and chin with his hands. He not only granted three days' leave but also handed Hulikunti five hundred rupees and said, 'Don't think of this as an advance, this is for your expense; if any money is left, put it in the collection box . . . Don't forget to bring two laddus, two vade, a Kashi-thread, and a photo of the Lord.'

Hulikunti was delighted that his problem was solved with such ease.

∾

Hulikunti's income is insufficient to make both ends meet, so Ramabai pitches in by making chakli, kodubale, nippattu and other fried snacks for sale. She does not bother to break her crispy chaklis into pieces just to make the weight precise; rather, she gives away some extra snacks to the buyers. This makes her customers extra loyal to her. It is also true that her products taste unique.

The fact that Hulikunti's boss had given him three days off from work and five hundred rupees for expenses made Ramabai very happy. She kneaded a bit more dough for the chaklis than usual. She felt that she needed to share her excitement as soon as possible, but she was concerned that if the trip got cancelled for some silly reason, she would have to face humiliation. She refrained from voluntarily disclosing any details to anyone.

She had just started dropping a few kodubales into the boiling oil, when lo, there came Kashavva along with her basket of cotton, ready for making wicks for the oil lamps. It was a standard practice for Kashavva to show up for her routine gossip session soon after Hulikunti left for the printing press in the afternoon.

After talking about some mundane things, Kashavva came straight to the point, 'Looks like you received someone's letter recently?' Ramabai replied, 'Yes, it is my brother's daughter's wedding. He is eager to go, even his boss has given permission. But, somehow, I am not so sure if I really want to go . . .' She pretended to not be interested.

'Oh, where did you say the wedding was?'

'Tirupati.'

Kashavva suddenly became alert. '*Le*, Rama, your family belongs to the "steal and offer" category! Didn't you know? You must steal something before going to Tirupati and offer the stolen money or object as dakshina, your contribution at Tirupati. Otherwise, the head of the household will throw up blood and die.' Her pronouncement scared the hell out of Ramabai, who had not heard of any families that belonged to this category of people nor about any such requirements to be followed by them.

'This is exactly why I am telling you. You see, you have no elders left in your family to tell you about such traditions. Poor you, how could you have known?' She began to give her the background to what she had said and told Ramabai stories about the families that were bound by this 'steal and offer' rule. Ramabai immediately reduced the flame-level on her stove and started listening intently to Kashavva.

'Hulikunti's great-grandfather's great-grandfather's name was Bheemasena, who was a bodybuilder and a wrestler. He was so strong that on Ramanavami day, he could drag the Lord's decorated teru chariot all by himself! This incredible hulk got married to a girl who was as delicate as a jasmine flower. Can you imagine how happy Bheemya must have been? He would take his new bride with him wherever he went. Once he took his wife, bedecked with gold ornaments, to the Gandi-Narasimhaswamy temple fair. There they had organized a contest, which involved climbing a pillar smeared with oil and lighting the lamp at its pinnacle. Most of the young men would slip and slide down after reaching half-way up the pillar. This Bheemya, though, wanted to show off his virtuosity to his new wife. He removed his shirt, tightened his dhoti, tied it between his legs, and started to climb the pillar. People started gathering to watch.

'He would climb a bit, get a little ahead and then slide down and lose whatever advance he had made, then repeat it and look at his wife, who would smile awkwardly. Her smile encouraged him to advance further. This way, he managed to climb to the top of the pillar, light the lamp, lift the victory garland and put it around his neck. The mob went wild and shouted slogans of victory. He looked proudly at his wife, who was fully immersed in the moment and was applauding excitedly. But from his vantage point, Bheemasena spotted a thief cutting off his wife's braid along with the gold ornament plaited into it. Bheemya slid down the oiled pillar with lightning speed and started running towards his wife, yelling and screaming. But it was too late by the time he reached her; the thief had snatched the gold ornament and was fleeing. The chopped braid lay on the ground. His wife, feeling her head unusually light, shook it. Her shortened, uneven hair spread out on either side, making her look weird. As soon as she realized what had happened, she started screaming in a frenzy.

'Although Bheemasena was running like a deer, the thief who was lean and fit ran even faster. But the humiliation inflicted on his wife right in front of him had enraged him enough to make him run like mad. He followed the thief along uneven ground and past wild bushes, where many birds, including peacocks, were nesting. A few of them got so startled by the unexpected entry of humans that they flew away making frantic noises. Bheemasena followed him all the way to Kanivelli village, when the thief ran out of wind, gave up and was caught. Bheemasena thrashed him soundly, tied him up using his own dhoti and dragged him along like a mace.

'He ran to his wife, who had been crying nonstop, threw the man at her feet and again started beating him with a cane until he started to bleed. His wife, now scared to see Bheemya's ferociousness, said, 'enough, enough' and stopped him from hitting the thief more. But soon a crowd gathered around; they had realized a thief had been caught and started landing blows on the man who had already been beaten up badly. Many of them had lost something to some thief somewhere some time, and felt justified in punishing any thief caught red-handed. Some of them thrashed him as if they were trying to settle an old score. Eventually, Bheemasena lost control of the situation and the mob took over. Some male dancers were so drunk by then, they went after the thief with a vengeance. Before things cooled off, the thief had breathed his last.

'"Sreeramulu" was the name of this thief, who belonged to distant Guntakal. He visited all the fairs in and around Bellary, mainly to steal, but he had a unique quality to him. He was a great devotee of Lord Tirupati Timmappa; he would donate half of whatever he stole to the collection box of the Lord's temple. Whether he stole gold ornaments or silk saris, he firmly believed that it was due to the Lord's mercy that he had not been caught stealing. Lord Timmappa too had shown him immense grace and love. So the Lord was none too pleased to see one of his favourite devotees face such a dire end. He waited for the right opportunity to teach a lesson to Bheemasena.

'With time, a good-looking child was born to Bheemasena. As there were some complications at the time of the child's delivery, Bheemasena had prayed to his favourite deity and pledged that he would conduct the first-hair-offering ceremony at the Tirupati temple if the baby were a boy; and if it were a girl he would perform a *kalyaanotsava*, the re-enactment and celebration of the Lord's wedding ceremony, at Tirupati. By God's grace, both mother and child survived the complications. The boy started to grow like the ascending moon. His hair grew so long that before he was three it would cover his eyes. Bheemasena's wife started complaining that the boy would be soon look like a girl as she would have to start braiding his hair. Finally, Bheemasena ventured to fulfil his pledge. That is when Lord Timmappa woke up and eagerly awaited the opportune moment that had finally arrived.

'On reaching Tirupati, Bheemasena lifted his feet to climb the hill, but . . . that was it, the entire step appeared like cooked rice! "What is going on," he wondered, rubbing his eyes to check if what he was seeing was real. His wife had gone ahead and climbed several steps by then. He tried again, but saw the same cooked rice again. He tried skipping a step and climbing the next, but it was no different this time. He saw nothing but rice on all the steps and stopped right there. His wife was calling out to him and asking him to climb up fast, "Come on, why did you stop right there?" He looks up, and what does he find? The whole hill is a monstrous mountain of cooked rice. The bushes, plants, rocks—they were all nothing but rice, and Bheemasena wasn't brave enough to step on Goddess Annapoorna, who blesses everyone with food. He simply collapsed and sat down there. His wife climbed down and joined him.

'Three days and three nights he struggled, but failed to climb the hill. How could he fulfil his pledge without climbing the hill? How could he think of returning without fulfilling the pledge? Devastated, Bheemasena went to consult a saint who was sitting deep in meditation nearby. Upon hearing his predicament, the saint surmised what must have happened and said, without opening his eyes, "He stole gold and you stole his life; your sin is bigger. Therefore, atonement is required, and a suitable reparation is a must." Bheemasena begged the saint to suggest to him a suitable reparation. "You need to offer something stolen by you in the form of charity; anything small is fine, but you need to steal and offer it to the Lord's collection box. And while doing so you must think of the life you have taken and repent for it," said the saint, and resumed his meditation.

'How could a man who had lived an aristocratic life steal? But there appeared to be no alternative to escaping the Lord's wrath. The following day, Bheemasena went to a shop that sold worship-miscellanea, purchased hundreds of rupees' worth of articles from there, and quickly stole a bell. He was sweating profusely; he couldn't help recalling the Sreeramulu incident.

'Look,' said Kashavva, 'This is the story of your ancestors; from that day onwards, anyone from your family, whenever they went to Tirupati, had to steal something for an offering, otherwise Timmappa won't give you way to climb the hill.' By the time she finished the story, she had twisted and spun a hundred cotton wicks for the lamp.

Now Ramabai got very worried. 'Where will I go to steal, Kashavva?' she agonized. '*Ayyayyamma*, why would you, a pious married woman, bother to do such petty things as stealing? Don't we have menfolk to do such rotten things? You see, they steal old and used stuff for burning during Kaamana Habba, the annual fire ritual to commemorate how the god of love, Manmatha, was turned to smoke by Lord Eshwara. This is also like that.'

By then Gururaja appeared, pretending to be driving a bus, making a 'burrrrr' sound. His mouth watered the moment he saw his mother frying kodubales. He swung his backpack off his with such force that it flew and landed on the pile of bedding in the corner. He quickly picked up a couple of kodubales and put them in his shirt pocket; he broke one and put it inside his mouth, trying to simultaneously sing a nursery rhyme with made-up words to suggest he was calling the parrots to eat the kodubales. The kodubale was fresh off the frying pan and was so hot that he was making strange noises while trying to toss it about with his tongue to avoid burning his mouth. 'The total weight of my kodubale packets will be low now,' said Ramabai in mock anger, giving him a gentle spank. Gururaja's reaction was to snatch one more and place it in his knicker pocket. Kashavva scolded him for touching the snacks without washing his hands and feet after returning from school. Gururaja made her even angrier by squatting in front of her and eating the kodubales, making crunchy sounds. And on top of that, he made fun of her shaven head by singing, 'Granny is a baldy, granny is a baldy,' and scampered away.

～

First thing the next morning, the father–son duo went on a stealing adventure after a quick breakfast of spicy puffed rice. 'Don't you be scared, I have informed Paddakka about the whole scheme, OK?' Ramabai assured him, but Hulikunti wasn't convinced one bit and continued to complain. He was getting fed up of this entire Tirupati project.

Yenkannachar was sitting in his courtyard with several items of worship and other miscellanea spread before him. Paddakka was preparing hulipalya, a sour curry with dal and methi leaves, and the pleasant aroma was all-pervading. 'What brings you here?' asked Yenkannachar, looking at Hulikunti and his son. 'Is Paddakka home?' asked Hulikunti; Paddakka came out as soon as she heard his voice.

'Come, come, Ramabai has told me all about your need to . . . you know . . . stea . . . l' she said with a smile. Yenkannachar was shocked. 'What? Why would they want to steal . . .?' he babbled in confusion. 'I will tell you all about it later, first, leave everything and go away for a while,' she ordered her husband.

'Hulikunti, take whatever you like, don't hesitate, but please don't touch the silver articles, OK? They are all prescriptively cleansed for worship and their sanctity must be maintained,' she said, showing her magnanimity and setting limits at the same time. Having said this, she too walked out, leaving father and son to themselves.

Hulikunti felt a slight chill and shivered inside. He looked around to decide what he should steal: the metallic gong that was hanging on a peg, the grinding stone set up in the corner, the clothes hung to dry on the horizontal bamboo staves, the shining utensils of bronze and copper, the sticks with hanging dry noodles, the boiling hulipalya on the stove, the rangoli mould on the pedestal near God's abode, and so on; he couldn't decide! Up on the attic, he saw a pack of cigarettes hidden by Yenkannachar's son, which he felt would be a lot more fun to steal.

Gururaja was thinking of taking what they didn't have: the radio sitting in a corner, a wall clock that strikes hourly, a bag full of marbles, a colourful Ganesha idol on a pedestal, a pack of colourful paper parrots hanging from the ceiling, the swing set in the courtyard and, more than anything else, a toothbrush and toothpaste found in the bathroom, which his father would never buy for him!

Hulikunti, though, was looking for the least expensive and most insignificant thing of all. Finally, he sighted a steel tumbler filled with rangoli powder, which had a distinct crack in its otherwise nice body. He decided that it was the most suitable item for stealing; he emptied out all the rangoli powder in a corner and placed that tiny tumbler into his pyjama pocket. Gururaja tempted his father to steal the coloured sunglasses, but he refused. 'You see, they decorate Tirupati Timmappa with three wide white stripes so large that they almost cover both his eyes and make it impossible for him to see, what will he do with sunglasses?' he said, and taking his son's hand, walked out.

Paddakka and Yenkanna, who stood just outside the house, stared closely at them when the two walked past. Paddakka went in and examined the entire house to determine what they might have stolen. When she saw the rangoli powder spilled in the corner, it became obvious. 'Stupid ass, what a naïve fool . . .' she cursed him affectionately, and praised his innocence.

As soon as he reached home, Hulikunti handed the tumbler to Ramabai and went out to the courtyard to smoke a beedi, squatting in his usual spot. Ramabai was amazed to see the rarest of rare items that her husband had found to steal, and slapped her own forehead in exasperation and disgust.

'Did you think of anyone when you stole this tumbler?' she asked him promptly.

'Yes. I could only think of the police and nothing else.'

'Oh, no! I completely forgot to remind you to think of Sreeramulu while stealing,' Ramabai lamented, as she wrung her hands.

~

After finishing all the chores, Ramabai packed a few kodubales, picked up a string of jasmine flowers that she had laced in the morning and started for Paddakka's house. She hid the kodubales within the folds of her sari so that the monkeys along the way would not see them. As soon as she reached Paddakka's house, she placed the flower string at the God's abode and the kodubales in a corner of the kitchen, washed her hands by sprinkling some water on them and went to the backyard.

As the maid Narasakka had not come to work that day, Paddakka was sitting with all the unwashed utensils spread before her. Ramabai said to her: 'Get up, Paddakka, why would you wash these, come on, get up.' She made her get up and started washing the utensils using rangoli powder and tamarind juice. Paddakka, who leaned against the tulasi-katte, said, 'If the Lord ever came alive and asked him, "What do you want?" he would probably ask for a pack of beedis,' as a way of appreciating Hulikunti's naiveté. Ramabai drew a few pots of water from the well, washed all the utensils, dried them using a cloth and put them away in their places in the kitchen, as naturally as if she were working in her own home.

After some small talk, Paddakka offered Ramabai a cup of panchamruta, a delicious mixture of milk, honey, sugar, curd and ghee. It had probably been 'sitting' since morning, and so had turned a bit sour, although it was still tasty. Ramabai washed the cup after finishing the drink and spoke with much hesitation: 'Paddakka, I want to ask you for something, give it if you want, or say no, it is okay . . .' Paddakka reassured her, not once but twice, 'Why do you hesitate so much, go ahead and ask.' Finally, Ramabai felt relaxed enough to say, 'You know, our Varadanna is a rich man. The wedding we are attending . . . you see, apparently the groom's side also is filthy rich. The wedding will undoubtedly be grand. See, I don't have any ornaments, except this black-bead necklace attached to my holy mangalasutra. I am concerned that all my relatives might look down upon me. That's why . . . if you could loan me your gold bangles, I will wear them during the wedding and return them to you when I get back. If you don't like the idea, it is okay . . . I will understand.' The woman who took the sun to task daily felt terribly small and cringed as she uttered these words. Paddakka removed two gold bangles from each hand without a hint of hesitation and said, 'Here, take these, why are you feeling so bad? Wear them and walk around with your head held high in the wedding hall.' She handed them to Ramabai. Ramabai had never expected Paddakka to part with her bangles and loan them to her so easily; she felt overwhelmed at her generosity and burst into tears looking at the bangles that had come into her possession so effortlessly. 'I thought you might not agree, Paddakka,' she wept tremulously. 'Please don't cry. A muttaide, a pious married woman like you, should not cry at the time of dusk, it is very unsettling for me,' consoled Paddakka, stroking Ramabai's back.

≈

The metal trunk lying under the heap of rolled-up beds was taken out and thoroughly dusted, wiped with a wet cloth and dried; its latch was opened by removing the temporary padlock made of light, corky wood. All the freshly washed clothes were packed in the suitcase, including Ramabai's wedding sari, of which she took extra care. Small packets of kodubales, rava laddus, chutney powder and methi-powder gojju also went in. As they had heard it could get chilly in the Tirupati hills, Gururaja's sweater too went into the box. A few mothballs, oil and comb for the hair, sacred threads, a small framed portrait of the Lord, some lemons and a couple of Kannada novels were among the things the family decided to carry along.

Kashavva, Gopanna, Radhakka, Yenkannachar and Paddakka accompanied Ramabai's family to the bus stand to send them off. Among them, Gopanna master was the only one who had done the Tirupati pilgrimage. He gave them instructions in a loud and authoritative voice about how to change trains, whom to trust and whom not to, what to see, and so on. Finally, he didn't forget to say, 'See, Hulikunti, you need to be extra careful when it comes to money. In that town, it is not just the humans that like your money, but even the Lord has an eye on your pocket.' When the bus was about to leave, Paddakka untied the corner of her sari, in which she had brought some yellow rice grains as a blessing from the Rayara Mutth, and placed a few grains in each one's head and wished them: 'Have a safe and rewarding trip, we will see you soon after your return.' Kashavva took Ramabai to a corner of the bus and handed her her holy mangalasutra. She said: 'Please offer this in the collection box for me. Tell that Lord Timmappa whose debt never gets cleared that he should bless that poor, blasted mendicant, whoever it is that is going to be my husband in my next life, at least a few years of life after he marries me.'

They kept waving until the bus disappeared from view.

≈

The Hulikunti family reached Bellary railway station three hours before the train was to arrive. For Hulikunti and his son it was their maiden train journey, although Ramabai had taken the train a few times with her brother. Still, she felt a bit uneasy. She inquired from some people about when the train might arrive. Gururaja was asking why there were no boards in front of the trains mentioning their destination, the way buses had. Hulikunti was thrilled to see that one of the notices on the board had been printed at his press.

Gururaja saw a chocolate wrapped in purple paper at a store and demanded it. After scolding him a couple of times and failing to coax him out of his obstinacy to have it, Ramabai went to buy it for him. When the shopkeeper said that each chocolate cost a rupee, she was shocked beyond belief. 'You get two liters of milk for a rupee, how can a piece of chocolate cost a rupee? I will pay ten paise,' she told him. 'This chocolate is imported, that is why it costs a lot,' the man explained. She offered to buy Gururaja some other snack in its place, like a peppermint or biscuits, but to no avail. Ramabai spanked him on his behind a few times, and that made things even worse. Gururaj started to scream and roll about on the platform to arrest everyone's attention. Finally, seeing no alternative, she parted with a rupee and got her son a chocolate that was as wide as his palm.

She unwrapped the cover carefully, broke off a piece and gave it to Gururaja, who quickly put it into his mouth and tried to feel the taste by slowly chewing and rolling his tongue around it.

He didn't like it one bit; he ran to the edge of the platform and spat it out. He rinsed his mouth and rubbed his teeth and gums clean using his finger. 'Is it not good?' asked Ramabai. 'No, it tastes somewhat bitter and strange . . .' he said, and refused to eat the remaining portion. Ramabai lamented, 'I paid a rupee for that,' and turned to her husband and asked him, 'Why don't you try a piece?' Hulikunti, who had already lit a beedi and started to smoke, thought it would be not manly to try a chocolate meant for children and refused. Finally, Ramabai put a piece of it in her mouth. Gururaja thought she too would spit it out; Hulikunti was curious to see what she would do. Ramabai, however, kept it in her mouth, trying to melt it slowly, and made funny faces as she experienced the unfamiliar chocolate taste. She then took a second piece of the chocolate, and Gururaja asked her if she found it tasty. She replied, 'It is kind of soft and tastes strange.' She then ventured to eat a third piece. When Hulikunti asked if she was liking the chocolate, she said, 'I enjoyed the third piece more than the first.'

Having eaten the first three pieces one after the other, she ate the remaining portion all at once. Although Hulikunti too wanted to try a piece, he felt too shy to ask her because he had rejected her offer of it earlier. Gururaja was upset that his mother had eaten the chocolate that was originally bought for him and now started a fresh demand for a ginger-peppermint. Ramabai would not indulge him any more. She continued to enjoy the leftover taste of chocolate in her mouth.

In the meantime, the ground started to tremble and there was flurry of porters moving around on the platform. The third bell went off and the whisle of their train could be heard in the distance. People got up. Gururaja, who had been crying his lungs out, became quiet at once, got up and went to his mother and held her hand, watching with amazement the approaching bright light of the engine. Hulikunti threw away his half-smoked beedi and lifted the steel trunk on to his head.

When the loud whistle went off again, they all shivered lightly and drew even closer to one another. As the wheels chugged towards them, they could hear the thrum of their quickening heartbeats. The vendor boys serving snacks started yelling in high excited voices, 'Dosé idli, coffee, tea . . .'

The family went looking for the general compartment from one end of the platform to the other, and after much inquiring finally found where it was. The crowd was enormous, and they had no clue how to push themselves ahead in that rush. They stood back in hesitation, but soon they managed to hold on to each other and push themselves towards the middle of the crowd, which slowly moved into the compartment.

≈

It was already afternoon when they reached the foot of the hill and the sun was scorching. Ghantasala's song was playing in a loop from the store's stereo system: 'Om Namo Venkatesha, Om Namo Tirumalesha . . .' They were told that it would take about four hours to climb the hill and that there was an arrangement for having their luggage carried up, provided they locked it properly. They had only tied a rope around their steel trunk. When they looked for a lock in a nearby store, they found it cost around three rupees, which they thought was too much. So, they decided to carry their luggage themselves. Hulikunti, with the steel trunk on his head, Ramabai, with a bundle of miscellaneous things under one arm and Gururaja holding her other arm, they put their feet on the first step of the sacred hill. Ramabai suddenly remembered something and felt suspicious; she asked her husband if he could see the steps clearly. He said, 'Why? I can see the steps all right . . .' This reassured her.

Gururaja started to run up and climb several steps at a stretch and exclaimed delightedly, 'I am the first one, I am the first one.'

Hulikunti and Ramabai took their time and climbed at their own speed. After a while, Ramabai took the steel trunk on her head. All three were exhausted by the time they reached the windy tower called Gaali-Gopura. They rested for some time; the sun was getting a bit mild by then. A monk was narrating the story of Srinivasa Kalyaana, the Lord's wedding, in Telugu, and scores of devotees were sitting around and listening intently. He was describing how Lord Venkatesha met Padmavati when he had gone hunting. Not knowing Telugu, Hulikunti pestered Ramabai for a simultaneous translation of the narration into Kannada.

The monk completed that part of the story and ended the narration for the day. He performed the *mangalaarati* to conclude the event and distributed holy water and goodies to eat, and a sweet drink in a donne, a disposable cup made with banana leaves. Gururaja wanted a real cup instead of the leaf-cup and began to cry, which irritated Ramabai, but she had to oblige him. She untied her bundle and removed the only cup she had, which was the steel tumbler with the crack in it. When she collected the sweet and sour paanaka in that tumbler and offered it to Gururaja; it leaked all over him. She scolded him: 'You want to do things that I ask you not to and create a mess.'

They started climbing once again. Climbing across the seven hills is no joke. Just to pass the time, Ramabai re-narrated the story segment that had been narrated by the monk. After climbing for an hour, they decided to again rest for a while. Because of his knee problem, Hulikunti could not climb for a long time without a break. Gururaja, being thirsty, asked for water, and Ramabai looked for the tumbler again. But no, there was no tumbler! She went berserk; she looked again and again in her bundle, but unfortunately the cracked tumbler was missing. After drinking the paanaka, the boy had left it near the windy tower.

Ramabai set out to recover the tumbler; Hulikunti had a knee problem, the boy could not go alone, and the tumbler, which was to be offered at the temple, could not be abandoned either. The thought of going down all those steps and climbing back up again was indeed dreadful.

There was no human presence in the windy-tower area; all the used donnes were lying around with flies sitting on them. Ramabai looked and looked for the tumbler but could not find it. After some time, several climbers passing by had inquired what she was searching for. 'Don't you worry, lady. If the Lord made you bring it all the way to be offered to him, He will somehow make sure you find it,' they consoled her, and resumed climbing.

Attached to the wind-tower was a small shrine; some devotee had etched a portrait of Lord Venkataramana on it, and so climbers had converted that into a makeshift mini-temple of sorts. A lamp was burning in front of the shrine. Ramabai sat in front of the shrine and closed her eyes in silent meditation for a couple of minutes. She opened her eyes, lo . . . there was the tumbler! Someone had lit a ghee-lamp and placed it on top of the tumbler. Because of the darkness inside the shrine, she had not been able to spot it initially.

She waited until the flame in the lamp receded peacefully, picked up her tumbler, washed it with water, dried it with her own sari and climbed back up. Gururaja was crying, complaining of aching feet; Hulikunti had taken the boy's feet into his lap and was massaging them gently, telling him a story to distract him. Seeing Ramabai, they were ecstatic and asked with great anxiety if she was able to find the tumbler. After relaxing for a few moments, she narrated in detail how she had recovered the lost tumbler.

They climbed for two more hours. As the evening approached and the daylight faded, the moon soon appeared, lighting up the hill with its brightness. Even in that cool night, Ramabai was dripping sweat from exhaustion. As she tried to wipe it off with her sari end, there was a sudden flash at some distance. She rubbed her eyes and looked again. Yes, there was no doubt it was Lord Venkappa's tower of gold! She pointed it out to Hulikunti and

Gururaja. The three stood there enthralled; they had seen the view of their lives! It was so satisfying that Ramabai prostrated on the ground and exclaimed, 'Oh Lord, eventually you got us here.' Hulikunti and Gururaja followed with a saashtaanga namaskaara, prostrating themselves so that eight points of their body were in contact with Mother Earth.

≈

Varadanna was worshipping the decorated pandal entrance by tying a coconut to one of the pillars when he heard 'Anna,' a familiar voice indicating the arrival of his sister. He went to meet her, caressed her back and greeted her. He lifted up Gururaja. 'Why are you so late in arriving? I have been waiting for you since morning,' he said, his eyes turning misty with happiness.

The groom's party arrived late as their bus had to be repaired on the way when it broke down near Chittoor. By the time they all showered and got ready, it was almost eight in the evening. They had brought with them quite a few things needed for the ceremonial sixteen-step welcome. Varadanna too had made elaborate arrangements to welcome the groom and his family. Ramabai herself had brought with her artistically decorated dried coconut with engraved pictures of the stone-chariot at Hampi and the names of the bride and the groom etched neatly below. But the welcome ceremony got delayed as the groom's party would not take a single step without the express permission of a Swami who had accompanied them. Sukhananda Swami's words were no less than Vedic commands to them.

During the welcome party, the altar where the bride and groom were to sit was offered to the Swami, who sat on a deerskin. His feet were washed and worshipped with great care. Everybody, including the bride and groom, prostrated before him and received his blessings. Then started the mutual introduction ceremony. Ramabai eagerly awaited her turn. Finally, they called Ramabai and Hulikunti to introduce them to the bride's future in-laws. 'She is the only one from my side of the family, the rest are all from my wife's side,' said Varadanna. The groom's aunt was short and stout, bedecked with a lot of gold ornaments. A diamond necklace, along with strands of black beads, glittered on her chest. Compared with the brilliance of her necklace, Ramabai's borrowed gold bangles appeared to have lost their lustre entirely. They made mutual offers of haldi-kumkum, the auspicious symbols for married women, and fed each other a shredded-coconut-sugar mixture to signify the happy beginning of a new relationship. Later that night, before the dinner, Ramabai looked for an opportune moment and went to the stout lady; she touched and felt her diamond necklace, experiencing its thrill. She also satisfied her curiosity about the number of carats and what it cost, and so on.

At the dinner there were laddus for dessert. 'Why, Anna, could you not have ordered mandige instead?' asked Ramabai. 'Only we the people of Bellary know how to enjoy the extraordinary taste of mandige, these people have no such appreciation,' was his explanation. Since Gururaja was already asleep, Ramabai saved a couple of laddus for him.

≈

Waking up at the crack of dawn and getting ready quickly, Ramabai made sure that Hulikunti and Gururaja also awoke early and used the toilet and the bathrooms before the long queues would form. But even after all that there was no sign of the morning coffee, let alone breakfast, though it was time for breakfast already. Instead, a little girl appeared with some prasaada and offered it to all three and declared, 'This is being distributed as per Swamiji's wish. All of you must consume it, consider it a command.' Hulikunti refused it as he was in no mood to eat anything. But when the little girl insisted, he put it in his mouth.

Hulikunti had been complaining of a stomach ache since the previous night. Ramabai had silenced him as she was in no mood to look for any medicine for him at that late hour amidst the mad rush of the wedding party. 'Eating a wedding meal can lead to such stomach upsets; once you use the toilet in the morning, you will feel fine,' she said, and went to sleep. Now, early in the morning, Hulikunti complained of pain again, and he looked pale. She decided to administer a home remedy. She went to the kitchen-storage area looking for some fenugreek seeds and curd. Near the storeroom area, it became obvious to her that there was a murmur going on about something.

The store room was being guarded by vainy's younger brother; she asked for what she needed and he gave her the items readily. As if he was waiting to hear about Hulikunti's stomach ache, he announced loudly: 'It seems her husband has a stomach ache.' Ramabai found it extremely inappropriate. 'Your wife farted when she was eating dinner last night; would you like me to announce that news and bring it to everybody's attention?' she snapped at him. When she returned to her husband, there were a few people gathered already to inquire about his stomach ache. She couldn't figure why a silly-simple stomach ache should become such a big issue. Hulikunti gulped down the methi seeds with curd and chased it with some water, as he was concerned that some of it might come out of his mouth. Some water spilled all over him; he felt more pain and lay flat on the ground. The short, stout lady came into their room along with four others; she looked rather sad and her eyes were red. Hulikunti somehow hauled himself into a sitting position. Ramabai quickly realized that the matter must be serious if all these people felt it necessary to visit her.

One among them came straight to the point and disclosed the reason for their visit. 'Our sister-in-law's diamond necklace has been stolen.' The moment he made that statement, the short, stout lady started to weep and said in a choked voice, 'The necklace you touched and admired last night, that necklace.' Her husband shut her up. 'All night we have been looking for it in vain. When we consulted our Swamiji, he said someone among the relatives gathered here has stolen it for sure, and hidden it right here in the marriage hall. He has given prasaada after praying and chanting mantras, to be distributed to all. He has said that the person, whoever it is, will start suffering from utter pain in the stomach as soon as he or she eats the prasaada.' Having understood the purpose of their visit, Ramabai felt sick to her stomach; she took courage and said, 'My husband is not a thief. He already had a stomach ache last night and he keeps getting it frequently.' But they were not ready to listen to her pleas; they insisted on searching their belongings. She screamed back, 'I am going to complain to Varadanna! You can't insult guests who have come to attend the wedding.' 'Go ahead, complain. Who is objecting? He has given us permission to search anyone we suspect. Not only that, until we find the necklace we are not allowing the groom to enter the altar,' he said coolly.

Ramabai sat on her steel trunk, trying to prevent them from opening it, which increased their suspicion of her even more. In the meantime, Hulikunti started experiencing excruciating pain and was rolling on the ground. He felt unbearable pain when he touched a part of his abdomen. He could not follow the quarrel going on in Telugu. 'Our Swamiji is no ordinary man, his powers are unparalleled; if you don't return what you have stolen, this man will die oozing blood from his mouth.' They tried to scare her. Ramabai surrendered the steel trunk to them and went to attend to her husband.

They did not have the patience to untie the rope wound around the steel trunk, but just tore it off. They started throwing out all the items one by one. The two laddus Ramabai had saved for Gururaja were tossed out, the broken pieces spreading on the floor. The cracked tumbler went to a corner; Gururaja, who was watching all this with great fear, ran to it, fetched it and handed it to his mother. The stout lady went after the bundle of saris and tossed each piece helter-skelter in no time; their clothes were soon strewn across the room.

No one knew who had called the police, but before they knew it there was a police jeep in front of the wedding hall. When the khaki-clad inspector entered, the missing diamond necklace was reported and he was informed of the power of the Swamiji's prasaada distribution. The inspector sat next to Hulikunti and asked him if he had stolen the necklace. The man who was suffering untold misery vomited out everything he had in his stomach. All the curd and the methi seeds could be seen in the vomit. The next instalment of vomit contained a bit of blood too. The inspector's clothes were soiled.

The inspector ordered the men around to put Hulikunti in the police jeep. When they lifted him, Ramabai went into a frenzy and wept loudly, hitting her mouth with her hands. Gururaja, who was petrified, also began to wail at the top of his voice. The inspector went to Ramabai and said politely, 'Please don't cry, I won't do anything to your husband. If you wish, you may come with us.' Thus having consoled her, he took her and Gururaja along with Hulikunti in the jeep. When the jeep stopped in front of Sapthagiri Hospital, Hulikunti was still crying in pain. After the inspector went in and spoke to the authorities, a couple of ward boys came with a stretcher and carried Hulikunti inside. The inspector assured Ramabai that he had spoken to the doctors and that they would do what was needed. He told her before leaving the hospital that she could contact him if any help was needed and that everything would be all right.

≋

Ramabai went looking for a moneylender's shop, exploring several streets of Govindaraja Pattana. Gururaja walked along, holding on to her sari end. The doctor had told her in no uncertain terms via a nurse that it would cost her a thousand rupees for the surgery, half of which must be deposited in advance before he could operate on her husband. He had also informed her that if his appendix were to burst, it would be extremely dangerous for him. When Ramabai asked if there was any danger to his life, they were noncommittal in their response.

Ramabai had never entered a moneylender's shop nor dealt with a loan shark; so she stepped inside rather nervously. The Sethji, clad in a white dhoti, black coat and a cap, was sitting behind his desk, working on some old accounts. The round spectacles at the tip of his nose looked like they might fall off any time. The diamond studs in his ears shone prominently. As her shadow fell on his account book, he raised his head.

Ramabai took off the gold bangles from her wrists, kept them on the desk and sat looking down. Sethji understood her intent; he took one of the bangles and rubbed it on a grindstone to confirm if it was indeed made of pure gold; he did the same with the rest of the bangles. He put them on the pan of a little weighing scale that looked like a toy. Gururaja looked on with curiosity as the Sethji used the black-and-scarlet seeds of wild liquorice as standard weights.

Sethji agreed to lend her one thousand two hundred and thirty-two rupees if she pledged all the bangles. He wrote on a blank sheet of paper all the pertinent information after asking her for other details and made her sign on it. Ramabai had no memory of signing any paper except when she was quite young. Her hands trembled and her tears fell on the slanted signature, smudging all the letters. He wiped off the smudged signature and made her sign again after asking her to dry her eyes. She was ready to take his leave after taking the money, but the Sethji did not let her go without making her count the money in his presence. She counted wrong three times and finally got it right. The Sethji gave her a copy of the letter and told her that she needed to bring that letter when she came with the money to take her bangles back, and then sent her off.

On the way back, she saw a small temple on the roadside. She kneeled before it, took Gururaja's hand and placed it on her head and made him swear. 'See, even if your father and I worked all our lives we will never be able to buy back the gold bangles for Paddakka. If we die without being able to return her bangles, you should fulfil that task for us. We don't care whether you perform our annual shraaddha or not, but you must secure the release of the pledged bangles and hand them back to Paddakka.' It was not clear how much Gururaja had understood of she said; he simply stared at her, blinking his eyes. She folded up Sethji's letter and placed it in his pocket.

≈

They dressed Hulikunti in a green hospital gown and carried him towards the operation theatre. In extreme pain, he looked at his wife helplessly as Ramabai and Gururaja receded from view. Ramabai felt very nervous when she saw a nurse carry the shining surgical scissors, knives and syringes in an open stainless-steel basin. 'What kind of misery will these blasted people bring upon my husband?' she pondered sadly. She stopped the nurse and told her, 'My husband does not know Telugu. If he needs something, he will ask in Kannada, please call me if you need an interpreter.' The nurse laughed and said, 'Inside the operation theatre, they will give the patient anaesthesia and put him to sleep; whether someone knows Kannada, Telugu or they are deaf, mute or blind, everyone is treated alike.' Ramabai and Gururaja were the only two who remained in the hall. She spotted a large idol of

Lord Venkataramana adorned with piles of flower garlands. Someone
had lit incense sticks and placed them before it. Ramabai felt like
an orphan as she stood in front of the portrait.

'Hey, you, Venkatesha, we came here with complete trust in
you. Because you asked, my husband went and stole a tumbler, of
all things. If anything happens to my husband, I am not the kind
to keep quiet, you understand? I will take the tumbler back to my
place and declare to the whole world that there is no power in you
as people claim. Not only that, according to the story narrated by
the monk on our way up the hill, your Padmavati pelted stones at
you and hurt you in the forehead, right? I will take a huge block of
rock and drop it on your head, or I will change my name if I don't.
Beware!' she warned him. The Lord inside the sanctum sanctorum
started to sweat.

When Varadanna came to visit the hospital, Hulikunti had not
yet emerged from the operating room. He went straight to his
sister and held her hand gently, asking how Hulikunti was doing.
Ramabai could not control her emotions; she laid her head on her
brother's chest and wept like a child. He caressed her head and
consoled her. Then he went on to unburden himself by blurting
out all that was pent up. 'Evil bastards, why in the hell should they
wear such expensive jewellery to a wedding? If they cannot take
care of it, they should leave it at home. They have insulted you
beyond belief; on top of everything, that blasted Swamiji! I suspect
that he is the one who must have stolen it . . .' After crying for a
while and wetting her brother's shirt with her tears, she felt some
relief and reassurance. 'Let it go, Varadanna, being poor is a sin,
poverty is a curse,' she said, and fell silent.

A nurse came out with a porcelain dish filled with blood and
a piece of flesh as small as the tip of a pinky. She showed it to

Ramabai and said, 'Look, this was the reason for your husband's pain in the stomach.' It is hard to say what kind of pain it caused her. Ramabai spat at that bloody piece of flesh; she crushed her knuckles against each other and produced clicking sounds of joints coming apart, as a sign of wishing away the evil that had visited her husband. She cursed that blasted thing heartily: 'You were responsible for creating suspicion on my husband, they called him a thief all because of you; may you be destroyed forever, and may your offspring be destroyed forever.' The nurse who had not expected such a reaction became upset and scolded her, 'What kind of behaviour is this?' she said, as she walked away with the blood-filled dish. Varadanna was flabbergasted at Ramabai's words.

The doctor was still drying his hands with a washcloth as he came out of the operation theatre and said, 'He is doing just fine, you may go and talk to him.' Varadanna got up to go and talk to his brother-in-law, but Ramabai ran ahead of him and stood at the door of the operation theatre, preventing him from entering. 'Varadanna, please don't come inside,' she said in a resolute voice. Varadanna did not want to listen and tried to make his way in by pushing her aside. But she put her hands on his chest and pushed him out. 'I beg you, Varadanna, please leave us alone,' she pleaded with clasped hands. Varadanna retreated, feeling stupid, and Ramabai alone went inside to talk to Hulikunti.

Varadanna did not know what to do, so he went to Gururaja, who was watching the fight between his mother and uncle. He brought a calm smile on his own face and caressed Gururaja's chin and asked him, 'Where did the money for the operation come from, Gururaja?' In response, Gururaja pulled out the letter from his pocket and showed it to him. Varadanna and Gururaja set out to look for the moneylender's shop, where Varadanna had a talk with the Sethji, cleared the loan and recovered the bangles from him. He put those bangles in Gururaja's pocket and said, 'Give them to your mother. You must always look after her and make sure

she never faces any adversities, OK? I like my sister very much.'
He left Gururaja at the hospital entrance and went back to the
wedding hall.

≈

'*Edukondalavada—Resident of Seven Hills—Govindaaa . . .*' '*Govinda.*'
'*Venkataramanaa Govindaaa . . .*' '*Govinda*'

After standing in the queue for the 'general' admission for four
hours, they had their darshan of the Lord. Ramabai was concerned
that because of the huge congregation Gururaja might not get a
good view of the Lord, so she kept on instructing him, 'Take a
good look . . . look at the diamond crown . . . look at the floral
arrangements . . . look at the grand necklace, the kantheehaara,
look at the huge white naama on his face,' and so on. Hulikunti
was moving his hand all over his son's freshly shaven head, making
fun of him that his head was shining like a freshly made rava laddu
rich in ghee, while Ramabai was admiring the hitherto unfamiliar
curves of her husband's clean-shaven head.

They were getting darshan of the Lord amidst the constant
orders of 'move on, move on' and 'make space, make space', and
pushes from the eager crowd behind them. They were soaked in
sweat by the time they got out of the final queue. Ramabai was
questioning Gururaja in multiple ways to make sure that he did get
a good darshan of the Lord. She kept at it until she was convinced
that he had indeed had.

Even at the collection box there was a queue, where the
devotees dropped their pledges into the box according as their
ability. Ramabai lifted her son on her shoulders; he was carrying
the cracked tumbler with him. Upon his father's order, Gururaja
dropped it into the collection box. The cracked tumbler quietly
became a part of the collection box that contained countless other

offerings, such as, cash, gold, silver-tongue, a child's anklets, divorce agreements, property records, urns of cremation ash and so on.

'*Edukondalavada Govindaaa,*' shouted the devotees; Gururaja too joined in and yelled, 'Govinda!' After having put her son down from her shoulders, Ramabai untied the knot in the corner of her sari. She took out the mangalasutra given to her by Kashavva, touched it to her eyes in silent obeisance and dropped it in the box. '*Krishnaarpana,*' she uttered; eventually, everything must be offered to Lord Krishna. The mob yelled, '*Venkataramana Govindaaa,*' and this time all three said 'Govinda!' in unison. Venkatesha, inside the sanctum sanctorum, breathed a deep sigh of satisfaction, that finally everything that should have reached him had reached him.

20 August 2007

The Final Offering

The first thing Ankita did on waking up was to pick up her cell phone. She scanned her Facebook page to see the number of 'likes' she had received for her status message or the photo she had posted the previous night. She was thrilled by the many comments it had fetched. She checked her friends' status messages and new photos, and hit 'like' for one or two; she envied those with more likes than herself. She then went on to post a new photo, which she was sure would receive more likes than her friends' had. If there were new friend requests, she would investigate their personal details and check for mutual friends before accepting them. She did not easily add boys as friends and did so only after their pictures convinced her that they looked 'smart'. Anyone with a red dot between the eyebrows, those wearing glasses with broad, square frames, those who had accumulated fat on their bodies, and boys wearing old-fashioned clothes were rejected straight away. Ageing men were certainly kept out of her friends circle. But she was not that strict about women. Some elderly women, or 'auntys' of her friends, had found a place in her friends list. In the beginning, she would hesitate to accept friend requests from unknown people, but was now used to the protocol. However, if anyone posted dirty pictures or vulgar comments, she would mercilessly unfriend them. Forty-five minutes could easily pass this way each morning.

By which time her mother, Kusuma, would have screamed at her tens of times to wake her up, 'Ankee, get up! The sun has climbed to the mid-day position already. You will be late for work.' She would go on in this vein, scolding her for being so tardy. 'You should be looking at your palms to recite the morning prayer—"at the tip of my palm resides Lakshmi, in the middle, Saraswathi and at the bottom resides Gowri,"—like all traditional Hindus do. Instead, you keep your mobile phone on the tip of your palm, middle of your palm and bottom of your palm." Both of them knew that Kusuma hated nothing more than Ankita's mobile phone.

Kusuma did not use a cell phone. She mumbled to herself, 'Did my parents ever use a cell phone? Did they not live happily without it? These days people have started indulging in all these excesses by buying unnecessary products.' She used only her landline, and that too only when needed. That phone had been installed when her husband was alive. She hated everything that was modern; she still washed her clothes on a stone and refused to buy a washing machine. The only reason she used an electric blender was because there was no stone mortar in the house. Otherwise, she would have preferred to grind the dosé batter manually. She tried her best to avoid using any mechanical or electrical gadgets. On the other hand, Ankita avoided manual labour as much as she could. When it fell upon her to wash a pile of laundry, Ankita complained of body ache and resorted to long naps.

Ankita could not understand her mother's stance in these matters. She suspected the reason her mother did not use a cell phone was to express her anger. Sometime back, Ankita's mother had shown her an article published in a Kannada daily titled 'Did the sparrows vanish since the advent of mobile phones?' 'When we were young, hundreds of sparrows used to gather in front of our house, did you know? Because of the craze of people like you, see what kind of damage has been done,' she had said with utter disgust. Ankita was hit hard by her mother's words. Gathering herself, she had retorted awkwardly, 'In all these days, you never felt the absence of sparrows. Now, after reading this article, there seems to be a sudden burst of love towards the little birds! Today, dinosaurs are extinct from this planet but life goes on, right?' Ankita's response hurt her helpless mother, who had mumbled 'Stubborn people won't get it.'

Getting her mother to buy Ankita her first mobile phone was no easy task, as Kusuma was a firm believer that children would be spoiled by such things. She had firmly declared: 'Never shall I buy you a cell phone.' When it came to being obstinate, Ankita was no less so; after all she was her mother's daughter. She rattled off the names of all her friends who had cell phones and enumerated all its advantages. 'If I ever get into a difficult situation in this monster city, how would I ever get in touch with you?' But no amount of explanation made Kusuma budge. Finally, Ankita resorted to a hunger strike, but Kusuma held her own. She hoped that hunger would force Ankita to come around. But when Ankita did not touch food for two days and gave her the silent treatment, Kusuma became anxious. She began to feel helpless.

Eventually, her mother's heart could take it no more. Kusuma took some food for Ankita to her room and tried to cajole her with affectionate words. When Ankita would not remove the sheet covering her face, Kusuma lost her temper and tried to use parental authority, but to no avail. After having lost her husband, Kusuma could never escape the truth that she and her daughter had no one else to turn to and were stuck with each other. This realization drove Kusuma to acute anxiety, which manifested as anger, and which was what was happening now too. Kusuma put aside the plate filled with food and gave Ankita a good thrashing, after which she cried helplessly. Even this did not soften Ankita. She did not try to console her mother and took the beating without making a sound. The grown-up daughter finally won the battle. A cell phone arrived home the very next day, which plunged her in joy. Kusuma sank into misery, seeing her daughter delightedly exploring all the features of the phone.

In the beginning, whenever Ankita received a call or a message, Kusuma wanted to know who it was from and when, where and how Ankita had met that person. She would be agitated until she got a satisfactory response. Ankita's patience was being tested. 'How can Mother know everyone I know?' If Kusuma heard a male voice, all hell broke loose and wars were waged. 'What is your relationship with him?' she would ask, making Ankita uncomfortable. Ankita got smarter and started naming only the friends Kusuma already knew. But Kusuma was no dummy; she would call them back on some pretext from the landline, and after some casual talk ask if they had called Ankita lately. If she found out that they had not called, there would be battles at home followed by a hunger strike and a crying match. Kusuma realized they could not carry on like this as she was growing older and weaker. She felt her blood pressure rising whenever she heard the annoying *kuy-kuy* noise from her daughter's phone at all kinds of odd hours. Even though she was curious about the content of those text messages, she had to control her urge because she did not know how to check them. These days Ankita had started taking the mobile even to the toilet. Kusuma thought, 'How nice it would be if the phone slipped from her hand and fell into the pot.'

Ankita could never forget the fuss her mother made to buy her her first cell phone. That was why, as soon as she completed her BA, she found a receptionist's job. Soon after receiving her first month's salary, she bought a better phone and started using it without telling her mother. When Kusuma found out after two days there was no end to her fury. She yelled, 'Have you grown so big that you went and bought that mobile without even telling me about it?' Ankita smiled inwardly and retorted: 'You would have prevented me from buying it, wouldn't you?' 'What will you do with the old cell phone I bought you shelling out thousands of rupees? Will you dip it in pickle and lick it? Or, will you make dessert from it?' Kusuma screamed. To which Ankita responded with utmost calm, 'Amma, you should keep it . . . whenever you go out it will come in handy.' Kusuma would have none of it. 'I don't need any blasted gadget like that, you can enjoy that too,' she yelled, and stood before her husband's photo and started to cry. She now directed her wrath towards her late husband. 'I am incapable of dealing with this girl. You left me floating in the middle of this ocean,' she muttered. 'I swear on those cruel people who have kept me from participating in all religious family events simply because I am a widow. Damn those who believe in traditions that ban widows from taking part in auspicious rituals. They are my witness: I would rather die than buy that stupid cell phone,' she blurted loudly, and felt some relief.

The next day, when Ningamma the maid servant came to do the dishes, Ankita handed over her old cell phone to her. Ningamma was delighted. 'Kusumakka, no matter what you say about your daughter, she has a large heart, God should keep her happy, madam,' said Ningamma, adding insult to injury. 'Ankavva, please enter my daughter's number in this phone. I have heard you can set an alarm for waking up in the morning, is it true, madam?' Ningamma excitedly asked many questions about her new phone.

~≈~

A long weekend stretched ahead, with Independence Day and Varamahaalakshmi Pooja, the traditional festival of the goddess of wealth, stretching into the regular Saturday and Sunday. The harsh din of the traffic had subsided, and the pleasant chirping of birds floated on the air. The weather was cool because of the cloudy skies. The air was filled with the fragrance of the blooming champaka flowers on the roadside trees. It was a day perfect for lying around in bed. Kusuma had allowed a bit of flexibility to her daughter that day. Ankita found her mother sitting next to her on the bed, caressing her back and gently running her fingers along her hair, occasionally kissing her cheeks, cajoling her to wake up. Ankita was enjoying this display of motherly affection; she curled up close to her mother's thigh, cooing like a baby. Kusuma had already decided to make upmabhaath, Ankita's favourite, for breakfast. She prayed to God to prevent any quarrels between them.

With four holidays ahead, Kusuma knew that waking Ankita up would not be easy, but the temple folk had organized a special sacrificial ritual, Sudarshana Homa, to relieve the troubles of suffering devotees. The event was to take place in a faraway area of north Bengaluru, where new development had taken place. Kusuma was unfamiliar with that location, even after having lived for thirty years in the city. Who could claim to know every extension of this monster city anyway? Realizing that it would take a while to reach the temple, Kusuma had found out the details of the bus routes well in advance. She used all possible methods of loving persuasion to coax her daughter awake.

Kusuma was a woman of great devotion, which took her to many temples. She never missed an important religious event. She had not been like this when her husband was alive. Perhaps with his sudden departure she had to find a way to fill the void.

Her husband had left enough for Kusuma to get by, so money did not pose a challenge for her. But just the thought that he would no longer return home in the evenings shook her to the core and pushed her towards depression. She was advised to take up a job. It was not easy for her to find a job with her limited skills. Nor was it possible to obtain a job in her husband's company on the grounds of compassion alone. An acquaintance helped her get a teaching job in a convent school, which she was unable to handle because she was not fluent in English. On the very first day, she started shaking in her chappals while teaching the class, and felt like someone who had fallen from the frying pan into the fire. It took her only three days to quit that job. She faced loneliness and depression all over again, unable to overcome the memories of her husband. At this crucial time in her life, temples and religious events offered her some support and a lot of solace.

At that time, Ankita was still in fifth grade and not old enough to understand what it meant to be without a father. She stuck to her mother at all times. Kusuma had secured her own position with her daughter; she took on the role of her missing father as well and strove hard to shield her daughter from pain. Kusuma fondly recalled the days when Ankita was still small and close to her, in spite of the hardships they faced. But these days she had slipped from her firm grip. She argued over everything and showed no regard for her whatsoever, causing major headaches for Kusuma.

Kusuma had two important reasons for insisting that Ankita attend the Sudarshana Homa. First, Somayaaji, the priest in whom Kusuma had a lot of faith, had told her that Ankita would soften up once the holy smoke from the sacrificial ritual touched her. The touch of the final offering for the holy ritual would destroy all the evil effects on her of any unfavourable planetary formations. Somayaaji's predictions had turned out to be pretty accurate many times in the past. Kusuma had gone to him several times during her difficult days and had returned with renewed faith.

Second, Kusuma was now seriously searching for a proper groom for her daughter, although she suspected that Ankita might have already found someone. One day she mustered up the courage to ask her, but Ankita, without looking her in the eyes, said, 'OK, Mom, go ahead and find someone if you wish.' Kusuma thought perhaps Ankita had been through a relationship or two, but did not have the courage to ask her directly. Not that Ankita would disclose such details. Ankita's words came as a relief to Kusuma, who had begun her search, believing that time would heal everything. She hoped to see her daughter appear in the assemblies of her community, which might develop some contacts and lead to a suitable alliance in the future. Kusuma had no complaints against Ankita except for the way she routinely dressed in non-traditional outfits. 'If Ankita ever wore a sari, she would look like goddess Gowri. She is not short like me; she has grown like a juicy sugar cane—tall, just like her dad. These are tough days even for boys looking for suitable girls. It may not be so bad, after all, to find someone and marry her off. My husband passed away but he did not leave me totally helpless,' Kusuma would often ruminate.

After her husband's passing, money from several sources, like insurance, provident fund and gratuity, had reached Kusuma, and this also caused major headaches. Many relatives visited her in the garb of showing sympathy, but what they really wanted were loans. Even during those times of unending sorrow, Kusuma was cautious with money. She kept most of the relatives at a distance and firmly declared that she would not loan money to anyone. Such harshness led her to losing several relatives, but it did not bother her as she believed it saved her from being cheated. Now, only mother and daughter were left to fend for each other.

By the time Kusuma wrapped a nice sari around herself and got ready, Ankita was at the sink brushing her teeth. She told Ankita to eat her breakfast, reminded her twice about switching off the lights, the fan and the geyser. 'Be careful, Ankee, please come as early as possible, it is very important that you be there before the final ritual of the poornaahuti starts. I will try to call you when we are half-way through.'

When Kusuma was about to leave, Ankita made a sign with her hand asking her to stop—she could not speak as she had foam dripping from her mouth—and tried to set right the folds of her mother's sari. She then went to her room to get the perfume bottle; ignoring her mother's resistance, she squirted a couple of puffs on her. She sparingly applied light-coloured lipstick on her mother's lips, looked over her eyebrows and lashes and examined her from a couple of different angles. She then went to the sink and rinsed her mouth and said, imitating her mother, 'Be careful, Kusumee', and gave her approval with a smile and permission to leave. In mock anger, Kusuma tapped Ankita's head mildly and said, 'You never cease your impertinence. You are really stubborn, don't listen when I try to stop you. You know all this is too much for me. What will elderly people say when they see me dressed up like this? Don't you think they will get mad?' Ankita couldn't care less. She said, 'Let them.' Kusuma realized it was futile to argue with this girl and rushed to the city bus stop.

Even though Kusuma had bought a Honda scooter for her daughter, Ankita would hesitate to give her a ride on it because she could not balance the vehicle when her mother sat with both legs on one side. Kusuma would not agree to wearing a churidar pyjama so that she could straddle the pillion. Kusuma was also a little heavy, despite her continuous and numerous household chores through the day, and could be considered obese. The doctors had given up, saying, 'It is in your genes, what can anyone do?' Her genetic inheritance included high blood pressure and diabetes. She would rationalize all this to herself: 'These things are part of ageing. After all, with my husband gone, whom do I need to please anyway by looking slim? Once I find a nice groom for my Ankita and marry her off, I will be able to breathe my last peacefully.'

≈

Ankita had no desire to go to any temple, but any time she tried to suggest this, Kusuma would start to cry. Earlier, Ankita used to dread her mother's tears, but it did not take her long to realize that Kusuma was using it as a weapon to control her. Ankita stopped being threatened by them, as she realized that by yielding she would have to face defeat in every battle. But she felt sorry for her mother, as she knew she still suffered the memories of her father's passing. For Ankita, who had little or no memory of her father, her mother was everything and that made her relent once in a while. For the past one week Kusuma had been pestering her about this Sudarshana Homa, at times resorting to affectionate persuasion. Finally, Ankita agreed to show up at the temple.

But after Kusuma left, Ankita lost her enthusiasm. Sitting amidst grey-haired seniors for hours together was truly a boring prospect. 'Everybody thinks it is their right to know every personal detail. The moment a young girl wearing a sari sings a devotional song, they start pouring in their appreciation. They don't seem to care much about my talents like dancing passionately to the tunes of latest film hits like *'Sheela ki javani'*. They're a bunch of self-centred people who're deeply buried in their own ways. 'They really couldn't care less about others.' While she was thinking along these lines sipping coffee, she suddenly decided to consult her friends and picked up her phone. Putting her coffee aside, she started typing a status message on Facebook: 'My mom has instructed me that I must go to some temple which is extremely boring for me. Should I or shouldn't I go? Don't simply like, please also comment.' She received four likes immediately. She muttered 'stupid', throwing the mobile phone on the bed and went to take a shower. She knew that if she went too late it would upset her mother. Ankita didn't mind her mother getting angry, but it hurt her if she got upset.

It was hard for Ankita to understand her mother's stubbornness over little things. For instance, her mother could still not see the advantages of using a cell phone. Logical thinking was no match to her obduracy. Her mother was never like this before. She was like a reservoir of love that overflowed like a waterfall. Her behaviour changed after Ankita's father died. Kusuma lost her smile forever, and became so serious, as though a huge responsibility rested on her head. She suspected everything, trusted no one, hesitated to try anything new, and most of all, dreaded change.

As soon as Ankita came out of the shower, she went to her
cell phone and picked it up; there were 120 comments and 250
likes! She was overwhelmed and felt happy about her friends. Her
friends messaged: 'Don't go to the temple, it will be boring,' 'We
are all heading to Shivanasamudra, which is overflowing. We are
going on our bikes, why don't you also join? It will be fun to bathe
in the river,' 'We are going to have a party at Rohit's, please join,
forget the temple,' and so on. She was thrilled to see her friends'
concern and their eagerness for her company! Could she ever put
a value to friendship? The decision to skip the temple visit was
slowly crystallizing in her mind.

Ankita liked to look at her naked body in the mirror while
drying her hair. Viewing her body from several angles was a daily
routine, but today it led to a naughty thought. She took the cell
phone and composed a frame in her mind: 'My hair should be
spread out on my back, in the background should be the bed,
though a bit blurred. The used towel should be clearly visible,
thrown about casually. The setting should create an illusion of
revealing something without actually revealing anything.' Then she
clicked a selfie up to her cleavage. She did not smile, and put on
a somewhat serious yet provocative expression that suggested she
was looking for someone. She edited it to improve her complexion
and cropped it as needed. She thought: 'The boys who see this
must get a kick, imagining I have posed naked for the picture. It
will create some waves, making it the hottest topic for today.'

'Thank you all for your suggestions; you guys made up my
mind for me, I have decided against going to the temple! I am going
to tell a little lie to my mother that I have a stomach ache. I am
going to laze around at home alone until afternoon. I will decide
soon as to whose group I will join. Here is my gift: this picture to
you all for the nice suggestions and for helping me decide. How
do you like my gift?' She had hardly finished writing her status
and posted it along with the photo than she started receiving likes,

one after the other in quick succession. She felt as though she had thrown a stone at a beehive and felt a strange sense of pride in her own mischievousness. She could hardly resist a smile as she went to the kitchen to eat the upmabhaath her mother had prepared.

The upmabhaath was tasty. Ankita knew there was no one else who could equal her mother in cooking such tasty food. 'I am sure Amma will get upset when I tell her I am skipping this temple visit. She has been talking about this event nonstop for the past one week. She will start crying again; maybe it will make her happy if I just went to the temple for a short while? But I'm really not in the mood, what should I do! I should not yield to her crying-weapon which she uses on me all the time, trying to destroy my individuality. I should not soften, I must remain strong. I am different, mother is different . . .' thus the thoughts continued, while the mobile kept pinging. Likes and comments were accumulating. She held the upmabhaath in one hand and checked the phone using the other—316 likes! Oh my, the three-hundred-and-seventeenth just got added! More than fifty comments already, forty-three people had already shared the photo! Ankita's happiness knew no bounds. She relished it, smiling contentedly to herself. While she was thinking she must respond to all the comments the same day, there appeared the fifty-fourth comment: 'Our own Priyanka Chopra!!'

The doorbell rang, as if to end her loneliness. She walked to the door holding the upmabhaath in one hand and stuck her eye to the peephole to see who was there. Although it looked like a very familiar face, she could not immediately place it, and so she hesitated. 'Who is it?' she asked, and the boy smiled and answered, 'Uday, Uday Svaroop.' His dimple reminded her of his Facebook profile photo, which looked just like this. They had chatted a number of times, and he was among the first to put a like whenever Ankita posted a new photo. She suddenly remembered; sometime back when he had posted his bare-chested photo wearing blue jeans and showing off his 'Salman Khan-like six-pack abs', she had put a 'super-like' comment. But this was the first time she was seeing him in person. Still, she got the courage to open the door and asked in surprise, 'You . . . here . . . how come?' What transpired after that was something she could never have imagined. Uday pressed her mouth shut with his hand and pushed her inside with force, as the plate fell from her hand scattering the upmabhaath all over the entrance. Two young men rushed into the house with ropes in their hands and bolted the door behind them.

~

Because of the four-day weekend, all the roads were empty, and even the city buses. Kusuma reached the location earlier than expected. As she was not familiar with the northern part of Bangalore, she had to ask many people before she found the temple. Seeing a few familiar faces inside the temple put her at ease. When someone asked if she had come alone, she said her daughter would join her soon, even though she had her own doubts. 'Will she show up or con me?' she asked herself. 'I must ring her up and remind her. It is enough if she comes before the ritual of poornaahuti. Priest Somayaaji had said that the contact of the holy smoke would remove all evil.' As she was wondering about Ankita, people started congregating and the event started. They had an excellent sound system and the mantras recited could be heard loud and clear. The rangoli design near the sacrificial altar was intricately done. A young, handsome man was taking pictures of the designs. This boy must be a little taller than Ankita; Kusuma thought he could be a good suitor for her daughter and started making inquiries. Somayaaji was conducting the event wearing a grand red outfit. He chanted the mantras in his high-pitched voice and invited the gods one by one as he pronounced 'Svaaha,' declaring the intent of the offer: 'Please accept this for your consumption.' The couple who had donated the maximum amount for the event were seated prominently, holding the long wooden ladle to pour ghee into the sacrificial fire. After each offering of ghee, the holy fire god stretched his multiple red flaming tongues, as though to express his satisfaction.

Even after several invited gods came and went, there was no sign of Ankita, which made Kusuma highly suspicious. 'That obdurate devil will not come, I know. She does not give a damn for what her mother wants, as if I am a speck of dust under her foot. All the trouble I have taken to raise her has no value. All my effort has been futile, like the ghee being poured into the sacrificial fire! When she was young she used to show so much love, she accompanied me wherever I went and willingly received all my love without resistance. Girls should never grow up because they start hating their mothers. Before they grow up we must have another baby so that there is always a child to receive the love given to it.'

Just then the priest Somayaaji's cell phone rang and its sound boomed all over the hall through the speaker system. Whether he chanted mantras or spoke, Somayaaji was equally loud. He let all the gods wait in queue and chatted over the phone. After finishing the call he turned his attention back to the waiting gods. Kusuma guessed it might not take more than half an hour before they came to the poornaahuti part of the final rituals. She started getting concerned that there was still no sign of Ankita. The coconut that would be used for the final offering was already in circulation, to be touched by all the devotees.

Kusuma got up to call Ankita. She could see that almost everyone gathered there had their own cell phones, but felt uncomfortable asking anyone. They would invariably ask 'Why, did you forget your cell phone?' And she would feel miserable admitting that she did not own one. She was just not capable of bluffing that she had forgotten her phone at home. She decided to go out and find a telephone booth.

As she walked to the end of the lane she did not see any store or shop where there might be a telephone booth. She stopped a girl who was walking by and asked her about it. The girl seemed to be around the same age as Ankita. She said, 'I don't remember having seen one nearby. With mobile phones, telephone booths are becoming rather uncommon, right, Aunty?' Kusuma smiled sheepishly and said quietly, 'I had to make an urgent call, that is why I asked.' The girl said sweetly, 'Why do you hesitate, Aunty, please use my phone,' and offered it to her. It looked exactly like Ankita's! Kusuma's vanity immediately awakened. She said with pride, 'No, no! There must be a store close by, perhaps you don't know because you are not accustomed to using such booths.' The girl gave her an odd smile and walked away. After walking a few steps, however, she turned back and called out: 'Aunty, there is huge building on that third cross-road, a very old-looking building. It has a mobile tower on top. There is an STD booth on the fourth floor, which is actually a Xerox centre and they have a phone too. Not sure if the place is open as it is a four-day weekend.' Kusuma replied, 'Fine, I will see,' and started walking in the direction pointed by the girl. After the third crossing she found the building. From the names on the board outside, it was obvious that there were several offices inside the building. The road was empty and the building looked deserted, but Kusuma took courage and went in. She wondered if the shop would be open, but her need to call up Ankita forced her to proceed. Although there was an elevator, she did not want to use it, thinking of her doctor's advice. As she climbed the steps, owing to her heavy body she soon felt exhausted and sat on the landing of the second floor to relax for a few minutes. At that moment she heard a couple of men talking as they were climbing down the stairs; she asked them if the STD booth was open. They were not sure; one of them said it was, while the other said it wasn't. Kusuma felt a little hopeful that the Xerox centre would be open and continued her climb.

By the time she reached the fourth floor she was breathing heavily. Her heart rate went up and she could hear her heart pounding. As she held on to the railing and rested a while, she sighted the Xerox centre, which was shut. She felt very angry but did not know whom to direct her anger at. She felt sad at her own helplessness. Her eyes became moist as she blurted out, 'She will understand my love only after I die.' She did not dare climb down the four floors, and headed towards the elevator. It was an ancient elevator with a wooden door outside and an iron collapsible grille inside. She went in and shut the doors, and pressed '0'. The elevator did not budge, so she thought it might be faulty. She pressed the button again with extra pressure, which gave the elevator a jolt. Each time she had taken the elevator earlier, she would feel she was being thrown up before being thrown down. Because of the minor jolt, she got some courage that the elevator was working, after all. She consoled herself: 'It is a matter of just a minute before I reach the ground floor.' The elevator had barely moved a couple of seconds before it stopped, and the light inside went off. For a moment she wondered if she had already reached the ground floor and tried to open the collapsible door, which did not move one bit. But she could see the wall through the collapsible door. Out of concern, she pressed the buttons for all the floors but the elevator did not move. She shouted, 'The elevator is out of order, is anybody there?' There was no answer.

~

At the temple, the time for the final offering was approaching fast. The coconut, which had been touched by all the assembled devotees had now been handed to Somayaaji, who placed his hands on it and prayed. He started explaining the significance of the poornaahuti, or the final offering. 'This coconut is akin to our head; we are getting ready to offer this head to the sacred fire. When I say 'the head' it represents our ego, our desires, anger, attachment, greed, arrogance and jealousy—they all originate in this head. Let us separate such a head from our bodies and offer it to this fire, let the gods accept it, thus annihilating our desires, anger, greed, attachment, arrogance and envy.' Having said this he placed the coconut in the hands of the couple who represented the congregation in this ritual. He also passed on the remaining unused ghee to be poured into the fire at the final offering.

> *Om poorNamadaH poorNamidam*
> *poorNaat poorNamudacyate*
> *poorNasya poorNamaadaaya*
> *poorNamEvaavaSiShyate'*
> *Om shantiH shantiH shantiH*

> That is infinite and full, this is full and infinite
> And fullness originates from fullness
> As infinity is so unfathomably large
> If infinity is removed from the infinite
> What remains will still be infinite

'Let there be peace, nothing but peace, peace all around us and within us. Om!' the priest chanted.

The fire god, having consumed the final offering, stretched his thousand tongues in all directions and raised them high with utmost satisfaction when the devotees in the congregation chanted victory slogans and offered auspicious coloured rice at the altar. The naadaswara and the accompanying drums played the climactic music at the highest possible pitch. The oblations were now not only final but total.

≋

When Ankita came to, it was raining cats and dogs outside. Her body was hurting like hell. She was cold and shivering in fear, feeling as though some sort of worms were crawling and slithering all over her belly. She tried lifting her hands to ward them off but could not, as both her hands were tied to the cot. Her legs too were tied to the two ends of the cot to prevent her from moving. She felt even colder as she realized she was naked and tried to curl up, but in vain. She started to remember what had happened. She visualized the unbearable scene of those three hooligans jumping on her and remembered being hit by some sort of a heavy rod when she attempted to resist. The bitter memory made her scream 'Amma', but she could not as her mouth was stuffed with cloth. Her mobile phone was on her midriff and she could hear the *kuy-kuy* of comments or likes on Facebook. The phone rang, and she tried to bounce the phone closer to her mouth by moving her belly up and down, but the phone fell down instead. She looked at the clock on the wall; it was past one in the afternoon. 'It is almost time for Amma to return,' she remembered, and felt some courage that mother would appear any time now and save her from this hell.

'Amma, come soon, come and save me, help me please . . .' she pleaded inwardly, as tears continued to roll down her cheeks. She felt extreme pain and lost consciousness once again.

⁓

When Kusuma opened her eyes she could not understand where she was. She was hungry and her throat was parched. She had no strength to get up. She changed sides wherever she was lying. She slowly realized where she was when she hit her arm against the collapsible door. She felt sad that she was still inside that six-square-foot area of the elevator. She must have fallen unconscious after screaming for help several times. Now she tried to gather up her energy again to shout for help, but no sound came out of her dry throat. She closed her eyes and prayed. A blurry image of Ankita appeared before her eyes and that gave her some courage. She consoled herself thinking, 'Ankee will certainly show up, she will certainly come looking for me and rescue me.' 'Ankee, come quickly . . . rescue me from this hell . . .' As she was praying and calling out to her daughter for help, she felt more discomforting pain and closed her eyes. The tears that had filled her eyes squeezed out and rolled down her chin.

≈

It was four days later that the bodies were found.

On Monday, people started arriving one by one and the old building started filling up. People who tried to use the lift found that it was out of service and stuck in the middle of two floors. As it was a common problem, people started using the stairs, cursing the building owner. The Xerox centre opened for business. People started sipping coffee and sharing the stories of how they had spent the long weekend. A few aged employees, however, were furious at having to climb up to four floors and complained to the maintenance department. It was past twelve when the repairman showed up. He too had gone to his hometown for the long weekend. He had already received more than twenty calls and had stopped taking calls on his mobile phone. 'People don't leave me in peace even for a couple of days,' he grumbled. He was totally aware of the problems with that elevator. It was an old piece of junk. He had insisted several times in the past to the owner of the building that he must get a new lift installed, but the owner had not paid any attention. He cursed everyone as he repaired it for the umpteenth time. Finally, when he was done and was able to open the door, he jumped in fear. The sight of a fat, unknown woman's body made him shiver in his shoes. The body had turned dark and was stinking. Amidst that nasty stench-filled air was a faint whiff of fragrance from the perfume sprinkled on her sari.

Within half an hour the police arrived. They understood immediately that her body had been stuck inside for four days. The inspector examined the scene and wondered why the lady did not call anyone for help. Inside the lift it was written clearly: 'In case of emergency, do not lose your cool, please call this number . . .' He checked with his mobile if there was signal availability inside and found no issues. He asked his colleague to check with his phone, and he too had no problem connecting. He remembered that there was a mobile tower on the building. He picked up the handbag from next to the dead body and searched it. There was no cell phone in it. 'What kind of a foolish lady is she, she forgot to carry her mobile with her!' he muttered angrily before his colleagues. An innocent-looking constable remarked slyly: 'If there were a phone inside the elevator, this wouldn't have happened, right, sir? The government should never permit a lift without a phone.' The irritated inspector scolded the constable: 'We have thousands of elevators without phones, what do we do with them, then?' The constable had to shut up. With the help of a little notebook inside the deceased person's handbag, they were able to locate the house address as well as several telephone numbers. They found that her name was Kusuma and that she had a daughter. They documented all the information after proper confirmation and contacted the Bengaluru South police station, requesting them to visit the address to communicate the sad news. Some of the people they contacted readily agreed to come and help with the investigation.

~

As the inspector looked at the naked body of the victim, he figured she had been gang-raped. She must have hardly been in her mid-twenties. Her body showed several bloody wounds which had already turned dark. Houseflies were having a field day. It was a pathetic sign of the times. Since the house had an auto lock, the police had to break open the door to enter. They looked around for clues all over the house, like they always did, and found the mobile phone lying beside the cot. The battery was long dead. They looked around for the charger. When they switched on the phone they found that there were thousands of likes and messages on the Facebook icon. When they opened the app they saw a photo of her naked body—from her neck down to her knees— posted as a cover image on her profile page. They concluded that this must be the rapists' doing.

More than 2000 people had reacted to the photograph with likes. Many had posted tawdry comments, such as 'bold and beautiful'. The photo, being 'public', had been shared by thousands and was being circulated around the globe. The inspector looked at the other activities of that day on her account. He found the status message where she had declared that she would be alone in the house until afternoon, in addition to her naughty but beautiful picture she had posted herself, which had got more than a thousand likes. For someone who knew the world of crime intimately, it didn't take more than a moment to figure out that that one short sentence was the catalyst for the tragedy that had unfolded.

'If we advise parents not to buy mobile phones for young people, do they listen? No. Do youngsters know how to use them with care? No. See now, what all has happened because of this mobile phone!' As the inspector was waving the mobile phone angrily at his colleagues, he was really thinking about his own teenaged daughter who could not be separated from her cell phone for even a moment. 'Sir, can we not look at the friends list and inquire and catch the criminals?' asked the constable. 'This girl has more than 4000 friends; each time one guy writes a comment, his thousand other friends will be able to see this status. How many people will you question? Which son-of-a-whore will finance such a costly inquiry?' the inspector scolded the constable for his stupidity. Completely unaffected by his superior's humiliating tone, the constable expressed his wonder: 'Sir, of the so many thousand friends this girl had, how come in the last four days not even one came looking for her trying to find out why on earth she had posted a nude photo of herself on Facebook?'

21 August 2013

Nimmi

Initially, Srinivasa Rao did not like the puppy Nimmi one bit. As someone who had never ventured to keep a dog at home, he thought: 'Why bother now? Why all this headache at this ripe age of seventy?' But his son and daughter-in-law, who came to visit him from America, coaxed and cajoled him into keeping her. 'All these days, Amma was with you. Now you are alone; you need the company of a living being. We'll make arrangements by employing a caretaker for the dog.' They begged him, with tear-filled eyes, to keep the dog. Rao yielded to this emotional blackmail.

He had prepared himself rather well to face old age alone. When he saw that his wife's health was a lot more delicate than his own, he began to brace himself for these days of solitude. At first he had felt sad when his son left for America, but he no longer felt bitter. He consoled himself, thinking: 'Just as I left my village and settled in Bengaluru, so did my son leave India and settle in America. It is nothing but selfishness to expect that someone should come to your rescue when you grow old. If we lose our health because of our poor lifestyle, we should not transfer that misery to our children.'

He had named the Pomeranian pup 'Nimmi' because of his initial dislike for her. Actually, that was the name of the girl in high school who had rejected him. She was the daughter of the

Kannada teacher. One day in school, he had gathered all his strength and written a page-long love letter to her. He had placed it inside a notebook and handed it to her. He had not been able to sleep all night. He did not have the courage to look at her the following day at school. But that girl, Nimmi, had no confusion whatsoever in her mind; she had placed that letter in the same notebook and returned it to him. She had corrected all the errors in the letter using red ink and put a note at the end: 'I have found twenty-eight errors in this one-pager. You should first learn how to write Kannada properly. Then, maybe, you can attempt to write a love letter.' From that day onwards, whenever he got upset with anyone he would call that person Nimmi.

Nimmi was a cute little creature. She had silky silver hair covering her body, with scattered spots of golden blonde hair, as though someone had smeared sandalwood paste on her, little eyes like tamarind seeds and silky ears. How could one hate such a sweet thing that followed one around, making soft puppy sounds? In no time Nimmi became enmeshed in Rao's life, like his breath. It filled his heart to see her follow him everywhere, even when she made him stumble as she walked very close to him. He thought: 'Why did no one ever tell me that raising a puppy can bring such pleasure!' He grew quite attached to the pup.

Nimmi was no ordinary dog; Rao realized very quickly that she was a very smart puppy. Rao usually sat in the veranda to read the newspaper while the milk was put on the boil in the kitchen. He would sometimes forget about it, only to run to the kitchen after the milk had risen up and spilled over. But now Nimmi, who sat by his feet, would somehow figure that the milk was about to boil over. Before it could happen she would bark at him in warning. He thought perhaps the puppy could recognize the aroma of boiling milk about to spill over. In the same way, Nimmi would run to the mobile phone and start barking before its ringing could be heard by human ears.

Six days a week, Rao would get up early at five thirty in the morning, brush his teeth, wash his face and head out for a walk with Nimmi. But he took it easy on Sundays and spent time in bed until seven in the morning. Nimmi had understood his routine perfectly. She would wake him up regularly at 5.30 a.m., six days of the week, but not disturb him until seven on Sundays. It was truly incredible that a dog could keep track of the days of the week with such precision!

There were a few puddles of stagnant water around the area where Rao lived, because of which the residents in the building had to face a regular onslaught of mosquitoes. The mosquitoes would enter the houses soon after darkness fell. The residents tried to minimize the menace by shutting all the doors and windows before dark. But Rao would forget to do this some days, and Nimmi gladly took the responsibility of this task upon herself. She was smart enough to know to shut the door at five in the evening and open the door at six in the morning.

Soon Rao was witness to a much greater talent in Nimmi, a lot cleverer than any of the others he had seen so far.

Rao lived on the ground floor, while a Tamilian family lived on the third floor. They had a son who was studying engineering; Rao had noticed him now and then but had never had the chance to speak to him. The boy was learning to play the flute. Rao would hear him practise many times as he sat in the veranda. He enjoyed the lilting sounds of his flute in the background while he read. Whenever there was an 'Aha' moment after a nice display of melody by the young man, Rao would place his book down for a few minutes, close his eyes and let the raga envelop him.

One day the young man came down and rang the doorbell. 'Uncle, my name is Swaminadan. I live on the third floor, and I need to talk to you.' He was all smiles. He was wearing a white dhoti and kurta, and had conspicuously smeared bright white ash on his forehead. This somewhat dark-skinned slim boy

sporting a small moustache made an impression on Rao. But he
wondered to himself even as he welcomed him: 'What does he
have to talk to me about all of a sudden?' The boy came in and
sat on the sofa while Nimmi sat next to him on an empty seat,
wagging her tail.

'Uncle, what's your dog's name?' he asked, caressing Nimmi's
head.

'I call her Nimmi.'

'Your Nimmi seems to be very intelligent, Uncle,' he said with
excitement, while Rao wondered how on earth he could know
about Nimmi's intelligence.

'It has a good understanding of classical music. I am a student of
the classical flute, still learning, you know. Many times, I slip into
apaswara, the wrong notes, and go off-key, despite trying hard,
maybe due to an incorrect placement of the fingers or blowing
wrongly. Whenever that happens, your Nimmi comes to the
veranda and barks, as though to scold me. She relaxes as soon as I
play the right notes.'

Rao was flabbergasted. 'There is no such thing. Nimmi gets
bored staying cooped up inside the house and she has made it a
habit of going to the veranda and barking off and on. It is like
us getting up to stretch after sitting for a while. You seem to be
imagining things.'

Rao's explanation did not satisfy Swaminadan. 'I do not lie,
Uncle. In the beginning I too felt the same, but I have tested
Nimmi several times before coming to you. When I play any
melody, if there is a note that is apaswara, Nimmi will surely come
to the veranda to scold me.' Rao did not know how to respond
to his claim and became silent. Having realized that Rao was not
convinced, Swaminadan became restless.

'Okay, Uncle, I understand why you doubt what I'm saying.
Let's do one thing. I shall bring my flute to your place, here, and
play; you will see how Nimmi acts up as soon as she identifies a

note that does not belong there.' He was enthused by his own suggestion.

'All that is fine, Swaminadan, but how am I to know when a note being played does or does not belong in that melody? I don't know much about classical music.' Rao aired his doubts.

'Uncle, it is not so difficult. You don't have to be an expert musician to identify an off-key or a note that's off. Our guru says, those who can honestly identify what is natural and what is unnatural in life can also identify musical notes that do not belong in a melody. When someone is lying in a normal conversation, don't we get a hint of the deception? On occasion, when things don't seem to be going right, for instance, when you get up in the morning, some days you feel something is wrong, it is just like that, Uncle. In any case, I shall give you a hint with my eyes just before playing the wrong note.' Having said this, he ran upstairs to pick up his flute and the shruti-box that provided the drone support for his practice.

≈

It was again the Ramanavami season. A huge pandal was raised for the month-long music festival in the Fort High School grounds, which happened every year. The special event that Sunday evening was a concert by Manjula Namboodiri, who was well known throughout the country for her rich voice, her rendition of difficult ragas and her improvisation. It was no wonder that the entire ground was overflowing with people. But what was special that day was that Rao had taken Nimmi to the concert with him.

Recently, Swaminadan had drawn closer to Nimmi. He would bring his flute to Rao's house and practise before her. He would say with a sense of appreciation and pride, 'Anyone who corrects your mistakes, Uncle, is like a guru. Nimmi is like my guru, Uncle.' Nimmi had shown extraordinary talent for identifying mistakes in not only popular ragas like Kalyani, Shankaraabharana, Todi and Kaamboji, but also in some unusual ones like Suruti, Bindumaalini, Kokilapriya and Gaanamurthy.

Rao liked Swaminadan's company. Anyone would like the company of a young man who came on his own to his home and played the flute melodiously. Rao, having listened to his flute regularly, had now developed a taste for classical music. Although he was yet to develop the capability to identify ragas, he was now quite proficient in identifying apaswaras. He too realized that an apaswara was analogous to 'When you are walking with ease, your foot suddenly hits a piece of rock, and you stumble and fall'. He found that this process of detection of apaswaras in a musical rendition was less of an analytical exercise of the external senses and more of an internal experience for the listener. But he could not understand how Nimmi had mastered this. His respect for the canine species had suddenly soared, and he decided never to swear at anyone with a 'You dog!'

Swaminadan had gladly volunteered to take on some of the chores related to Nimmi's care. They included taking her out on mating trips, feeding her non-vegetarian food—something she enjoyed but never received from her master—taking her out to his friends' houses to play with other dogs, and so on. If any of his music-loving friends visited him, he would bring them over to Rao's residence and demonstrate Nimmi's talents and stun them. The friends invariably took selfies with Nimmi.

Swaminadan had insisted that Rao bring Nimmi to Manjula Namboodiri's concert. 'Nimmi has never ever attended a live concert, Uncle. If she hears Manjula Namboodiri's singing, she will be very pleased. Most of the auditoriums do not allow dogs inside the concert hall, but the Ramanavami concert takes place in an open-air pandal, where cars can be parked close by. So taking Nimmi would not cause any trouble, Uncle.' Being open to new ideas, Rao had readily agreed.

Manjula Namboodiri entered the stage wearing a Kanjeevaram
pattu sari, sunset-red with a moonlight-yellow border, a headful
of jasmine flowers, lots of gold jewellery and a noticeably large
dot of kumkum on her forehead. The large audience welcomed
her with a standing ovation, which she acknowledged respectfully
by bowing to the house. She occupied her spot and checked
the sound system, tuned the tamboora after taking it from the
boy who was to play it during the concert, made some casual
conversation with the accompanying artistes, giving them some
suggestions and instructions, and began to sing. Rao took two
chairs, one for himself and one for Nimmi, and sat down to enjoy
the evening.

Manjula started off with an Abhogi-varnam and went on to
sing Thyagaraja's *'Meru samaana'* in the raga Mayaamaalavagowla.
Both were rendered very well, and the audience expressed their
appreciation with what appeared to be unending applause. Rao
himself was very pleased and looked over at Nimmi, who appeared
to be quietly enjoying the music. Rao felt he could easily tell
by looking at her eyes that Nimmi liked Manjula Namboodiri's
singing. As a third piece, Manjula picked the twentieth melakarta,
a parent melody, Natabhairavi, and the famous composition of
Papanasam Sivan *'Sri Valli deva senaapate'*, which happened to be a
favourite composition of both Rao's and Nimmi's. In anticipation
of the aesthetic pleasure that was to come, Rao looked at Nimmi
and got ready to relish the experience.

The raga elaboration was providing the listeners a unique
experience. It was as if they were sent hiking in the magnificent
Himalayas, seeking uncharted territories to fathom the profound
expanse of the silver ranges. The Natabhairavi then effected a
sense of capturing the varied shapes of the early monsoon clouds,
which gradually expanded into the infinite sky to contain all living
beings. It was akin to witnessing the mesmerizing beauty of a small
mustard-sized seed falling on the earth and springing up in the

form of a huge tree, lush with green leaves. The reverberating elaboration made Rao go into a meditative state; he closed his eyes.

Amidst the perfect expressions of the traditional raga elaboration by Manjula Namboodiri, accidentally, an apaswara note that did not belong to the Natabhairavi raga was heard distinctly by the connoisseurs. It was as if a writer had penned a jarring line in the middle of a great novel. Rao too felt that a smooth walk had been disturbed by a sudden fall. He was forced to open his eyes and was about to blurt out 'Ayyo, apaswara!' when he heard Nimmi's loud barking, which was audible across the entire ground. 'How can Nimmi's barking be so loud?' wondered Rao. He looked down sideways at Nimmi's chair, but where was she? The chair was empty. As he began to worry about her, he realized that something terrible had happened. The barking sounds were coming from the loudspeakers. There was pandemonium in the pandal; Manjula Namboodiri had stopped singing. Having heard such loud barking, several stray dogs from the nearby area suddenly entered the pandal, running into it and barking. They might have been wondering who was this dog that could bark so loud.

Rao went running to the stage, wondering how Nimmi could be so nimble as to vanish from his side in a trice and reach the stage. He panicked hearing Nimmi's restless barking and seeing the audience also rushing towards the stage. He ignored the volunteers who were attempting to control the crowd and ran to catch his dog. He was afraid they might hurt Nimmi badly or even kill her. Manjula and the accompanying artistes were standing awestruck to one side, not knowing what to do. When a few members from the audience advanced towards Nimmi, she jumped off the stage and escaped through a small gap she found among the audience, running away towards Makkala Koota, the building next to the auditorium.

'Where is my dog? Where did you chase her to?' Rao was pleading with the people near the stage. 'So, it's your dog, is it?

Why the hell did you bring a dog to a music concert? Didn't you know that it would disturb the performance?' someone was heard chastising Rao.

Rao tried to explain the situation: 'My Nimmi loves music, that is why I brought her. I was sitting with her at the edge—way back there, but by some magic she appeared on stage. She can identify faulty musical notes, you see, that is the reason for her barking.'

'You mean to say that a senior artiste like Manjula sings apaswara notes? How dare you? Look at his arrogance, who is this old man . . .?' People started saying all kinds of things about Rao. In the meantime, Swaminadan came running towards them and asked for pardon on Rao's behalf. Most of the people in the audience knew Swaminadan; they accepted his apologies and let Rao go. Swaminadan encouraged Rao to return home quietly.

Rao was very upset that Nimmi had run away from him. 'No matter where she is, I will go and find her,' he told himself. All those people had driven away that poor dog; where could he go looking for her at this hour? Who knows how scared she might be? Nimmi was not familiar with the area. Rao was worried that the stray dogs might attack her. 'Why on earth did I bring her to the concert? I could have played a few good CDs for her at home. That poor thing was yelled at by hundreds of people because of me. How could I have known that an eminent musician like Manjula Namboodiri would sing an apaswara note?' Rao was cursing himself again and again.

Rao went to his car and sat there, feeling very sad. 'No matter where Nimmi is, I shall find her,' he swore to himself, as he started the car and tried to exit the parking area. Just before his car reached the signal near the Makkala Koota, Nimmi, who had been sitting quietly in the back seat all this time, jumped to the front seat. Rao got so excited seeing her right next to him, he pulled his car to the side and stopped. With tears of joy, he said to her, 'When did you come in, Nimmi?' What could she say? She just licked his hand.

Luckily, Rao had left the windows lowered while parking his car. Amidst all that commotion, Nimmi had quietly come and sat inside the car. Thank goodness for that! Otherwise, where could he have gone looking for her in the dark of the night? Rao was ecstatic. Once his excitement and agitation calmed down, he asked Nimmi, 'Did such an eminent musician sing an apaswara?' Nimmi stretched her tongue out all the way and said '*Huh . . . huh . . .*'

≈

Nimmi's photo appeared in many newspapers the following day. The baffled faces of the artistes on one side and the barking Nimmi near the microphones on the other, brightened by the stage-lights, had been clicked from various angles by different photographers. Details of the incident were also reported. However, what was most surprising was that Manjula Namboodiri had nothing but praise for Nimmi.

Manjula Namboodiri had no fear of dogs as she had a couple of her own at home. She had simply been stunned by Nimmi's appearance on stage. She had resumed her singing once the commotion was over, and continued to elaborate Natabhairavi in all its glory even after the interruption. She could tell in the depths of her heart that the pup had been truly enjoying her singing with rapt attention. So, she continued looking fondly at Nimmi, who was sitting upright with her front legs raised.

Manjula had not slept properly for two nights as she had taken late flights two days in a row. After the delayed flights, she could not fall asleep easily in a hotel in an unfamiliar town; she was exhausted after the previous evening's concert. It had brought on a headache and body ache, and she felt a kind of restlessness overall. That was perhaps how the rare apaswara in her concert had

stolen into her rendition. Perhaps it was the angry expression of an
exhausted body that badly needed and desired some rest. The dog
had suddenly reminded her of her guru, who used to keep a small
cane with him to slam the ground with, to indicate his disapproval
whenever a wrong note appeared in the middle of his disciples'
smooth singing. Nimmi's lightning-speed reaction to the apaswara
had reminded her of her guru's 'cane-slamming' reaction. It made
Manjula quiver. She felt she was insulting the goddess of music
by accepting too many concerts too frequently, out of monetary
greed. She repented with tears in her eyes, thinking her guru had
appeared before her in the form of Nimmi to caution her. It was
at that time that an elderly gentleman had appeared on stage to tell
her that it was his dog and it had this unique talent of identifying
apaswaras. She was amazed and even thrilled by this possibility.

The pandemonium had ended in ten minutes; things came
under control and the concert continued. Manjula Namboodiri
spoke to the audience before she resumed her singing. 'I beg your
pardon for the interruption, but I am amazed at the unique talent of
this dog. I honestly admit to the audience that accidentally a wrong
note had appeared in my rendition. The question is, how after
listening intently for nearly fifteen minutes did that little puppy
identify that this one note did not belong there? This to me is the
greatest wonder. There are so many wonders in this world. I truly
believe that this puppy is a special creation.'

All this was reported in detail in the papers; someone had
recorded the entire incident and the video was floating on the
internet. Hundreds of thousands had viewed the video as it went
viral.

Greg Jones is among the top fifty richest men in America; at forty-
five, he is still a bachelor. His software company has branches all

over the world. The interesting fact about him is, he is a high
school dropout because he couldn't get passing grades; but today he
is a billionaire. He has made so much money that he has absolutely
no value for it; no one can arrest his attention by flaunting their
wealth. Nowadays he spends most of his wealth on charity, serving
the poor and downtrodden in various countries in Africa and Asia.

In order to feel special and superior, he has started collecting
things other than money. He collects dogs with unique
characteristics from different corners of the globe. He has a Chinese
dog that helped the police identify his master's murderer after five
years of the crime; a Russian dog that recognized in advance that
an earthquake was imminent and drove all the members of the
family out into the open and saved them from being crushed by
the rubble; a Kenyan dog that administered a rare medicine made
out of crushed greens to an ill boy—who had been written off even
by doctors—saving his life; an English dog that uses a commode to
relieve itself, and so on. In his interviews he never fails to talk about
his dogs; he flaunts them, making them sit around him during his
interviews.

An employee of Jones's company in San Jose had shared a video
in which a Pomeranian puppy was seen identifying faulty musical
notes. He shared some notes on the dog too. He said this unique
dog was his father's pet and it was his gift to his father who lived all
alone in Bengaluru. Although his father had told him earlier about
this unique ability of the puppy, he had paid no attention to it.
Now that he had shared the video, he received many compliments
from co-workers from different parts of the world.

Greg Jones was astonished by the video; he might have seen
it at least thirty times. He knew that dogs could understand and
appreciate music, but he felt great excitement and curiosity about
this little puppy which could not only identify misplaced musical
notes but also bark at the one who had committed the blunder.
He was convinced that such a dog should belong in his collection.

The fact that such an exceptional dog was owned by a retired old Indian made him very sad; it was like a rare diamond buried in the mud. 'I must get it in my possession somehow,' he resolved to himself. Once Greg makes up his mind, it is final; he knows from previous experience that he will fulfil his wish at any cost.

As a first step, Greg summoned Ramakant, who had shared the video, to his office for a meeting.

≈

Srinivasa Rao was very upset and was also getting very irritated. 'Why on earth does he have his eyes on a poor man's dog?' Ramakant couldn't figure how to make his father understand.

'Appa, it is not like that. He is a rich man, and it is a matter of privilege that we possess something that he desires to have. If you say no, it is going to pose some problems for me. In any case, it is I who got you Nimmi. Remember you had opposed the idea?' Ramakant tried to use his idea of logic.

'Yes, I had opposed your idea. If you had not compelled me, this problem would not have arisen. You didn't listen to me then; you are not listening to me now. I can't live without Nimmi.'

'Appa, I will get you an almost identical dog, if you wish.'

'Why don't you go look for an identical father and tell him that?'

'Why are you talking like this, Appa? See, if Nimmi lives in a tycoon's home, wouldn't that be nice for her too? Are you telling me you don't want that for Nimmi?'

'Who told you that a dog in a tycoon's home will be happy? For a dog to be happy, all you need is a morsel of food, a handful of love. Do you think dogs demand gold jewellery? If you show it a heap of cash, it will lift its leg and piss on it.'

'When I insisted on getting you a dog, you refused. Now again you are being stubborn. Don't you ever forget that it was I who got you Nimmi.'

'How could I ever forget? You are the one who gave me that puppy. No doubt about it. Along the same lines, do not ever forget that it was your mother and I that brought you into this world.'

Ramakant hung up; he had run out of ways to convince his father. At this end, Rao was very disturbed; he shared his grief with Nimmi all day.

'They want me to give you away—how is that even conceivable? All these days I have taken you out whenever you needed to go out, I have bathed you, combed your hair and removed fleas from your body, fed you, loved you . . . now all of a sudden, if they demand that you be given away, what does it mean? You tell me, Nimmi, why children these days seem to have no wisdom whatsoever, they don't seem to get it, do they?' What could poor Nimmi say? She just hung out her long tongue and followed him around as her expression of love.

But Greg Jones was not about to give up so easily. Around 10 p.m., when Rao was just getting ready to go to sleep, Ramakant called again.

The tone in which he addressed him, 'Appaaaa . . .', it was clear to Rao that his son was quite subdued and way down in the duel. So he remained silent.

'He must have the dog, he is just not quitting,' pleaded Ramakant, 'and he is willing to offer one hundred thousand dollars. Do you know what it means in our currency? Seventy lakh rupees.'

'What will I do with that kind of money at my age, Ramakant?' Rao too was yielding slowly.

'I know that you don't need or want any money, Appa.'

'. . .'

'In addition, he has promised me two promotions; I don't think I have achieved so much greatness as to refuse it. Appa, I am sure you know that after Trump came to power it has been extremely hard for Indians to keep our jobs. Please, Appa, don't act as if a dog is more important than your own son.'

Ramakant knew exactly what effect these words would have on his father even before he uttered them. They shattered Rao like a hail of bullets.

'Okay, son, tell him to come and take the dog. I lost my wife, I couldn't save her, now this puppy. Why would I show stubbornness? For what?' Rao had lost all energy to extend the argument.

'Thanks, Appa, thank you so much . . .' said Ramakant, with exuberance and in a flood of relief. Rao hung up.

Nimmi, who was listening to their dialogue, came and slept by Rao's thigh. 'We don't have many days left between us, Nimmi; they are coming to get you,' he said to her, his eyes moist.

Although Greg Jones's company had its development centre in India, he had never visited India. He would simply issue the necessary instructions to his subordinates via videoconferencing and get things done. Whenever opportunities arose for visits to India, he hesitated, out of fear of mosquitoes. He knew about the mosquito menace in Bengaluru. He believed that if he was bitten by even one mosquito he would get infected with malaria and die. This fear of malaria had developed into a major phobia as a result of the stories his grandmother told him when he was growing up. She had narrated creepy stories, in which 'Indians convert humans into parrots by witchcraft and imprison them in cages'; 'there are cannibals in that country'; 'mosquitoes the size of a corn are so nasty that their bites cause death', and so on. As he grew up, he realized of course that her stories were not true, but he was still unable to get rid of the phobia. Although his colleagues assured him several times over that India was safe to visit, he would google for evidence of an abundance of mosquitoes in the country. A search like 'mosquitoes in Bangalore' would easily yield thousands of articles and hundreds of pictures instantly. If it is a fact that mosquitoes exist, then they will certainly bite; then, according to Google, some of them could infect you with malaria, dengue, chikungunya and such other debilitating and life-threatening diseases. All this made him resolve that he would not visit India, no matter what. But this puppy, which was so talented as to identify faults in music, had forced him to relax his resolve. Finally, he reluctantly agreed to visit India.

The two conditions laid down by Rao had caused some discomfort to Greg Jones. First, he insisted that Greg should personally come to Rao's place, hand over the money and receive the puppy. 'I am not putting my Nimmi up for sale, it is he who is showing off his wealth and taking my puppy away from me. Therefore, he should come,' Rao had told his son firmly.

It wasn't so hard to fulfil the first condition. By making the visit during the day, Greg could easily avoid the mosquito problem. But the second condition imposed by Rao would not let that happen. 'This transaction should take place only after sunset', was the second condition.

'Appa, when you have agreed to part with your dog, whether it is during the day or night what difference does it make? Why are you imposing such conditions?' Ramakant was angry. But Rao couldn't care less.

'Selling a pet that you have raised with love is nothing less than a filthy transaction. No honourable man would ever do such a deal in daylight. How, after committing such a horrible sin in daylight, will an honest man have the courage to face the sun the following day? All such evil transactions in the world happen in the dark of night. Tell your boss to come after dark.' Rao didn't mince his words. Ramakant, realizing that he couldn't change his father's mind, went to Greg Jones and pleaded with him: 'I am really sorry for putting you through all this trouble.' But Greg was not upset in the least, and he readily agreed to Rao's conditions. Being a smart businessman, Greg Jones knew that if he got upset he would never be able to make the deal. His immediate goal was to get Nimmi in his possession; he could worry about other matters later.

Srinivasa Rao's residence was located near Bannerghatta Road, around which there are several ponds, once filled with fresh water. Now they have very little water but contain enough filth to produce a rotten smell. The nearby factories had added their wastes to the ponds to make matters worse. Real estate companies were waiting for the water bodies to dry up, while the elected officials of the city corporation, who had received kickbacks from every side, were sitting tight. Thus, every evening, armies of mosquitoes would attack the nearby apartment complexes.

Several management meetings were held at Greg Jones's company to discuss 'how to save Greg from such potential mosquito onslaughts'. Greg was not ready to apply any repellents on his body; he was afraid of skin reactions to them. He had no faith in the devices made in India, such as repellents plugged into electrical outlets. Also, uninterrupted power supply was not guaranteed in Rao's apartment complex, which did not have a back-up generator. After serious discussions, they decided to place non-electrical repellent coils next to Greg during his visit to Rao's residence. Several such spiral coils were packed by Greg's security guards, along with their guns.

Finally, Greg boarded his private jet and left for Bengaluru, India.

≈

By the time Greg Jones stepped inside Rao's residence, it was around seven in the evening. After landing at the Devanahalli airport, he had boarded a private helicopter, landed on the Apollo Hospital helipad and taken a ride in a BMW to reach Rao's apartment. He had instructed his employees to keep his travel under wraps as far as the public was concerned so that there would be no uninvited crowds to deal with. He made sure that only the security officials in India were informed about his visit.

Around five in the evening, Rao made sure that all windows and doors were shut, as Ramakant had briefed him about his boss's fear of mosquitoes. Rao took enough care to prevent any discomfort to his guest. He had been burning the insect-repellent fluid continuously since early evening; and luckily the electricity had not deceived him. Rao was worried what to offer such a rich man when he arrived, although his son had made it crystal clear that Greg wouldn't touch even water in his house. What Greg wanted to do was to test Nimmi's talent once before taking her into his possession, so Rao had made the necessary arrangements.

Leaving all his other work aside, Swaminadan, clad in a kurta-pyjama, was ready with his flute and shruti-box, sitting in the living room. He had decided to play the raga Hamsadhwani. Rao had briefed him about the kind of wealth the guest had, and that had created some unease in Swaminadan. But he was very confident, because even if he played apaswara notes by accident, that would be no problem! 'The entire exercise *was* to play apaswara, then why bother about playing perfectly? This was his consolation. Still, somewhere in Swaminadan's mind, he was worried, 'What do I do if I am unable to produce a faulty note?'

Greg Jones entered, along with two security guards, like Jaya and Vijaya flanking Lord Vishnu. A boy was walking in front of him, holding a burning mosquito repellent coil that produced a lot of smoke. He looked just like the incense-carrying boy in front of the Lord's procession. It appeared as though he had stolen Vishnu's lethal disc weapon, the Sudarshana Chakra. The security guards knew their limitation as far as mosquitoes were concerned; they could not shoot them with their guns. But they kept strict vigil to make sure no flying insect came near their boss. If they happened to see one in the room, they would run and slap it between their palms. They were shocked that a clap could be more powerful than a machine gun.

Having received a two-hour-long coaching and orientation in Indian culture, Greg brought his palms together and greeted Rao with a 'Namaste'; Rao returned the courtesy by saying 'Namaskaara'. Greg was mighty pleased to see Nimmi, who was sitting upright. He ran to her and said, 'O my sweetheart,' as he caressed her lush hair. Nimmi seemed unmoved by his show of affection and simply stared at him. The boy carrying the sudarshana Chakra hurried after Greg, spreading the smoke around him. Greg put his hand inside one of his pockets and removed a diamond necklace from it. He made Nimmi wear it, exclaiming excitedly, 'I love you, honey,' as he wiped his moist eyes. Slightly irritated by the prickliness of the necklace, Nimmi shook her neck this way and that.

Rao showed Greg to his seat and he occupied it gracefully. The smoke-producing red 'Sudarshana Chakra' was placed on the side table next to Greg. As if he just remembered something, Greg brought out his cheque book, wrote out Rao's name and an amount of one hundred thousand dollars, signed his name using a fine gold pen and handed it to Rao. Rao didn't care to even read it. He simply placed it on the side table where the mosquito repellent was kept. Some ash particles from the coil fell on the cheque.

'Let us start,' commanded Greg Jones. Having waited for this moment all this while, Swaminadan put his palms together and showed his respects; he tuned his shruti box and placed his flute on his lips. Greg knew nothing about Indian classical music, although he was well versed in western classical; he could play the piano very well. With that in mind, Ramakant had briefed Greg that it would not be a problem for him to identify an off-key note. If a company that made money year after year suddenly went off track, Greg was able to quickly sense it. If someone were to ask him how he could do that, it would be hard for him to explain.

Swaminadan started playing the highly popular 'vaathaapi Ganapatim bhaje' in the raga Hamsadhwani. At that very moment there was a power cut—the lights went off and the room went dark. Nimmi's two shining eyes were seen moving back and forth in the dark. The burning coil appeared much brighter. The smoke was spreading feebly but steadily. The security guards brightened the room with their flashlights; Rao went in and brought candles and lit them. Swaminadan felt it was a bad omen for the lights to go off right at the start of the piece. But it was hard to predict who might be at the receiving end. In any case, he continued with the Hamsadhwani composition.

Nimmi, after being quiet for a while, started behaving abnormally. She started barking at Greg non-stop. Swaminadan had not struck any musical notes that could be considered out of place in the melody being played. Greg realized Nimmi's error, but remained silent. Swaminadan resumed playing, and again Nimmi barked at Rao, although the flute music was flawless. Rao was surprised at Nimmi's conduct, but Swaminadan was convinced that Nimmi was not listening to his flute at all.

Nimmi's barking went on and on; she would alternatively look at Greg and Rao and bark at them, ignoring Rao's commands to her to keeping quiet. Nimmi seemed to be getting angrier and angrier and her barking and growling became more and more intense.

Finally, Nimmi's irritation reached its climax. She stopped barking and took a serious look at everything around. She jumped on the side table where the burning coil was placed. Remember the one-hundred-thousand-dollar cheque placed close to the burning repellent on the side table? Nimmi pissed all over it. The coil was put off by the wet stream and the ink signature on the cheque was washed out. Nimmi didn't stop at that, she ran to the door and jumped at the bolt, unlocked it with all her force and pushed the door open. Thousands of mosquitoes rushed inside Rao's apartment, humming and droning, like enemy soldiers pouring into a fort once its gates have been breached.

It took Greg a few moments to realize what had just happened. The moment the mosquitoes went on a rampage on his body, he started shivering in fear. 'Devil dog, devil dog . . . it's conspiring to finish me,' he cried, and ran out of the house shouting. Behind him ran the security guards carrying their guns, and the boy carrying the Sudarshana Chakra. The Hamsadhwani raga ended before the complete rendering of the composition, but, in a strange coincidence, the electricity revived and the lights came back on!

～

The next morning Ramakant called Rao on his cell phone.

'Appa, what's all this, how could Nimmi cheat him like that?'

'Who told you she cheated?'

'My boss called me and told me everything that happened. He said we had lied about her talent and had taken him for a ride.'

'Stop it, son. Do you think faulty notes occur only in music? They exist in life too. Look at your boss, who thinks everything can be bought with money, and look at me, who was stupid enough to agree to sell such a precious thing for money. Nimmi was able to recognize apaswaras in both of us. Don't underestimate her ability to realize that life is even more precious than music. That is why she stopped listening to the flute and started barking at both of us. Couldn't you understand that much?'

Ramakant cut the phone.

(A tribute to Satyajit Ray)
13 September 2017

Two Rupees

The Madras–Bombay train came to a stop at Guntakal station. When a chameleon halts suddenly after a neck-and-neck race, it is as though it is pretending it forgot how to move. The motion of the breath in its neck is the only sign that the chameleon is alive. Similarly, the engine was exhibiting signs of life by hissing. When people started alighting and boarding, the train changed its colours and the entire scene was transformed, just the way a chameleon changes its colours to match its surroundings. Porters wearing red turbans were moving in and out of the compartments, looking for potential clients. They were like the spots on a chameleon's body. It was ten in the night, and even though the city of Guntakal had already fallen asleep, the railway station was wide awake and aglow with life.

Kashavva stayed put in the general compartment. Putta and Gowri, who had fallen asleep, were now half awake because of all the noise and commotion generated by the passengers, and were rubbing their eyes. They could easily hear the announcements coming from the loudspeaker, piercing through all the background noise. The announcer was shouting that the train had arrived at Guntakal station. Although Kashavva knew that she was to get down at Guntakal and board the Bellary train, she had decided not to get down until Koteshwara Rao came to help her. Her holdall, a large steel trunk, a basket made of plastic wire and a rail-chombu—a specially-shaped bronze water container—were at her feet.

As the passengers got down one by one and the compartment became empty, Kashavva started to lose courage. She started shivering as she thought the train might start moving and carry her away to an unknown, distant town. But she did not want to get down on her own. Kashavva felt that the entire world was conspiring against her. Her bitter experience in Madras had taught her that a childless, helpless widow like her would never receive kindness or love from anyone. On the other hand, people would wait for opportunities to hurt and exploit her.

Gopanna had cautioned her, not once, not twice, but three times, that she must not trust anyone in an unknown place like Guntakal and that his friend Koteshwara Rao would be there to receive her and help her switch trains. When she went to Madras, Gopanna himself had come with her up to Guntakal and had helped the three of them to board the Madras train. But he was unable to accompany her on her return journey owing to some important work at his office. Since he couldn't come he had requested a friend to help her. Kashavva had never seen Koteshwara Rao, but Gopanna had assured her, saying it would not be very hard for Rao to identify a widowed woman with a shaved head wearing a red sari.

A porter wearing a dirty white dhoti and a blood-red shirt, with a towel thrown over his shoulder, appeared and asked politely, 'Ajji, where to?' 'Maybe to the graveyard, why do you care,' Kashavva responded irritatedly. The porter laughed and asked the little girl Gowri, 'Where to, little sister?' She replied, 'To Bellary,' enthusiastically. Kashavva got upset with her and slapped her on the back and took her to task: 'Shut up, don't you try to act like an adult.' 'Let go, Ajji, why do you spank the little girl? The train going to Bellary is standing on platform number one, it is somewhat far; if you wish, I can take you there. I shall carry all your belongings, you just have to pay three rupees,' said the porter. Assuming the transaction was over, he started collecting the bedding and the trunk. Suddenly afraid that this guy too was out to exploit her, Kashavva took the newspaper from Gowri's hand, rolled it up and hit the porter's wrist with it. The unexpected attack made him exclaim 'haa', and quickly retract his hands. 'Even after my objecting, you place your hands on my belongings? I won't just sit and watch, do you understand? Our Koteshwara Rao is coming to take us to the Bellary train . . .' she blurted out. Massaging his wrist to relieve the pain, he said, 'Ajji, if you say no, why should I care?' he mumbled to her and moved on to the next compartment. As he moved away, Putta called him by his name, 'Sreeramanjaneyulu!', making him look back. Putta squeezed his eyes and pointed to the large metallic name plate on the porter's arm, containing his name written in English letters. The porter was mighty pleased to note that this little boy was able to read such a long name as his, written in English, without making any mistakes. He went to him and stroked his head, saying, 'Quite a smart boy, your grandson, Ajji . . . my child too is roughly of the same age . . . I have also put him in school . . . he has started learning ABC . . .' Having said this, he went away.

There were no more passengers to get in or get out. Kashavva's compartment was now empty and the train got ready to move. Kashavva's anxiety was growing by the minute; she put her head out of the unprotected window and started looking for anyone who might be approaching her. When she saw someone walking towards the compartment, she yelled 'Koteshwara Rao . . .' but to no avail. There was no one coming for her. Seeing Ajji's anxiety, the children too became desperate and started yelling out Koteshwara Rao's name. Many people looked back at the call but went their way. Kashavva started chanting the *'Navagraha japa'*, a prayer to the planets, wondering which planet might have prevented Koteshwara

Rao from reaching the train station on time. The train whistled, Kashavva felt helpless and began to cry; seeing her, the children too began to cry.

In the meantime, Sreeramanjaneyulu appeared again, carrying some other client's belongings. Putta called out to him. The porter was astonished to see the old lady and the children still inside the compartment. He knew the train was about to leave. He asked 'Why, Ajji? Your folks didn't show up, yet?' Kashavva was dismayed. She responded, 'No, he did not . . . our Gopya had told me that he knew the man, you see? He too has duped me . . .' 'Wait, you wait' said the porter, and placed the load he was carrying on his head to a side and came back.

By the time he carried the bedding and the trunk on his head, the wire basket on his shoulder, and assisted them to alight from the compartment, the train whistled again, making noises as it started moving out of the platform. The very thought that even a minute's delay would have taken her to the unknown city of Mumbai made her shiver; she felt as though she had escaped from some monster's cave.

The wind that blew with the departing train brought Kashavva back to earth. As soon as the porter picked up the luggage and started marching towards platform-number-one, Kashavva became alert and started haggling about his fare. 'First let's talk about how much I should pay.' 'I told you already, Ajji, three rupees' said the porter. '*Ayyayyappa*, which fool will pay you three rupees just for carrying the luggage a few steps? This is cheating. I will pay one rupee, take it or leave it,' Kashavva bargained. 'Ajji, if you try to save two rupees and start bargaining with me, the Bellary train will also leave, and you will be sitting here all night. I am a poor man; I have put my son in school. By paying two more rupees you won't become poor,' he started pleading. 'Do you think I am a moneylender? I am poor myself. Do you know, just to earn two rupees, I must work all night preparing shaavige vermicelli.

Come on, let us agree on what I must pay.' She stood her ground. Finally, they agreed on two rupees. Sreeramanjaneyulu was more concerned than Kashavva about the Bellary train leaving the platform, so he started running with the luggage and Kashavva ran behind him along with the children, carrying her rail-chombu in one hand. The leaky lid of the rail-chombu dripped water along the way and formed a zig-zag pattern on the platform.

The Bellary train had blown its whistle, the green light was showing the way and the general compartment was swarming with passengers. Sreeramanjaneyulu managed to push the bedding and trunk into the compartment, the train started to move as soon as the children had boarded it. He literally had to lift Kashavva and drop her into the compartment. The train started to pick up speed as the porter ran beside it, yelling 'Two rupees . . .' Kashavva had stuffed her money in a pouch. It seemed a banana was concealed in her sari next to where the pleats were tucked. In her rush to open the pouch to get the money, the pleats had come undone. Scared that she may get exposed, she sat down, holding on to her sari. Sreeramanjaneyulu was running along with the train, yelling louder and louder. The wind got brisker as the train picked up speed. Kashavva somehow recovered a two-rupee note; she slid on her buttocks towards the door, stretching out her hand and holding on to it tightly. The note fluttered in the wind. No matter how fast Sreeramanjaneyulu ran, he could not keep pace with the train. She could not muster the courage to let go of the note as she feared the high wind might carry it away. He ran as far as was possible and stopped helplessly at the end of the platform. The note remained in Kashavva's hand like a heavy load.

～

It was truly a miracle that they had found a groom from Madras for Kashavva. For the thirteen-year-old girl running around the house

like a little calf, it wouldn't have been much of a problem for the
parents to find a nice match in or around Bellary. But fate had
something else in store for her.

Kashavva's father, Pranesha Rao, was an employee of the
revenue department. Bellary was under the Madras Presidency
during those days. Maybe that was why Carnatic music was
the favourite form of classical music for all art lovers in Bellary.
Kashavva too had learnt the basics—like the Dasa-compositions,
Devaranamas, and Thyagaraja compositions from the local teacher,
Subbayya Pandith.

It so happened that a gentleman by the name of Raghottama
Rao once came for an inspection to the revenue department. He was
such a stickler for Brahminical principles he wouldn't touch hotel
food. He wouldn't even touch water from the houses of Brahmins
who did not follow strict ritualistic routines. How could anyone
have their house ready for him? Kashavva's father agreed to host the
officer. More than preparing for the audit at the office, Kashavva's
father spent all his energies in making flawless arrangements at his
residence for all manner of rituals. For his efforts, Raghottama Rao
praised him in the presence of his colleagues.

Rao noticed the teenaged girl running around like a little deer
in the house and immediately concluded that Kashavva would be a
suitable bride for his son Parthasarathy. Pranesha Rao's excitement
knew no bounds. He was overcome by emotion as he folded his
hands respectfully and gave his consent in a trembling voice. He
looked just like Anjaneya swami—Mukhyaprana Devaru, at that
time. Giving away one's daughter to the son of a highly placed
officer living in a big city like Madras was nothing short of good
fortune falling into one's lap. But Kashavva's mother cried and
cried, saying, 'I don't want to send my daughter to a strange place.'
Pranesha Rao yelled impatiently at her: 'How stupid can you be?
You don't have the sense to distinguish between what is good and
what is bad. How can we say no to a high-level officer who is

literally begging for this marriage?' Kashavva herself was too young to know whether it was going to be good or bad for her.

The wedding band sounded high at the Satyanarayana Temple and all the attendees enjoyed a festive meal with mandige as the main sweet dish. Pranesha Rao boasted proudly to all his friends and relatives that his son-in-law lived in Madras.

Within six months, unfortunately, Kashavva had to shave her head. Apparently, Parthasarathy was afflicted with countless 'secret infections' long before the wedding. The infection soon spread all over and killed him. He had infected Kashavva too before he died. Pranesha Rao had to struggle hard to get her cured.

As long as her parents were alive, Kashavva received a lot of help. But once they were gone she had to resort to working in the households of strangers as a domestic help. She had to face untold humiliations. Finally, she found refuge in a little room which was her nephew's outhouse. Gopanna's residence was where she lived, all alone. A small old-age pension and any assistance provided by Gopanna were all she had to get by. She would make shaavige, cotton wicks and condiments, and sell them to earn a little extra here and there. She also accepted assignments as a chef for special occasions.

Nearly forty years after her return from Madras as a young widow, she received a letter from her in-laws. The letter, written in English, had insisted that Kashavva's presence there was a must. This generated a sort of strange hope in her. On her way to Madras, she made mental calculations about how much money she might get if her late husband's family had decided to give her her share of her husband's ancestral properties by selling the lands they owned and the house they lived in.

As Kashavva had picked up some Tamil during her short stay of six months in Madras years ago, she felt confident about going there by herself. But Gopanna's children, Gowri and Putta, had insisted on joining her.

Kashavva felt very proud when she saw that folks from her in-laws' side had come to the railway station to receive her. The members of the family introduced themselves after reaching home and demonstrated their respect by touching her feet. That was enough for Kashavva to soften up. She started to weep, remembering her husband and in-laws who were no more. She showed a picture of her husband hanging in a corner of the house to Putta and Gowri and praised him, remarking on how handsome he was.

The relatives made her sign many papers; she signed in Kannada—'Kashavva'—without a single mistake, wherever there was an 'x' mark; they took her thumb impression too. Finally, they gave her one hundred rupees along with taamboola as a parting gift of betel leaves and areca nuts, and bid her goodbye.

By the time she realized that what had happened was all a show to dupe her, it was too late. The entire extended family had gobbled up the family property. She had no idea what the real value of her property was, nor did they tell her. She sat there bawling, insisting that she would not leave town until justice was done to her. Eventually, someone physically hauled her into a rickshaw and dropped her off at the railway station. She wept and cursed herself for not bringing Gopanna with her and shared her grief with the children. But how long could she sit there in an unknown city where they spoke a language she had little knowledge of? She decided to return to Bellary, not knowing what else to do.

~

Gopanna came in a jeep to receive her at Bellary railway station. As soon as they got down from the train, the children ran to their father and hugged him. Kashavva was angry. When asked, 'How was your journey, Kashavva?' she yelled at him: 'Your so-called friend, Kotesha the bastard, duped me thoroughly! What kind of friends do you have?' On the way home in the jeep, she cursed Kotesha, the bastard, at least a million times.

On reaching home, she described in colourful language how the in-laws' family had cheated her and how a porter named Sreeramanjaneyulu had helped her at Guntakal junction. For Kashavva, who lived a life of poverty, the deceit on the part of her in-laws' family did not remain in her mind for too long. But she could never ever forget Sreeramanjaneyulu.

If she heard that someone was going to Tirupati via Guntakal, she would ask if they could take two rupees and pay off Sreeramanjaneyulu. How do you pay someone whom you have never seen before? On what grounds should they pay? So everybody refused to take on the task. 'At least tell your friend Kotesha the bastard to help me to pay off Sreeramanjaneyulu . . .' she pleaded with Gopanna, but he never took her seriously.

Gopanna's wife Radhakka got tired of listening to Kashavva's 'two-rupees' story and gave her some free advice. 'Just to return a measly two rupees, why do you keep pleading with so many people? Why not drop two rupees into the collection box at the Rayara Mutth, prostrate and pray that it reaches the right person?' This suggestion was totally unacceptable to Kashavva. 'Why would I drop two rupees in the collection box? Understand, it was Sreeramanjaneyulu who took me from one train and put me in the other, not Rayaru,' she said.

Around twenty years later, there arose another opportunity for Kashavva to travel through Guntakal station. Gopanna's son Putta was now working as a software engineer in Bengaluru, earning plenty of money. She pleaded with Putta, 'It seems I was born after my parents visited Kashi and that is why they had named me Kashavva. Before I die, please take me to Kashi and help me get darshan of Kashi Vishveshwara. In the same stretch, take me to Gaya too, where one can perform one's own *shraaddha* while still alive. There are priests in Gaya who perform the Ghatashraddha

ritual, prescribed for those who don't have any children.' Putta had
readily agreed, and Kashavva tucked away two rupees in a corner
of her sari.

~

The Bellary train always arrived at Guntakal at the hour of dusk;
the station was swarming with people. The sounds of Telugu
movie songs being played somewhere in the distance merged with
the frequent announcements of arrivals and departures of trains.
People from different parts of the country were waiting there to
change trains. Books in various languages were being sold at the
bookstores. As soon as any train arrived, there would be a sudden
gush of people and a mad rush of activity at the stores; just as
suddenly, it would all recede, making the platform silent and dull
again.

Kashavva was confident that she would see Sreeramanjaneyulu
there. Putta thought it was foolish even to venture to hope
for something like this. He had no memory of how the porter
looked, but Kashavva behaved as though she had seen him just
the other day. 'Round face, huge moustache, pearl ornament
in his ears, a small birthmark on the face; it won't be a problem
to identify him, we will certainly meet him,' she declared self-
assuredly.

The two started their search; first they inquired with a couple of
porters, but no one had heard of that name. Putta went hesitatingly
and asked the station master about Sreeramanjaneyulu. He laughed
and ridiculed him, 'How do you expect to meet someone who
worked here twenty years ago?' They inquired at some of the
stores on the platforms, but they had no idea either about a porter
with that name. In the end, Putta became quite exhausted. He sat
down, having given up on the possibility of finding the porter. But
Kashavva would not give up; she kept looking around. The train

going to Kashi was about to arrive. It was getting dark, the nascent moon was barely showing in the sky and there was a pleasant coolness surrounding everyone on the platform.

Another random train arrived on the platform, inducing the usual rush of people trying to get in or out. The loudspeakers started blaring and the vendors were yelling, trying to attract the attention of passersby to the commodities they were selling.

In that mad rush, Kashavva spotted Sreeramanjaneyulu!

'Yes, that's him, that's him!' she yelled loudly. Putta could not make out whom she was pointing to. 'There, the man carrying three suitcases on his head . . . he is the one, I saw his face,' she said, with breathless excitement. He was going out through the gate at a distance and Putta could only see his back. 'Kashavva, how could you identify him from such a long distance?' Putta was suspicious. 'I am not joking, it is true, and it's him all right. I haven't forgotten his face. This blasted widow's life might have stolen lots of things from me, but the one thing I have is health. I am hale and hearty, my eyes never lie,' she said with great confidence. Impressed by her certainty, Putta started walking towards the gate and Kashavva followed him.

The man had disappeared by the time they reached the gate. Kashavva repeatedly called out his name, but it was probably never heard in all the noise. He did not turn back, but they hoped he might return to the station once he had deposited the luggage wherever he had to, and waited with curiosity near the gate.

In a short time they could see him, though not too clearly. Kashavva's pulse quickened with anxiety while Putta's curiosity rose. The porter shook off his towel and lighted a beedi; the spark in that dark looked like like a kumkum on his forehead. The spark started walking towards them; the man's face could barely be seen in the darkness. As he came closer, the streetlight fell on his face; Putta was disappointed as he realized a twenty-five-year-old man could not be Sreeramanjaneyulu. He felt completely misled and let down by Kashavva's excitement. But Kashavva went to the man without an iota of doubt.

'Are you the son of Sreeramanjaneyulu?' she asked him. Hearing his father's name from an unknown old lady, the man was stunned. 'Who are you? What do you need?' he asked. 'Come, sit down, I need to talk to you . . .' pleaded Kashavva. Feeling a strange respect for the old lady, the porter threw away his beedi and sat down on the bench next to her. Putta too went to them.

'What's your name?'

'Sundarayya,' he said. Putta had already read that on his label.

'Where is your father?'

'He is no more, he passed away long back.'

'What happened? He looked like he was in good shape.'

'He was fine, but one day he slipped and fell under the train.'

'Ayyo, that's terrible! What about your mother? Is she all right?'

'Yes, she is doing fine.'

'Why do you work as a porter? Didn't your father admit you in school?'

'No, mam, I was not good in studies. In addition, after Father passed away, it was difficult to pay the school fees. So my mother sent me to work as a porter.'

Kashavva narrated the story of the two rupees in detail. She removed the old two-rupee note that she had tucked inside her sari and offered it to him. He refused it at first, but when she pleaded again and again, saying that it would give her peace of mind, he took it and placed it in his pocket. He came with them to the platform, deposited their luggage in their compartment and bid them goodbye as the train started moving. Putta wanted to pay him for his service, but he refused to take anything, even though Putta tried to force some money on him. Kashavva told Putta not to push him too much.

After the train had gone some distance, Kashavva mumbled as if she were talking to herself, but was really addressing Putta. 'If the son of a musician becomes a musician, or a writer's son becomes a writer, we feel happy. But if a porter's son becomes a porter, it makes us sad.' Her eyes were moist.

6 October 2007

The Gift

Little Phaniraja was not going to give up. 'I too want to go, Appa,' he bawled. He would always insist on accompanying visiting relatives whenever they got ready to return. Now, when his own father was about to travel to a faraway town in Andhra, would he miss such an opportunity? Phani has rarely, if ever, set foot outside Bellary district in Karnataka. So far his father has taken him only to Dharmasthala and Mantralayam. Now he is about to visit a town called Rajahmundry. From Bellary, it would take almost a day by train. You need to change trains at a place known as Vijayawada. Apparently, the Godavari, a major river, as wide as Phaniraja's town, flows through Rajahmundry. They say they have built a long bridge over the river. Whenever a train moves over the bridge, it produces a lot of scary sounds. That stretch is full of water whichever way you look. For Phani, a child growing up in a town where even gathering a potful of water is a major difficulty, such a large waterbody was far beyond his imagination.

All these scenes were described to him in detail by Narayan-Kaka, lovingly called Nani-Kaka. Nani-Kaka visited them every year without fail, no matter what, to observe grandpa's and grandma's death anniversaries right here with them. He generally spent a couple more days after the ceremony, and during those days he would narrate to Phani numerous stories about Rajahmundry.

Most of those stories had to do with that river; how major ships sail on the river; how one could sit on those ships and travel to Bhadrachalam for a darshan of Sri Rama; how Goutami—a Rishi's wife—became a river and started to flow as a result of her husband Goutama's curse; how a smart English officer had built a dam across the river and made all the farmers rich . . . so on and so forth. He would narrate stories in such interesting ways that Phani never left Nani-Kaka's side from the time he arrived until the time he left. He slept next to his Kaka and would often fall asleep listening to his stories.

One of those nights, Phani woke up to go to the bathroom. He had forgotten to relieve himself before going to bed although his mother had reminded him. Earlier, he would wet his bed and his mother would complain to her friends about how tired she was of washing the sheets. Now that he was in fifth standard, he felt embarrassed and insulted if his mother reminded him of those mishaps. He had started waking up whenever he felt the urge, and although he was frightened of the dark he would somehow manage to reach the bathroom on his own. That night when he woke up to pee, he got scared when he realized that Nani-Kaka was missing from his bed. When he looked around, he saw Kaka sitting near the window gazing at the moon. He went towards him quietly and asked, 'Kaka, aren't you sleepy?' Kaka replied with a smile, 'Can't sleep, what to do? That is why I am watching the moon, who remains up all night and sleeps only one night in a month.' 'Which day of the month does he sleep?' Phani asked innocently; Nani-Kaka laughed: 'Isn't it the new moon day?' As Phani returned to his bed he heard the loud snoring of his parents, sounds that resembled the sawing of a huge log of wood. 'How could anyone sleep amidst such noise?' Phani wondered, as he tried to go back to sleep. He dreamt that the snoring was the roar of a tiger and that Kaka fought the tiger as Phani watched fearfully from behind a tree.

Phani's mother had not allowed him to learn to ride a bicycle as she feared for her only son's safety. His father had little time to teach him to ride one. Phani used to feel a sense of anger, shame and jealousy that all his friends already knew how to ride one. Phani took his grievance to his Kaka, who assured him: 'Don't worry, this Saturday I shall teach you, don't tell anyone.' Just as promised, Kaka took Phani to the Gandi-Narasimhaswamy temple field with a rented bicycle. Before letting him step on the pedal, Kaka gave him a piece of advice: 'More than being smart, you need to be brave, my dear. If you are brave, you can even fly a plane.' First Phani learnt cross-pedal cycling, then to step on the pedal while pushing and running and jumping on to the seat, and so on. Phani was learning fast. Suddenly, Kaka let go of his grip on the cycle as Phani pedalled on, and Phani kept pedalling on, knowing that Kaka was no longer holding the bike. A lorry carrying mined products was coming from the opposite direction and was making 'pom-pom' sounds. Phani froze in fear. He knew Kaka was running behind him to catch him; the honking of the lorry grew louder and louder as Phani totally forgot to pedal. He headed straight into a fence covered by thorny bush and fell into it.

Amma created a huge hue and cry when she came to know. She yelled at Nani-Kaka and mercilessly took him to task; Appa, however, was quiet. Amma tried saying, 'My only child, if he had fallen under the lorry . . .' but couldn't even complete the sentence as she sobbed. Nani-Kaka couldn't say a word. He had no choice but to silently listen to her non-stop scolding. Nani had taken Phani to the hospital, where he received treatment for a number of minor cuts and scratches, and his leg and forearms were bandaged. Nani-Kaka had shown a lot of concern by taking him back to the hospital two days in a row to get him re-bandaged. He also took the wounded patient to school and brought him back. Phani's wounds had healed within a couple of days, but left some scars before healing entirely.

The following Saturday, Nani-Kaka coaxed Phani to restart his cycling lessons, but Phani had bad memories of his fall and hesitated. 'Are you afraid of the bike? Or, should the bike be afraid of you?' asked Kaka. 'Me? Scared . . . of that stupid bike? No way!' said Phani, and readily agreed to continue where he had left off. That day he showed some courage, and lo! He got it! Now he thought it was a piece of cake! Even when a car came in front of him he knew how to avoid it and move forward. The next day, Sunday, Phani went and rented a bicycle on his own and came riding home making a 'trin-trin' sound from his bicycle bell, stopping barely inches from his mother, almost touching her as she prepared to go to the Raghavendra Swamy temple carrying a lamp with wicks dipped in ghee. She was startled and dropped the lamp. She looked up and saw it was her son who had caused the accident. She yelled: 'You? Rascal!' as she raised her hands to give him a good thrashing. But he was too fast for her and escaped quickly on his bike! She was still scolding her son while serving dinner that night: 'You are so stubborn . . . so stubborn.' Nani-Kaka and Phani looked at each other, smiling quietly. Before returning to his place, Nani-Kaka bought Phani a used bicycle.

Nani-Kaka came alone most of the time; he never brought his wife and children with him. Amma used to say, just for formality's sake, 'You should have brought Gangoobai and the children.' Kaka would remain silent for a moment, but then say with a touch of sadness, 'You know how she is, neither does she come, nor does she send the kids with me. For me it is a matter of duty, I cannot miss my parents' *shraaddha*. I have to come, I always do.' Amma would not raise the matter again, but start her bickering with Appa when Kaka left. 'Your brother should get a bit stronger with her. You see, she is spinning him like a top, does not even have a bit of respect for her poor husband. She is putting up with him simply because he has a job with the bank and earns some money. Otherwise she would have thrown him out of the house long ago.

I have not seen a wretched woman like her anywhere, I say.' It was too much to swallow for Appa. Not that he did not know about the fate of his own brother, but how could he set things right? A woman who scolded her own husband, would she listen to advice from her husband's brother? 'This is all our own karma. Each person has to suffer the consequences of sins from his past . . .' Thus saying, Appa would sigh deeply.

Nani-Kaka had not visited for the past three years; the only information Phani's family had was through the fifteen-paise letters that indicated his inability to attend the annual ceremony. 'Dear Seenanna and sister-in-law, my regards to you both. Somehow, I am not feeling well these days. I cannot sleep well at night and I am afraid to travel. I have started to suspect that, maybe, our dear departed parents have no desire to receive the annual ritual feedings from my hands any more. Life is becoming unbearable; I am unable to manage even the measly bank job. Don't know what is in Raghavendra Swamy's mind and what is in store for me. Please give my blessings to dear Phaniraja.' Appa would feel sad and become morose out of concern for his younger brother after reading these letters. But Amma did not stop complaining: 'That Gangoobai is no ordinary woman, she doesn't let him live in peace. She criticizes him at every step, every moment, making his life a living hell. How on earth can anyone, that too a meek person like your brother, get any sleep in that household where there is no trace of tranquillity? She won't rest until she drives him crazy, you watch my word.' Phaniraja, who had by now learnt how to ride a bicycle with his hands hanging free, had also picked up driving a Luna that his friend had bought. He was so eager to show it off to Kaka; but, alas, his letters would disappoint him a lot.

After three years of this, Appa had begun to feel a deep sense of urgency to go and see his younger brother, but would get discouraged thinking how far his town was from his. For someone who had spent all his life in Bellary, the mere thought of travelling was outside his comfort zone. But Nani was his sibling, with the same blood running in his veins. Appa was unable to decide what to do. 'You seemed to have stopped thinking. Is travelling to such a faraway place cheap? Your brother works for a bank and earns a huge salary, unlike you. By month's end we won't have money even to light lamps for the Lord unless we borrow. Do not try to show how great you are,' was Amma's verdict in the matter.

But finally, a letter came that compelled her to reconsider her decree. This time it was Gangoobai who wrote. The contents were: 'Dear Respected Brother-in-law, I hope you are all safe and things are going well for you all. But things here are totally out of control, as it has become extremely difficult to manage your brother. He has stopped going to work for quite some time. I am finding it very hard to run the household and manage the children. I humbly request you, through this letter, to visit us once and help us. I have written our address on the other side of the letter, will send my son to the station to receive you if you inform me the date and time of your arrival. Please say hello to dear sister-in-law for me. My best wishes and blessings to Phaniraja.' Appa reckoned that she must have dictated the letter to her son as Gangoobai did not know how to read or write.

Appa imagined the worst and made up his mind to visit his brother. Amma too did not object this time. Finally, he wrote to Gangoobai about his arrival schedule. That was when Phani insisted that he too would accompany Appa. Amma felt it would have been okay to take him along if it were a happy occasion, but now, when it was a stressful situation? She was totally against it, but Phani would not budge. He created a scene by throwing himself on the ground and rolling around and crying. Amma spanked him a few times, but he would not listen. 'You will fail the exam if you miss a week's worth of school. As it is you are so bad in English and have done poorly in the last examination,' she said, trying a different tactic. It was of no use. He stopped eating. Finally, Appa gave in and said, 'Let it be, when does he get a chance to see a faraway place like that? Anyway, it is half-price for his rail ticket. Let me take him with me.' Phani could barely contain his excitement; he went around the town a few times on his bicycle announcing to everyone that he was going to Rajahmundry.

He wanted to offer something very valuable as a gift to Nani-Kaka but could not quite figure out what.

~

Nani-Kaka's son, Prakash, had come to the railway station. Phani had no memory of having seen him, although he could see the resemblance. Seenanna, however, recognized him readily. Seenanna, along with his wife, had visited them to attend Prakash's *upanayana*, the thread ceremony. After the upanayana, though, despite Narayana's requests, he had somehow decided not to stay even for a day because of the way Gangoobai had treated them. Phaniraja was yet to be born; he was born years after they were married. This was the first time that Phani and Prakash were seeing each other. Prakash was in the second year of his bachelor's degree programme in commerce. He had a younger sister too. When Seenanna asked, 'How is Appa?' 'Same as before, Doddappa,' was his answer. When Prakash said, 'For some reason, nothing seems to work, Doddappa,' Seenanna suspected that things could be far worse than what he had imagined.

Prakash took Phani on the rear seat of his bicycle while he arranged for a rickshaw for Seenanna. The sunlight was quite intense as early as eight in the morning. Phani announced to his new-found elder brother that he too knew how to ride a bicycle. The town, which was much bigger than his own, created a feeling of awe in Phani. Every wall was filled with posters from the movies. Phani decided in his mind to see at least three or four movies after convincing Nani-kaka. He also wanted to go to the riverside in the evening by persuading Prakash to take him.

Their house was situated in a compound that could only be accessed by means of small unnamed roads. The house did not have proper light or ventilation. The heat was wretched and there was no question of switching on the lights as they had no power. It took a while to get used to the dim light inside the house. Gangoobai alone was home and the little girl was at school. Seenanna assumed that his brother Narayana must be at the bank where he worked. Gangoobai spread a mat on the floor and asked them to be seated and offered them cold water to drink and pieces of jaggery to Phani. She caressed Phani's chin and exclaimed 'Look at you, how big you have grown!' She asked, 'What grade are you studying in?' Phani realized that, after all, she was not as bad a woman as his mother had made her out to be.

The house was bare, in fact near-empty, without even a couple of chairs in the veranda. A few mattresses were placed on top of each other in a corner, and red chillies were spread on an old sari to dry in the sun. From the ceiling, bamboo staves were hanging horizontally next to each other; they were used for hanging clothes to dry. A few light beams emanating through holes somewhere up in the wall were struggling to pierce through the space between the hanging clothes on the staves. One could see framed pictures of Lord Venkateshwara and Goddess Padmavati, adorned with garlands woven around a wire. The garlands though, had become so dark from the kitchen smoke that no one could tell what the original colours of the flowers might have been. Behind the photo frame was a lizard that was playing hide and seek. Gangoobai, who was leaning against the mound of beds, started beating her own forehead and cried 'It is all our fate, Bhava.' Phani was shocked at the speed with which she knocked her own forehead. Prakash, who was wearing a lungi, came and squatted on his butt with his knees drawn close to his chin, near the wall opposite her.

'Nani was just fine, what exactly happened to him?' asked Seenanna. She replied, 'At first, he used to complain "I can't sleep, I can't sleep at all."' Phani recollected that night when Nani-Kaka sat near the window gazing at the moon.

'I had told him, "If you cannot sleep one night, that is okay, you will be able to sleep the next." Many a night, if I worry about family problems, I cannot sleep either. If we make a mountain out of a molehill, how can we survive? Please tell me. He used to spend weeks together without sleeping. Both the body and the mind got tired. You know his job at the bank is that of counting cash; he started to make mistakes almost on a daily basis. We were then asked to make up for the loss with our savings. Once an honest man had returned the excess cash he had given away and had advised him to be careful with money. But you cannot expect such honesty from everybody, right? I won't ever lie to you, Bhava, once there was a shortage of eight thousand rupees and the manager insisted that he make up the loss or lose the job. To save his job, I had to dispose of my two gold bangles and the two-string gold necklace that was made for my daughter's wedding. I consoled myself thinking, why get attached to that blasted gold jewellery; if God is kind, I can always get them made again. I went to the bank and begged them to give him some other easy job, but they refused, saying, "We can't give him some other job when his experience is that of a cashier." I am not an educated woman; I don't feel comfortable going to an office like that and arguing with senior officials. Still, I somehow gathered all my strength and did all that to save my family, Bhava.' She wiped her tears as she narrated her plight. Seenanna too had tears in his eyes when he said, 'Gangoobai, please gather yourself.' Prakash got up from his squatting position near the wall and went to the backyard to attend to his daily chores. Phani was observing the lizard on the wall behind the photo frame; the creature had remained immobile, as if lifeless, but suddenly made its move and gulped an insect.

'It has been nearly six months since he stopped going to the bank. They somehow paid him for three months, but how long could they continue to pay? We are deep in debt. I wonder where he got this fear from, Bhava. Afraid of everything, afraid of doing anything. Forget about working, he is even afraid to take a bath or eat! Amidst such fear, how can anyone sleep? He behaves like a crazy person, talks like a madman. Sometimes, I have to send the children to friends' houses to sleep. For me, it is my fate, I am suffering the consequences of my karma. I am so scared that I might turn out to be like him, Seenanna Bhava.' She wept as she described her husband's condition and wiped her tears with the corner of her sari. Seenanna asked if they had taken him to a good doctor. 'Of course, we did; they prescribe sleeping pills. He would sleep through the nights but sit like a zombie by day, showing no interest in anything. This works for about four days and then the pills don't work any more. He then demands more pills; how long can we go on like this? We have no money to feed ourselves. My parents did extend their helping hand, what little they could afford, but they too got tired and stopped. We visited temples, prayed to gods, even consulted mystics and magicians. I applied all my knowledge and did all I could, but nothing seems to yield any results. Where do you think I should run away to? Please tell me, Bhava.'

Seenanna was at a loss as to what he could say to her. But he could feel her pain. If Nani had lived close to him, maybe he could have done something, but he lived in such a faraway place. Growing up in Bellary, as students, they had the option of studying either in Kannada- or Telugu-medium schools. They spoke Kannada at home, so Seenanna had studied in the Kannada-medium school and remained in Karnataka. Narayana was crazy about movies; he used to harass his mother for money and frequent the movie theatres a lot. Those were the days when theatres showed mostly Telugu movies in Bellary. N.T. Rama Rao and Nageswara Rao were considered demi-gods! Kannada movies paled in comparison to these Telugu movies. Maybe that was the reason Nani insisted on studying in a Telugu-medium school. After his schooling, he mostly worked in Telugu lands and Seenanna stayed back in Karnataka. It was a matter of distress to Seenanna that their language of instruction in school had created such a distance between them.

Phani was getting totally bored as he could not make head or tail of what they were discussing. He was thinking of catching a movie with Prakash-Anna. At the same time he was feeling famished as he had eaten nothing since the morning. He was sitting there squirming, afraid of getting scolded by his father if he tried to raise his silly problems when they were dealing with such serious issues. The mat he sat on was old and damaged, with the cane poking out. He started pulling some of them out one by one, breaking them into pieces. Noticing his restlessness, Seenanna slapped him on the wrist and warned him silently with a dirty look.

'What time is Narayana coming home, Gangoobai? I feel like talking to him,' said Seenanna. She did not respond, but called her son, 'Prakashu, hey Prakashu.' Prakash came running; she told him, 'Kaka wants to see Appa, please take him to his room.' Prakash went to the room where Nani was sleeping and opened the door and let Seenanna in. Seenanna was shocked. 'Was Nani right here at home all this while? I have been talking outside, did he not feel like coming out to see me and talk to me?' he wondered. What has happened to him? Seenanna stepped in quietly, Phani after him. The room was dark, Prakash opened the window shutters and allowed the light to rush in. Seenanna's eyes slowly got accustomed to the dim light in the room. Other than a steel cot on which lay a torn mattress and a dirty pillow without a case, there was nothing else. Narayana was sleeping in a sitting posture, with his back resting on the cot. His hands were tied to the frame with an old sari of Gangoobai's. Other than a torn undershirt and a striped pair of undershorts, he wasn't wearing any clothes. He hadn't shaved in many days, and his hair was completely grey. The room was filled with a stale stench. Seenanna was overcome by grief at the scene and tears fell from his eyes. He had not imagined that his brother's condition could be this bad. Phani got so scared that he hid himself behind his father's legs. 'Even after giving him several pills last night, he did not sleep; it looks like he is falling asleep just now,' said Prakash. He tried to shake him and wake him up, 'Appa . . . see who has come to see you.' Seenanna wanted to say, 'Why do you disturb him, let him be,' but the words never left his lips. Narayana opened his eyes slowly, he looked exhausted, and his eyes looked lifeless. He barely attempted to look at his brother for a few moments. Seenanna went close to him saying, 'Hey, Narayana, it is me, your elder brother.' Nani recognized him. 'Seenanna . . .' he called out, in a pathetic feeble voice. An expression of sadness or happiness flashed on Nani's face; Seenanna started untying his hands. 'Don't, Kaka, please . . .' Prakash started to say something, but Seenanna gestured to him to stop.

Narayana raised his hands in despair and shook them, saying, 'It's over, it's all over,' in a feeble voice that had no sign of life in it. Seenanna felt a deep sadness within on hearing such words from his brother, who was younger than him by two years. 'Why do you talk with such pessimism? Take your words back, you should live for a hundred years,' Seenanna said in a mock scolding tone. But as he blurted out those words, he could sense the fear in his own frail voice. At this point, Narayana's sight shifted towards Phani, who seemed to be shrinking in the corner where he stood. 'Come, touch Kaka's feet,' said Seenanna to his son. Phani came hesitatingly and prostrated before his kaka, who raised his wobbly hand and caressed his head and chin. Phani was convinced that this was not the same man who had come to his town and taught him how to ride a bicycle.

Seenanna tried to smile as he said, 'Now, he rides without holding the bicycle handle . . . it looks like all that Bellary sunlight is meant for him, these days.' A hint of a smile flashed on Nani-Kaka's face. Seenanna said, 'Phani has brought something for you. Hey, Phani, why don't you give it to your Kaka?' Phani quickly ran out of the room and brought his backpack. He pulled out a notebook and gave it to his Kaka. Nani-Kaka started to turn the pages one by one. It was an old, used notebook. Unique pictures peeled off from used matchboxes were glued on the pages over the old writing. A sunrise, a Bahubali, an Olympian running with a burning torch in his hand, a beautiful rooster, a chrysanthemum, a farmer couple carrying a load of fodder and going homewards with a couple of sheep, jumping deer, an upright posing lion, and so on. It was an album of several rare pictures collected over four years by Phani while loitering in the streets of Bellary. Some of those beautiful pictures were won in marble games played with matchboxes as bets. If you soaked the matchbox in water overnight, it would allow you to carefully peel off the picture. Then you dried them in the sun and glued them on to your notebook. Phani could hardly resist the temptation of browsing through all those pages at least once or twice each day. This was the utterly valuable gift he had brought for Nani-Kaka, who had taught him how to ride a bicycle. On the first page he had written in red bold letters: 'To Nani-Kaka' and drawn the picture of a bicycle next to it. Narayan-Kaka kept leafing through the album, page by page, intermittently looking at Phani with pride. After leafing through a few pages, he started to yawn. Prakash understood the signal. Immediately, he went close to him, and Narayana very matter-of-factly held forward both his wrists for Prakash to tie. Prakash tied his father's hands tightly to the cot using the same old sari of his mother's. Kaka slipped into sleep in his sitting position.

≈

Phaniraja woke up suddenly in the middle of the night. It was clear from the noises that there was pandemonium outside. It took him a while to realize where he was; he extended his hand towards his father where he was supposed to have been sleeping but found the spot empty. They had been given the larger sleeping area in the kitchen, while the only bedroom was set aside for Nani-Kaka. The wife and children slept in the veranda. The worship area was in a corner of the kitchen; the lamp had already burnt out after exhausting the oil in it, leaving the entire kitchen dark. However, one could see the light in the veranda through the gaps in the door. Phani felt some panic and an urge to pee, but had forgotten where the bathroom was. He got up slowly and pushed open the door slightly, and what he saw in the veranda created a pounding in his chest.

Now, Nani-Kaka was wearing nothing more than the striped undershorts and had thrown away his undershirt; he was pacing back and forth from one corner to the other, breathing heavily. The expression of fear in his face was as if he had just seen the devil. Prakash and his sister were standing in a corner, and Kaka was in the opposite corner. Gangoobai was making all sorts of efforts to stop him from pacing back and forth, but if she went close to him he would push her away and resist vehemently. 'Please sit in one place; see, your brother has come, what do you think the impression of your behaviour would be on him?' She was also yelling and trying to force him to sit. This infuriated him so much that he pushed her away with force. Gangoobai crashed against a pillar, which resulted in a bloody wound on her forehead. Prakash's sister Geeta screamed 'Ammaaaaa' and ran to her, held Gangoobai and tried to stop the bleeding by pressing hard against the wound with the edge of her long skirt. Prakash ran into the kitchen, saw Phani watching everything through the door, but showed no reaction at all. He went to the worship area, collected the turmeric container and ran out. He applied the turmeric on his mother's wound on the forehead while Geeta tied an old piece of cloth around it. All the while, Nani-Kaka was pacing back and forth without any regard to what was happening around him. Seenanna paced with him and asked him, 'What is this, Narayana, why are you behaving like this? You have turned the house into a living hell . . .' Nani-Kaka was waving both hands and shouting 'You don't know . . . you don't know . . ., she is the one, she is the one who has done all this . . . she has ruined my life, she has left me incapable of sleeping, demoness, demoness.' Thus saying, he ran to Gangoobai and began to thrash her. Having received several blows, Gangoobai tried to escape. Prakash was angry; he used all his strength and pushed his father away. Although Nani-Kaka was pushed far away and he fell too, he got up as if nothing had happened and started pacing back and forth all over again.

After several rounds of pacing, Nani-Kaka got exhausted. He was sweating. He went inside the kitchen, knelt before the god in the alcove and started repenting and praying; 'Forgive me, oh Lord . . . please save me from this torment, my father, Tirupati Timmappa, Manchali Raaghappa . . . someone, anyone, please protect me . . . please grant me some sleep . . .' he continued to plead and beg as he stroked his cheeks and chin. Phani, who was watching this scene, could hear his own heart beating loudly. Nani-Kaka did not seem to have the persistence to rest there either; he walked out, yelling 'It's too hot in here, it's too hot . . .' He went straight to the main gate and attempted to open it, only to find it locked. He went to his wife, shouting, 'Give me the key, give me the key, I must go out.' When Gangoobai did not yield, he begged her again and again, 'Please Gangoo . . . I plead with my palms folded, kindly give me the key, I cannot stand this heat any more, Gangoo, please.' Gangoobai put her palms together and begged him in return, 'This pandemonium inside the house is bad enough, please don't embarrass us in the middle of the night . . . I have had enough . . .' 'Will you give it me or not?' he yelled like a demon, while Gangoobai kept insisting she wouldn't.

Nani-Kaka raced into his bedroom and brought with him the notebook that Phani had gifted to him. He tore out page after page from it and cut them into hundreds of bits and pieces and started pouring the pieces over his own head. The rare and beautiful pictures, collected by picking up discarded matchboxes and by winning many marble games, were destroyed in the matter of a few moments. The entire veranda was strewn with colourful pieces of paper. One piece fell near Phani's feet. When he picked it up, it happened to be that of Bahubali, the rarest of them all. Now only the head remained. None of his friends had ever possessed even one picture of Bahubali. It had truly been a symbol of his pride; he started to cry, looking at the pathetic shred of the destroyed figure.

Geeta ran into the kitchen and dropped three or four pills into a glass of water, mixing them in using a spoon. She brought the glass containing the mix, and Prakash held his father's hands tightly so that she could forcibly administer the sleeping dose. They pressed his nose shut. Whenever Nani-Kaka opened his mouth to breathe they poured a part of the mixture into his mouth. Even though some of it spilled out, enough of the mixture had been consumed, and Geeta loosened her grip on his nose. This stressful operation caused Nani-Kaka to cough a lot. He was now exhausted. When a little of the mixture was found left, Geeta shut his nose again and he opened his mouth without much resistance. Geeta shook the glass with the leftover water, mixed it once more and poured it into his mouth. He gulped it all down. Geeta went into the kitchen, hoping her job was done for that night, while Prakash stood steadily holding his father's hands tightly for about ten minutes. Slowly, Nani-Kaka collapsed. Prakash quickly dragged him and tied him to the cot using the same old sari and jammed the door shut.

Gangoobai told Seenanna, 'Let us go, Bhava, please sleep now, he won't wake up until morning. Unfortunately, we have ruined your sleep . . .' Having witnessed it all, Seenanna was devastated.

He said, '*Che, che*, my sleep be damned, what a critical state you are in. I had no idea the situation had reached this stage . . .' 'You are so shocked from just one night's exposure, I am going through this for almost a year, Bhava. I am his wife; I have no choice and I will put up with it somehow. But what about the children? Just imagining the possible effect of all this on the children breaks my heart into pieces.' Not knowing what to say or how to respond, Seenanna walked into the kitchen where his sleeping mat was. He pulled Phani back to their mat. Phani, who was overwhelmed, hugged his father tightly and started to sob. 'No, Raja, do not cry, nothing will happen, come sleep.' Phani kept waking up in fear. He had nightmares all night, even though he was hugging his father tightly. Seenanna couldn't sleep a wink; he stared at the ceiling all night. Geeta swept the veranda and collected all the pieces of paper and threw them out. The veranda light was switched off and the entire house became pitch dark. Seenanna could hear whispers among the mother and children followed by sounds of the rolling around of bodies. Although Phani was asleep, he saw only pestering demons in his dream.

≈

Seenanna wanted to stay back another day or two and return to Bellary after offering some solace and saying a few words of courage to the family. To do anything more was beyond his capabilities. For someone who had to resort to taking loans just to make ends meet, it was unthinkable for Seenanna to arrange for a doctor's visit for his younger brother in an unfamiliar big town. But Phani created a scene, which made it impossible to stay there. As soon as he woke up in the morning he started insisting on returning home. 'Raja, we will spend a couple of days here with Kaka and then return,' Seenanna tried to convince him, but he was in no mood to listen. He refused to drink his milk in the morning and kept crying and repeating, 'Let us go home.' Seenanna got quite frustrated with Phani's stubbornness and whacked him on his back. That was enough for Phani to lie on the ground and roll around, kicking and beating the ground with his feet and hands. Gangoobai could not take it; she said, 'Why do you hit him, Bhava? After all, he is a young boy and is visibly shaken. You should prepare to return. Let us avoid any bad impact on the child.' 'How can I leave you in this mess, Gangoobai?' Seenanna lamented. 'We have to suffer the consequences of what we have accumulated from the past; no one can do anything for anyone in this world, Bhava,' was her sad verdict. It was decided that they would leave that very day, and that pacified Phaniraja.

Gangoobai prepared some kheer as a treat for the relatives who had come from far away. Seenanna could not enjoy the meal, and the kheer tasted bitter. Tears rolled down from his eyes, which he wiped silently using his scarf, trying not to make it very obvious. When Gangoobai came to serve the vegetable curry, he recollected the old times. 'When Nani was young, he chose Telugu medium for his studies. Had he chosen Kannada medium instead, he would be working somewhere close to Bellary. And we would be there for each other during good and bad times.' 'When our luck is bad, what can a language do, Bhava? Many who studied in Telugu medium in Bellary are serving here with well-paying jobs; just to console ourselves, we can say all that,' she responded.

As Phani was visiting their house for the very first time, Gangoobai made him sit on a wooden pedestal, applied kumkum on his forehead and gave him a gift of ten rupees. 'Why all this under such circumstances?' said Seenanna, and tried to stop her. 'Under all circumstances, one must follow the customs and do what needs to be done, Bhava. You can't say no to a small gift; unfortunately, we are not in a position to get the boy a new shirt,' Gangoobai replied. Just before departing, Seenanna went into Kaka's room once more and saw his brother sitting upright, squeezing and blinking his eyes. Seenanna sat next to him and caressed his head and chin saying, 'I will be back, Narayana, don't be scared . . . meditate and pray to God . . . everything will turn out to be fine.' Seenanna did not believe his own words. Nani-Kaka did not react; he just kept squeezing and blinking his eyes. Seenanna asked Phani, who stood near the door, to come in and touch Kaka's feet, seek his blessings and bid him goodbye. Phaniraja, however, did not show any signs of coming close to Kaka. 'Come, Raja, he won't harm you . . .' Seenanna called him in again, but Phani ran to the pillar in the veranda and stood there, ready to leave.

Prakash did not come to the railway station this time; he had already left for college as the train departure time was in the afternoon. Seenanna and Phani hired a cycle rickshaw on their own. Gangoobai bargained with the rickshaw-wala and instructed him to take the straight route to the station. Seenanna searched his pocket and found some spare cash, which he offered to Gangoobai. She said, 'No, please, Bhava,' her eyes moist. 'Please keep it, may come in handy to purchase medicine or something.' He forced the money into her hands as the rickshaw pulled away. When Seenanna looked back from the end of the alley, Gangoobai was still standing at the front door looking at their moving rickshaw. In the sunshine he saw that the bandage on her forehead had turned yellow and red in spots. He felt a shockwave of cowardice pass though his entire body. Sitting next to him was Phaniraja, swearing that he would never ever set foot in this town again.

~

Some six months later, a fifteen-paise-stamped letter with black ink applied to its edges arrived, carrying the tragic news that Narayana had jumped into the Godavari River and killed himself. All attempts to save him had failed. As per Gangoobai's instructions, it was written that all the final rites would be conducted in Rajahmundry in the Uttaraadi Mutth situated on the banks of the Godavari and that elders should join in the ceremonies. Seenanna was grief-stricken for a long time after this. His wife, having read the letter, said, 'I knew it . . . that Gangoo is a stubbornly wretched woman . . . finally, she finished him . . . you watch my words, she will grab her husband's bank job for her son . . .' His wife's words sounded extremely cruel to his ears. He scolded her, 'Shut up for a while at least, don't talk nonsense and reserve a place in hell for yourself.' She was not the type to admit defeat so easily, 'You won't understand how women work, and you better stop scolding me. I know quite well what a loudmouth that Gangoobai is. Didn't I see what happened when our ancestral property was to be distributed? How she insisted that the coin necklace must be hers and grabbed it, which actually should have been mine?' Seenanna made her stop, 'You are talking about the coin necklace, I doubt if they have anything left to cover the expenses of Narayana's final rites.'

This time around, Phani refused to join his parents to go to Rajahmundry; he convinced them that he would be okay to stay with the neighbours during their absence. The parents decided to go by themselves; Seenanna borrowed some money from a friend to meet any incidental expenses. Nani-Kaka's death made Phani very sad. But after a couple of days he forgot everything and was engaged in playing with his friends. He had no more interest in collecting thrown-away matchboxes as he felt it was a pastime for small children.

After this incident, Gangoobai and her children completely lost touch with Seenanna's family; their whereabouts were now unknown. They heard through some second- or third-hand sources that Prakash had been given his father's job at the bank. They did not even receive an invitation for Geeta's wedding. Seenanna's wife decided to stay away from them. 'If they don't care for blood relationships, what can we do? We too will think the same and cut them off.'

~

Phaniraja had smoked three cigarettes already and was lighting the fourth, but still Tanmayee had not shown up. She had not answered the phone even though he had called her three or four times already; she had not bothered to send a text either. Getting a parking spot on weekends in Koramangala is not easy; the lot at Forum mall was full and they had mercilessly sent people away to park elsewhere. He had bought the tickets for the movies four days in advance. You can book a ticket online but there is no such facility for reserving a parking spot. He had to go around a few times before he could find a spot for his car. He stood there, leaning against it and smoking one cigarette after another.

He thought, 'She may not show up, she is just playing me,' and felt the urge to cry. If he were inside his house, he would have wept, for sure, but here, out in the open, he somehow managed to control himself. He had booked the tickets only after checking with her at least twice; she had said yes, but a noncommittal yes. No wonder she was missing in action now. The starting time of the movie had come and gone; he was getting angry and ready to beat her up if she showed up that very moment. But Phani knew that he would not do any such thing if she did really show up. He had never lost his temper with her so far in all these six years he had known her. He knew his own nature and his limits. All decisions were made by her; his role was merely to abide by the decisions, as though they were commandments.

Phani understands that six years ago, when they started liking each other, this was not the situation. It seems like a dream now . . . the memories of all those trips they took—hiking, climbing, staying at resorts, and their visits to other tourist attractions. Phani spent money like water, without any hesitation; he would never let Tanmayee spend even a paisa. He did not have a car then; they always went on his bike. He did not like to race his bike, but she was different. 'Faster, faster . . . more, more . . .' she would urge him, and he would press the accelerator further, while his heart pounded amidst Tanmayee's screams of excitement.

Once Phani had gone to Delhi on work and had lost all his luggage. He had to urgently use the bathroom and he had left his luggage unattended in a corner for a few minutes. Afraid he might lose his cell phone and credit cards in the toilet, he had put them away in the suitcase. He had locked it up and secured the key by attaching it to the bunch of keys in his sacred thread. By the time he returned, everything had disappeared, leaving him nothing but the clothes he was wearing and the bunch of keys hanging from his sacred thread. The watchman looking after the toilets had said 'How could I say who has taken it, sir? Thousands keep coming and going . . .' He had simply shaken his hands and had said, 'Please pay five rupees for using the toilet.' Phani did not have a single paisa on him. The man rebuked him, saying, 'I hear the same story, every day, go now . . .' The train Phani was supposed to board was ready for departure, but he had lost his ticket along with money, and he hesitated to board the train. Finally, someone who heard his plight suggested that he complain at the Railway Police Station, which he promptly did.

He received a patient hearing at the police station, where they said such incidents were increasing in frequency. When he said he did not have even a single paisa, they assured him that suitable arrangements would be made to transport him to Bengaluru. They asked him if he wished to speak to anyone at home. That was when he realized the real problem he had; he could not remember his parents' cell phone number, nor his younger sister's, and he had doubts about even the landline number of his own office. The one and only number he could remember clearly was Tanmayee's.

The police allowed him to use their phone and he spoke to her. She gave him courage and asked him to reach home safely first and that the rest of the things could be sorted out later.

~~

All the way to Bengaluru, Phani could think of only one thing; that he remembered just one person's phone number in the world and that was Tanmayee's. What other proof was required to establish his love for her? This realization made him so emotional that he went to the toilet and wept. As soon as he arrived in Bengaluru, he tenderly narrated all this to Tanmayee. She simply laughed. 'When you call me, you don't use your cell phone, but stealthily use the office landline and dial my number repeatedly. So, no wonder you remember my number,' she explained. She had so easily burst his emotion-filled balloon by pricking it with the needle of truth. Outwardly he showed mock anger, but his feelings were hurt.

Phaniraja realized that nothing had been going well for the past six months between them. Earlier she used to meet him a couple of times a week, but now he hardly saw her even once a month. She would get furious if he asked for a reason. Lately, he was even afraid to ask for one, and resorted to silence. As the meetings had become so infrequent, he did not want to waste time in silly quarrels. Even if he tried hard to avoid quarrelling, they ended up arguing on other inconsequential matters. Once, when he said he liked a movie that they had seen, that became the reason for a fight. 'Don't you have anything called "taste"? How could you like a stupid movie like that? Such a bad movie it was, you have no appreciation for subtle aspects whatsoever,' she shouted. As a last resort he said, 'Sorry, dear, I just wanted to tease you, that is why I said I liked the movie, but in reality I too did not like it.' He tried to appease her by showing his affection. That led to an even bigger fight. She said, 'Don't you have your own conviction?

If you really liked it, you should have stuck to your view. That would have made me respect you more. Why do you say you dislike something simply because I dislike it? I hate this quality of yours.' He said 'sorry', like a little boy who had committed a crime. That was like pouring ghee over a fire, and things became worse. 'What have you done to say sorry?' Having run out of all ammunition, Phani was left with no option but to fall silent, as he always did. These days he struggled, worrying what was okay to do and not okay to do, whether to say something or not, and so on. Even the few times that they met, during their time together he would feel he was walking on needles and become full of fear and anxiety.

If this was his misery while in her company, when not with her he would suffer in a different way. 'How do I make her happy? What am I doing wrong, how should I deal with her? What should I do to make her behave the way she used to when I first met her?' He would recollect each incident with her, which had come and gone for the thousandth time in his mind, as he inwardly argued with himself to the point of exhaustion. He started losing interest in eating; he totally lost interest in his work. The man who had been awarded the 'Best Employee' title several times was now the subject of grievance for his project managers. He thought of Tanmayee twenty-four hours a day, her words, his own anxiety to talk to her on the phone and her lack of interest in their relationship . . . and so on. Gradually, he began to have breakdowns.

Finally, one day, he practised in front of a mirror what to say to Tanmayee and how to say it. He mustered up all his courage and asked Tanmayee when they met, 'Why do you do this to me? Don't you like me?' She laughed it off. 'People change, you know. Don't our feelings change? Growing means changing, right?' Her response sounded definitive to Phani. He asked, 'Then, should we stop seeing each other? Should we split up?' He was almost shivering when he asked her. 'Oh, my God! Did I say anything

like that? Today this change, tomorrow there might be some other
change in me; I might start liking you a lot more, is that not a
possibility?' she counter-questioned him. He thought there might
be some truth in what she was saying. 'Why not? What is wrong in
her statement?' he consoled himself. But she continued to behave
the way she did—not picking up the phone even if he called several
times, then giving him some lame excuse for it. Phani could tell
she was lying, but was afraid of saying it to her face. He was getting
frustrated with himself for being unable to figure out what it was
that he felt towards Tanmayee, love or fear.

He was under a lot of pressure from the family to get married.
Appa, Amma, cousins . . . no matter whom he spoke to, they all
seemed to sing the same tune: 'When is the wedding?' One of his
female colleagues asked him directly, 'Are you gay?' which made
him squirm like hell. 'If you have crossed thirty, what else does
it mean!' she said, appending a rude comment to her question.
His sister was more direct: 'Are you in love with someone? Don't
worry if she is not of the same caste, you can go ahead with the
marriage.' What could he say? It was true he was in love with
someone. But was it easy to convince Tanmayee and bring her
home to introduce her to his family? Once he did try that and
proposed the idea of her coming to meet his family. Tanmayee's
response was curt. She cut his enthusiasm down by saying, 'Don't
do any such crazy thing, yet.'

Phani felt as though his pulse had stopped when he began to
think that Tanmayee might not love him at all and that he was
the one imposing himself on her and making her miserable. 'Just
because she showed some affection, did I interpret it as love? She
might have felt some attraction in the beginning and then lost
interest after some time. But does that mean the fault lies entirely
with me? Does she have no role in all this?' he wondered.

When his mind started wandering in the opposite direction, he
felt as though everything was becoming crystal clear. The fear he felt

quickly turned into a chill in his body. The chill was magnified by the wind that was blowing around him. Evaluating his relationship with Tanmayee and holding her guilty, he felt a sense of fury burn within him. But sometimes, and rarely, when he attributed the fault in their relationship to himself, he would start shivering in fear.

Phaniraja was struggling like a little mouse caught inside a trap.

≈

After burning the sixth cigarette, he had little hope left, so he decided to return home. He texted a message to Tanmayee: 'I am really hurt', and waited for her response. Instead, he got a call from a bank. The voice on the other end said, 'Our bank has approved to grant you a personal loan. If you visit our bank, it will only take one day to . . .' Who knows what else she was going to say. 'You stupid bitch, who the hell are you to give me a loan? Come to me if you want a personal loan, I can arrange for one, you stupid arsehole,' he shouted. The caller at the other end got so scared she said 'I am sorry' and hung up. Phani was still hissing away.

At that point he suddenly heard a familiar voice. 'Hey, Phani, you? Here?' The man put his hand on Phani's shoulder and asked him, 'How are you?' which brought Phani back to reality. It was Rajendra, with whom Phani had worked for five years. Rajendra had then left to set up his own private company. They had lost touch with each other. After having been sucked into Tanmayee's vortex, Phani had paid little attention to his friends. He had vague memories of having occasionally seen Rajendra's picture, either on LinkedIn or on Facebook.

'How long has it been? How have you been, Rajendra?' asked Phani, smiling. The boiling rage in his heart subsided on seeing his old friend. They had worked closely with great understanding, had seen movies together, and Phani even remembered a fun-filled trip to Goa that they had taken together.

'Do you have some time? We can go for a cup of coffee somewhere close by and talk peacefully.' His friend's invitation was enticing. Phani thought that a bit of casual conversation with an old friend over a cup of good coffee might do wonders to distract his agitated mind and agreed readily. They entered a café close by and settled in a corner where there was not much noise from the loud music. Rajendra ordered green tea and Phani his usual cappuccino. When the girl serving the coffee moved away, Rajendra said, 'Isn't she gorgeous?' Phani, who was immersed in his own world, had not paid any attention to her. But he was not about to admit it, and quickly said, 'Super.' He removed a cigarette pack from his pocket and offered one to Rajendra. Rajendra said, 'Ayyappo, I quit smoking long ago.' Phani could hardly believe him, because it was Rajendra who had initiated Phani into smoking during their Goa trip. 'Why this detachment?' Phani asked him.

Rajendra's voice was heavy when he started talking about his plight. 'You know, Phani, I have suffered a lot in life; I got cheated with my health.' Phani could hardly believe him, as he appeared to be in perfect health. 'What could have gone wrong with you, my friend? You had run the TCS 10K marathon,' Phani reminded him. 'Nothing was wrong, physically, but the mind had gone haywire.' He could barely continue. The girl came with the green tea and cappuccino and said, 'Have a good time, guys,' in her sweet voice and walked away coquettishly. Rajendra continued.

'Not sure if you remember: I had started my own company. You know you can't earn much working for others all your life. So, I thought I would invest everything I have and start a company, but . . . you know what? I lost my shirt. Everything was gone. In addition, I had all that loan sitting on my head. My parents, my wife, all of them thought it was my stupidity. I couldn't just join some job either. What could I have done? I was going crazy worrying about my plight all day. I could not sleep all night. I did not even know that I was suffering from mental health issues.

There was a time when I did not sleep a wink for five continuous days! It was my wife who finally insisted that I see a psychiatrist, and I did. He diagnosed my condition as 'clinical depression'. That was the beginning of trouble for me. Because I was overcome by fear I could not sleep. I used to roll this way and that in my bed all night. The next morning, I would be filled with fear. I started feeling so helpless that I thought I was unfit for anything. I was afraid even of going to a store to buy something, I was afraid to respond to an email. I was caught in the vice grip of distress; it took me almost six months before I could emerge from it.'

Phani was alarmed and asked fearfully, 'Does lack of sleep cause all that much trouble? I don't sleep several nights . . .' Rajendra was startled. He asked, 'What do you mean, you don't sleep several nights? How many nights, really?' Phani admitted that he would often not sleep for four to five nights in a row. When Rajendra wanted to know if Phani was stuck in some serious problem, Phani realized that he had never shared his problems with anyone. Now he felt like sharing everything with Rajendra. He narrated in detail everything that had transpired from the day he met Tanmayee to the present. He was in tears when he said, 'I cry a lot, my friend.'

Rajendra suggested: 'This is something that must be taken care of immediately, please see a psychiatrist right away. Spending sleepless nights like this is not a sign of good health.' Phani resisted, 'No, no, I don't have any such issues,' but Rajendra said, 'OK, let's assume there are no issues, but what is the harm in consulting an expert for his opinion? Is it not important for a man to have peace of mind? Don't let it go out of control, like I did. I suffered like anything. I thought I had reached a stage of believing that life was futile.' Phani was silent for a while. He was tearing up the sugar packet to shreds after pouring its contents into his cappuccino. 'Phani, they say this problem is often hereditary. Tell me, did anybody in your family have this problem?' Rajendra inquired. Phani said, 'No, I don't believe there was any such thing. Both my

parents are still quite healthy.' 'Not just parents,' said Rajendra,
'any close relatives from either your mother's side or father's side
who suffered sleeplessness?'

Immediately Phani remembered Nani-Kaka; he started
to sweat profusely. Even in that air-conditioned room, he felt
as though he was inside an oven. 'I had an uncle who used to
complain about not being able to sleep. He eventually jumped into
a river and committed suicide.' Before he could finish the sentence
he had started to shiver uncontrollably. Rajendra was shocked to
see this. He held Phani's hands and tried to console him, 'Don't
be so alarmed, it is not necessary that you should have the same
disease. Just because one person in the family had it, it does not
mean that everybody in the next generation would also have it.'
For a while both were silent. Rajendra came and sat next to Phani,
put his arm around Phani's shoulder and gave him a few words of
courage. Phani visualized Nani-Kaka pacing back and forth in his
veranda and asked Rajendra, 'Will I too become like Nani-Kaka?'
'*Che, che*, this is a different era altogether; medical science has
advanced so much,' said Rajendra. He reassured him, 'There are
powerful drugs that can control severe depression. Don't imagine
any problems; just go to a doctor once and consult with him. First,
let us understand the problem, if there is one.'

The well-dressed waitress brought the bill. Phani did not care
to pick up the tab but Rajendra casually did. Phani was lost in
recollecting the days after Nani-Kaka's passing. Phani's mother had
declared, referring to Nani-Kaka's family: 'If they so desire, we too
will cut off the blood relationship.' But Phani was realizing that
blood relationship was not something that could be 'cut off' or
wished away.

19 July 2015

Rare Blood

That was a Monday; I had overslept as I'd returned home late after a party the previous night. It was getting late for office. I could see my boss's angry eyes glaring at me. As though this wasn't enough, my driver had sent me a crisp message, written in Kannada using English script: 'Not coming to work today, sir, feeling sick.' He had also switched off his phone. He knew not to disturb my sleep by calling me. Well, I was driving to work cursing myself and swearing, 'I should never ever depend on others.' To avoid traffic, I passed through several nameless streets and was finally feeling victorious as I reached the final stretch near the Marathahalli Bridge. The view that met my eyes was horrific. Cars were everywhere, looking like worms surrounding a rotten corpse. Bikes and autos were making their way ahead somehow, squeezing themselves in between cars. It made me feel very nervous. I was afraid someone might hit me as I shifted gears often; I felt like an acrobat walking a tightrope. At that 'divine' moment my phone started to vibrate. It was a call from Rinda Aunty. I could neither pull over to the side to answer the call nor talk to her while driving as several cops were watching and directing the traffic. I could only helplessly watch the vibrating phone and try to guess what the news might be.

By the time I crossed the bridge and turned towards Whitefield, Rinda Aunty had called me at least ten times. I knew she had neither the wisdom nor the intelligence to imagine the conditions under which I might be driving. In addition, she thinks that she is the boss and I owe her my time, no matter what. She often told me, 'I was the one who took care of your mother and attended to her needs soon after your birth. You have peed and pooped all over my saris and I have cleaned you up without a word. Now that you are grown up, don't try to show off wearing your phony pants and shirts, OK? Even now I can spank you.' She had assumed this authority over me by openly saying such things in public. In any case, by the time I could pull over to the side and call her back, she had called me for the eleventh time.

It has been two years since Rao Uncle and Rinda Aunty have moved to Bengaluru. Angada, their son, had tried and failed at first to get them over to the city. 'We can't get used to any place other than Bellary, please don't force us, you take care of yourself, OK?' They had told him curtly. They had simply paid him a flying visit once, just to appease him, but Aunty had complained to me relentlessly before returning to Bellary: 'What kind of cold city is this? Even after eight in the morning, there is no sign of sunlight; I don't think we can take this weather. You see, it has been three days since your uncle has had a clear bowel movement. While in Bellary, you would see him running to the toilet with a bucketful of water as soon as he wakes up. You can digest what you eat only if the sunlight hits your body on a regular basis.' She had exhibited her knowledge of medical science as a prelude to returning to the burning Bellary heat. She did not forget to call me after reaching Bellary. She said, 'Today your uncle's bathroom visit was one of the most satisfying ones,' and went on to celebrate the grandeur of Bellary. In the meanwhile, poor Angada developed jaundice after eating at the roadside eateries in blasted Bengaluru. It took almost six months of Rinda Aunty's nursing for him recover and for the white lustre in his eyes to return. Eventually, Rao Uncle and Rinda Aunty had to come to Bengaluru. They constantly grumbled to me, 'We need to get him married as soon as possible.'

Angada showed a bit of smartness this time; he moved from his residence in Electronic City to the Vidyapeetha area. He had rented the house in Electronic City to be close to his workplace. Now that his parents were here, he realized they had nothing to do nearby in the Electronic City area. This change had a positive impact on Rinda Aunty and Rao Uncle. There were two Raghavendra Swamy mutths within walking distance of the new location, where they could attend the daily religious discourses in the evenings. They were also close to the Gandhi Bazar area, where they could find everything from ready-to-use cotton wicks for oil lamps to sugar-cubes (for Sankranti). This made easy their daily, weekly, monthly and yearly rituals and festival observances. Thus, the two started getting used to Bengaluru life gradually, so much so that they became Bangaloreans. 'Whatever you say, the Brahmins in this city are unique. We don't see their type in Bellary. You see, when Swameeji visited the Uttaradi Mutth the other day, there were hundreds of them, like flies on a fruit—men, women, children and even those young boys who work in big companies and earn lakhs of rupees came to receive his blessings. They got themselves the mudre. It was amazing to see the devotees smilingly accept that sacred imprint from the hot metallic seal applied by the Swameeji, even though it seared their skin! Swameeji, too, was so quick and dexterous in his brisk action of applying the seal on the devotees. He was faster than even a printing machine.' She praised the scene no end. Rinda Aunty, who would sport the nine-yard sari only occasionally during special religious events while in Bellary, had now resorted to the regular garb of the muttaide, the traditional married woman. If I teased her, 'What is this new costume, Aunty?' she would explain the nuances of religiosity, 'We must maintain our status of respectability among the community members, my dear boy; we should be second to none in our observances of ritualistic rules and regulations related to purity and impurity.' Poor Rao Uncle, however, would grumble sitting in his corner, 'No matter what you say, Kaveri water does not agree with my tummy the way Tunga water does. I have a hell of a time moving my bowels every morning.' Rinda Aunty would react curtly and take Uncle to task, 'You are among those who look for lame excuses like finding stones in curd. You see, if you sit at home doing nothing, how can your tummy agree with anything you eat? If you go to the Rayara Mutth every day and do circumambulations and prostrations, everything will be fine.' Despite these minor issues, somehow the two had adjusted to their new surroundings and their new routines, but it was Angada who was facing a real problem. He had developed piles from driving nearly thirty kilometres every day on his bike; initially; he only had pricking and irritation, but lately had also started bleeding occasionally. He hesitated to tell his parents about it, but shared his problem with me. 'I need to quickly find a girl and get married so that I can ship my parents back to Bellary, where they belong, and rent a place close to work. Somehow, I must save my ass.' I could see the pain in his face.

Such was Rinda Aunty. Now, wouldn't such a person be upset if I didn't take her call?

'Hello, Aunty, what is the matter?'

'What have you been doing? Praying? I must have called you a hundred times so far . . .'

'I was stuck in traffic, Aunty. Traffic cops are everywhere watching.'

'So what if the cops are watching? Are they more important than your Rinda Aunty?'

How could I respond to such questions?

'OK, let it go, tell me why you are calling.'

'Do you remember Narayanachar who used to visit us often . . .?'

'What about Narayanachar? Did he pass away?

'*Thoo*, what do you mean, pass away? You have a foul mouth. Take it back. By God's grace he is alive and well.'

'Then what happened to him?'

'Yesterday, when he was giving his daily discourse, he was demonstrating how Anjaneya carried the Sanjivani Mountain. Suddenly he felt as if he was truly carrying the load of the mountain himself and started sweating profusely, and eventually passed out. He was admitted to Narayana Heart Institute. They have kept him in the ICU. They are saying they must operate on his heart this afternoon. Both of us are here since morning. We haven't eaten breakfast or lunch. We are simply chanting the *"Vayu stuti"*—glory of the wind-god.'

'*Che, che*, Rinda Aunty, he seemed to be doing just fine just the other day when he gave a discourse on the Sundara Kaanda at your place.'

'My dear boy, that happened nearly eight months ago. Yesterday he had officiated the Satyanarayana pooja in the morning at the Balehonnur family residence. It seems he ate four holiges at lunch with ghee and milk.'

'Do you think he needs any money for the operation, Aunty?'

'Ayyo, my boy, he is a person who sings the glory of the Lord, there is no shortage of money for him. Just the other day, all his devotees performed a ceremony, of pouring gold coins on him and presented him with solid gold bangles to wear on his wrist.'

'Then why are you calling me, Aunty?'

'Need your blood, my boy.'

'Ayyayyo!'

'Why don't you listen first? It appears his blood is also of a rare type, just like yours, not easily available, according to the hospital. They have asked for people with the same blood group to be readied, just in case. That is why I called you. Have your lunch and come over here directly. If you donate blood for a great devotee like him, you can accumulate lots of punya, religious credit.'

'OK, Rinda Aunty, I don't have much work today anyway,' I gave her my assurance. Rinda Aunty put the phone down.

I too had had the opportunity to listen to a discourse by this Narayanachar once. It was during the Sundara Kanda that Rinda Aunty had organized at her place. He had narrated the story with great emotion. He was describing the sequence when all the monkeys started praising Anjaneya and how Anjaneya grew and became huge before crossing the ocean. In the flow of the moment, Narayanachar had stood up, made a swollen face like Anjaneya, and raised his right hand as though carrying a mace. He had brought a really dramatic grandeur to his narrative performance. Those who were listening to the discourse were so moved by the vivid depiction, they felt as though they had experienced the presence of the great Hanuman and prostrated before Narayanachar with utmost devotion. When he narrated the sequence of Seetadevi receiving the chudaamani, her crest jewel, Narayanachar shed tears, and the listeners too were overcome with emotion, imagining the agony experienced by Seeta. It seemed only natural that such a man with a heart full of emotion would have a disease related to the heart.

Such a devotee had seen difficult days too. His only daughter, twenty-one years old, had fallen in love with a Muslim boy and had married him. There was much outcry among the devotees, including Rinda Aunty. She had cried over the phone to me, 'Could she not have fallen in love with one of those nice-looking boys that attended her father's discourses? Did this evil witch have to select a Muslim boy, of all the people? What sort of a disgrace has she brought to her own father! Who would ever invite him to deliver discourses anymore?' Narayanachar, a widower, was both mother and father to this girl. He wept and wept over what had happened, and finally declared to the devotees that he had nothing to do with her any more and had cut her off totally. Only then did they allow him to deliver his discourses at the mutths. 'Parents own the sins of their children only up to the time they are fourteen, and not after that. This girl is twenty-one; Narayanachar does not bear the responsibility of her sins and therefore will not receive any shaapa, punitive retribution, as a result of her actions,' Rinda Aunty explained. When I asked her who had given her this logic, she said it was Narayanachar himself who had explained it to the devotees. He had said that one could see this in the Puranas: Sage Mandavya had raised this very question to the god of death, Yama. Rinda Aunty was convinced about this logic.

I had once had a chance meeting with this Narayanachar under a strange set of circumstances. I had to attend a wedding reception that was scheduled to take place in a wedding hall located in Yeshwanthpur, beyond Malleshwaram. I did not want to return very late in the night, so I had reached the party hall early—so early that even the bride and groom had not yet arrived. I saw a senior member there and casually inquired if the buffet was ready and if I could eat and leave. He looked at me angrily and said, 'We won't start the buffet until the bride and groom appear on the stage.' Not knowing what to do, I went out for a stroll and entered the park next to the reception hall to while away some time. I saw a person there sitting on a bench, smoking a cigarette. I was able to clearly identify him as Rinda Aunty's hero, Narayanachar! It was quite a sight to see this pious man smoking. I stepped forward and greeted him with folded hands, 'Namaskaara to Narayanachar!' He could not recognize me, but I said, 'You know, Brundavanamma and Subba Rao from Bellary, who live near Vidyapeetha—they are my aunt and uncle. I have heard your discourse at their place.' He quickly brought his cigarette pack out of his pocket and offered it to me. I politely declined. 'I don't smoke,' I said. 'I do not understand the behaviour of boys in this modern age,' he said rather philosophically. He said he was expecting someone who would be meeting him to discuss a potential invite for a discourse. I told him about the reception next door.

Around that time, a young woman clad in a burqa arrived with two glasses of lassi in her hands, gave one to Narayanachar and sat next to him. He, in turn, offered the glass of lassi to me, 'I hope you will accept this, at least,' he said. I smiled and accepted the drink. The woman in the burqa slid her head-cover behind her head and introduced herself, 'I am Zubeida Begum, his daughter.' Narayanachar quickly said Vedaavati was her original name from her previous avatar. I realized that it would cause them much embarrassment if I continued to stay there. I quickly drank the lassi and took their leave. The Acharya walked with me to the park's exit, threw the cigarette butt into a ditch and mumbled, 'She is my daughter who grew up with her hand in mine, and He'—pointing upwards—'is my Lord who holds my hand and leads me. I can't give up either of them. Please do not tell anyone about us, please . . .' he begged me with folded hands. I took his hands in mine and assured him, 'Please do not worry, I will not tell anyone.'

I kept my promise.

≈

When I parked my car near my office, a doubt arose in my mind: how did Rinda Aunty know my blood group? I couldn't remember ever having disclosed it to her. I suspected Mother might have informed her, but still I had to verify, so I called her.

'See, I took your call just after a single ring, unlike you. That is how important you are to me. You make me call you so many times before you answer . . .' Aunty went on and on. I just laughed.

When I asked her, 'How did you know what my blood type was?' she simply laughed.

'Remember, I told you that I came for your mother's post-delivery care; you were still a little baby, eight days old. You had developed jaundice and were crying nonstop. You would throw up all the milk you were fed. You see, you were delivered at home by a midwife who had no idea what to do with a jaundiced baby. So we had to take you to a doctor. As your mother was still weak after the delivery, it was I who took you to the doctor. I rolled you up in a blanket and carried you close to my chest; you looked like a little sparrow! The doctor had told us we should get your blood tested, for that too I was the one who went. The boy who did the testing was someone from my mother's town. He was the one who told me that your blood group was the rare kind. I haven't forgotten that, see.'

For some reason, I felt very emotional. 'Your memory is amazing!' I said.

'Ayyo, my dear boy, if you were to ask me what Angada's blood group is, I wouldn't be able to say. In fact, I did not know what my own blood group was until recently when I developed diabetes and the doctors insisted that I get my blood tested, you see.' We both had a good laugh. I promised Rinda Aunty that I would be at the Narayana Heart Institute exactly at two and entered my office.

~

Something happened that afternoon that prevented me from going to the hospital. I had been pestering one of our clients in the UK to arrange for a telephone conference for the past two months. He had ignored my emails, never bothering to respond to them all these days, but now, suddenly, he had sent me an email saying that this afternoon 3 p.m. would suit him for a meeting with us. He was an important client, and there was already a pandemonium about the issues that needed to be discussed. Under the circumstances, I realized that no one would understand my need to go to the hospital to give blood to this random guy, Narayanachar, to satisfy Rinda Aunty's desire. If I told Rinda Aunty that I couldn't come to the hospital, she would get angry; more than that, I would feel

terribly guilty to have disappointed her. After much deliberation,
I thought of a plan; I looked up the database of the office staff and
identified two co-workers who had the same blood group as mine.
Luckily for me, they both worked on my project—Janardan, a
team leader, and Mohammad Hussain, a trainee. I thought sending
two instead of one might please Rinda Aunty. I summoned them
both to my chamber and explained the situation. Janardan readily
agreed, while Mohammad expressed some reservations.

He said, 'Sir, I feel dizzy if I see blood. I had passed out once
when I went to donate it.' I wanted to laugh at the thought of this
six-foot giant feeling scared at the sight of blood.

'But, sir, there is a way to deal with this,' he said, but hesitated
to elaborate. When I insisted, he said 'When I am giving blood,
if Ranjani stands next to me I can do it.' He had let the cat
out of the bag. Everyone knew he was in love with Ranjani.
Although I was not happy about his cheap trick, I had no choice
but to call Ranjani to get her to agree to the plan. I explained the
situation all over again to Ranjani and proposed the approach.
She consented readily, though she hit Mohammad lightly on
the back and said, 'You idiot,' in mock anger. I felt extremely
relieved and thanked all three profusely, promising them a party
as a token of my appreciation. They all decided to go on their
bikes to Narayana Heart Institute after lunch and took Rinda
Aunty's mobile number from me. Mohammad Hussain and
Ranjani did not speak Kannada; he was from UP while Ranjani
was from Tamil Nadu. But Janardan was from Bellary, so he said
he would be the one doing the talking with Rinda Aunty. All
three left my office.

I called Rinda Aunty and tried to explain my predicament.

'When a man is dying, and you want to help, they insist on
having a meeting? What kind of a company do you work for, my
boy? Go look for another good job,' Rinda Aunty was trying to
disgrace the entire world of MNCs!

'Don't you worry, Aunty, I have a plan. I am sending two boys from my office, both of them have the same blood group as mine.' I tried to get some brownie points for my ability to handle the situation effectively.

'What are their names?'

'One is Mohammad Hussain . . . and the second . . .' She did not even let me complete the second name, and exclaimed, 'Shree Hari, Shree Hari!'

'What happened, Rinda Aunty?'

'Are you recommending Muslim blood to be mixed into a great Maadhva scholar's body? You will enter the worst kind of hell just for thinking about it.' She had given a new twist to the story of blood transfusion. I was enraged.

'What are you talking about, Aunty? There is no caste or religion for blood. Do you think your Maadhva scholar will convert to Islam if he received blood from a Muslim boy?'

'Don't you try to teach me; boys like you don't understand Brahminism. If we wanted to resort to such irreligious actions, we would have sent word to Vedaavati, his daughter, who shares his blood group. All devotees have sworn not to inform that girl at any cost, do you know?'

'You should have asked Acharya about this.'

'What is there to ask him? He is as great as Dharmaraya of Mahabharata, he has long cut her off from his life.'

'Then, it is up to you, I just cannot be there, what do you want me to do?'

'Who is that second boy?'

'His name is Janardan.'

'Doesn't his name sound like he is one of us?'

'I don't know, Rinda Aunty. He too is from Bellary side, that is all I know. For all you know he might even be a Maadhva, but that is not important. He is volunteering to donate blood, that is important.'

'That will be so good, if he turns out to be one of us!'

I could only laugh.

'Do me a favour, just ask him what his caste is.'

'That is something I just cannot do. In such companies, no one asks anyone about his or her caste. People will certainly be offended if they are asked.'

'There is no sin in asking anyone's caste. Such questions can be asked when you are about to save someone's life.'

'I will not ask him about his caste, even if you give me one crore rupees. That is a matter of my honour. He has worked for me for the past five years; he doesn't know my caste and I don't know his. Neither of us has ever raised such questions.'

'If you feel so hesitant to ask, do this, he must have written in his job application about his town and caste. Find out from his personnel file.'

'How do I explain, Rinda Aunty? No one cares about the employees' caste in such companies. If the employee performs, he will be retained, otherwise he will be sent home, it is as simple as that. When they are employed, it is prohibited to write down such information as it is not needed.'

'What kind of companies are these, my boy? Your uncle, when he joined his job, had to write down "Maadhva Brahmin" in his application. As a matter of fact, they had recognized us a respectable Brahmin couple; some of them would invite us and feed us and give us dakshine, a coin as a post-dinner gift, to show their respect. They used to prostrate at our feet and take our blessings.'

'Uncle worked for the government; they need all such information there, but here all they care is whether the employee performs or not.'

'OK, let it go, just tell me whether you will come or not.'

'Please forgive me, Rinda Aunty, I just cannot avoid this meeting.'

'All right, let us look at other options.'

'You say that Narayanachar is in trouble. Instead of thinking about how to save him, you are worrying about caste, religion and such other irrelevant matters. What if something happens to him?'

'Ayyo, wretched fellow, who cannot sacrifice a lousy meeting, why are you worrying about him? He is such a pious man who has dedicated his entire life in the service of the Lord. He has been spreading the glory of the Lord all his life. God will never give up on his devotees. Just because you can't make it, that is not the end of the world, the Lord will show the way. Don't you worry, just take care of your meeting.'

'It is not like that Rinda Aunty . . .' but before I could complete my sentence, she had disconnected the call. I just sat there helplessly.

I did not have the strength or the courage to find out if the Lord saved his devotee or not.

25 October 2011

The Unforgiving City

Who could imagine such a name? The name of that famous apartment complex situated on Bannerughatta Road in Bengaluru is 'River Side'. For those who occupy the 500-and-odd cage-like apartments, the never-ending traffic below must seem like a flowing river. Their daily immersion in the dust billowing from the traffic must be their sacred bath in the River Ganga! Driving in the middle of such traffic must feel like partaking in the festival of floats on the Ganga!

It is an irony that such an apartment complex should suffer chronic water shortage. The water allotted to this complex by the Cauvery River Corporation doesn't even satisfy its toilet-flushing needs and its occupants are left with no choice but to purchase water by the truckload every day. Excel spreadsheets with details of how much each occupant owes the water supplier reaches them via e-mail every month. A pleasant image of the bathing ghats of Banaras cleverly adorns a corner of the spreadsheet. All the occupants pay their dues online.

In this famous complex, there is a huge swimming pool which is put to use only during the summer; and only by a limited number of occupants, maybe twenty or thirty. Although the pool maintenance fee is rather expensive, the non-users too end up sharing the cost. They pay their share without complaining, because of the prestige associated with the pool. They make it a point to take their visitors and guests to the pool, and swell with pride to see the admiration flashing in their eyes. The reserving of separate swimming hours based on gender is specifically forbidden in this complex. This allows the residents of the penthouse apartments to sit in their balconies and sip their beer while taking a good peek at the commingling swimmers splashing away in the pool below.

Rekha Joshi, a resident of E-Block, Apartment Number 208, had taken her three-year-old daughter Rishika to the swimming pool that afternoon. The little girl had no interest whatsoever in getting into the cold water. This upset Rekha immensely. She spanked her daughter and got her ready to go into the pool. Rekha did not know how to swim, which perhaps made her angrier. 'You should know everything,' she would admonish Rishi often.

Suja Srinivasan from Apartment Number 306 in K-Block was the only one swimming in the pool at that time. To Suja, a woman from Kerala, swimming was as natural as breathing. She was swimming to and fro in the deep end of the pool and waved with a smile when she saw Rekha at the other end. Rekha felt a surge of jealousy at Suja's ease at swimming. She commanded her daughter emphatically, 'Rishi, you should be able to swim like that aunty, you understand?' However, the poor little three-year-old had no inclination whatsoever to enter the pool.

There is a kiddy pool attached to the main pool, especially for toddlers, just about a foot deep, which has a steel railing all around as a safety measure. Rekha made Rishi change into a swimsuit and made her enter the kiddy pool. After resisting for a while, Rishi got into it gingerly. She felt the chill of the cold water and instantly forgot all about swimming and began to shiver. She felt a sudden urge to pee. The blue water mixed with the yellow urine and suddenly turned the surrounding water green. Realizing what had happened, Rekha got quite mad, but scolded her daughter in an indulgent way. 'Yuck, you dirty girl!' Rishi smiled and gave a proud chuckle. Suja, who heard the commotion, came closer to see what the matter was. 'Look Suja, I don't know how to teach pool manners to such kids, do you?' Rekha said casually, to which Suja gave her a blank smile, not knowing what else to say. She quietly got out of the pool, put on her clothes and left, disgusted at what had happened. Seeing this, Rekha regretted having disclosed her daughter's mistake.

≈≈

Srinivasan Namboodri was screaming on his cell phone. He had purchased a pink diamond ring over the internet for his close friend who was getting married. They delivered the ring as promised, within twenty-four hours of his ordering, but when he opened the package he found a blue diamond ring instead. He had tried at least ten times to reach the seller's call centre and had failed. There was no showroom to go to and talk to the seller's representatives. He had spent more than fifteen minutes since the morning pressing his dialpad keys for different options and following the instructions of numerous recorded voices in vain, and it was such a relief when a human voice finally replied. 'How may I help you, this is Catherine speaking.' That artificial sweet voice was enough for him to lose his cool. All the anger pent up since the morning came surging out, and he yelled at the girl at the top of his voice. The more he shouted the calmer she got, and that drove him crazier. Luckily, she was not physically accessible to him.

As soon as Suja entered, she realized what could have gone wrong but was in no mood to listen to the yelling and screaming. She went straight into her bedroom and rolled into her bed. She had gone to enjoy a relaxing swim on that summer morning but it had ended in such a disgusting episode. She started to think: 'It was a little kid, all right, but who can tolerate urine in the pool? OK, the child does not know enough, but what about the mother?

Should she not have taken her daughter to the toilet and given her a thorough wash before allowing her to enter the pool? On top of that, she had the nerve to show off what her daughter had done, as if that was some kind of a joke. If I had tried to say something, I am sure she wouldn't have taken it well.'

Even though Srinivasan was really mad and fuming on the phone, he realized that Suja had returned within a few minutes of going to the pool. Besides, she'd normally go to the fridge and take out some orange juice soon after returning from a swim. But today she just went to the bedroom and was lying on the bed. He quickly understood there must be something wrong. 'Send me a replacement as quickly as possible,' he shouted at the girl on the other end of the phone. She asked in the same deceptive sweet voice again, 'Is there anything else I can do to help you?' He yelled back 'Why don't you just shut up, lady,' as he cut her off.

He went into the bedroom to inquire what was wrong, but Suja was in no mood to talk. She said there wasn't anything wrong and simply turned to the other side, breathing silently. That did not satisfy Srinivasan. He moved closer to Suja, and caressing her hair with great care and love said, 'Suji, if you don't tell me, how on earth will I know what is wrong?' Having realized that he was not going to accept silence, she sat up in bed and said, 'I am not even sure why I am telling you all this . . .' and proceeded to describe the entire episode in detail. This was more than enough to excite Srinivasan all over again.

'Why did you not tell Rekha? If you don't tell her, how will she know what she did was wrong?' When he went on yelling, Suja said, 'What is the use of telling just her? Who is going to tell everybody else?'

'Why worry about that, darling, just wait, I know what to do to tell everybody else!' He jumped to the corner where the computer was. Using Suja's password, he tried to login to the Yahoo! group to write to the River Side residents, but failed.

'Have you changed your password?' he asked her, but she did not like the idea of sharing her password with him and said, 'Why don't you send the message using your ID?' He did not give in and said, 'You are the witness to what happened and the message would be more effective going from you.' Seeing no other alternative, she told him her new password—'SRIJA'. He knew 'SRI' was from his name, but 'JA' caused him some discomfort, 'You haven't forgotten Jagan still?' he sighed, rather quietly. 'How could I?' she said, as though she was just talking to herself.

In his message to the residents, under the title 'We are all swimming in urine', he described the entire episode as though he had witnessed it himself. 'I am not writing all this to complain about Mrs Rekha Joshi or her daughter Rishika. We are all educated people in important professions and we have seen different parts of the world. What good is it if we cannot keep our surroundings clean? I am sure none of you would like to rinse your mouths with urine. My suggestion to all is that we not allow children under five to enter the pool henceforth. Signed: Suja Srinivasan (K-306).'

'Just wait and see the fun that unfolds, now that I have sent this message out to the residents; see how this spark will grow into a volcano.' As he said this he went into the living room, hardly able to suppress his glee.

≈

Although Rishika had initially refused to get into the pool, once inside she started enjoying herself, splashing the water, kicking and striking her arms about, inviting her mother to also jump in. After a couple of kids joined her in the kiddy pool, her enthusiasm knew no bounds and she refused to get out even after an hour of playing. Rekha got worried that her daughter might catch a cold and began to cajole her to get out, but to no avail. Finally, she had to spank her and pick her up and return to her apartment. Rishika sneezed a couple of times after returning home as she was being dried. Rekha took her to task for not having listened to her. Rishika couldn't care less; she shook her hair and splashed and sprinkled water all over Rekha, tickling her mothers' chin with her wet little hands, giggling happily all the while.

After drying off, Rishika sat in the midst of her toys and played, while Rekha trimmed her finger and toe nails as though she was plucking flowers gently from a plant. Rishika was quite sleepy, but was resisting sleep while making her cute Barbie and teddy bear fight each other. That was the exact time when Rekha's cell phone rang. It was a call from Akruti Sharma, the lady who lived in the apartment right below Rekha's, in E-108. Feeling happy after her daughter's successful swimming session, Rekha started with a cheerful 'What is the new gossip, Akruti?' Akruti was dead serious; she simply asked, 'Have you visited Yahoo! lately?' From the tone of her voice Rekha figured that something related to her must have been written up there. She asked, 'What have they written?' Akruti was not ready to spoil the suspense. She said, 'Why don't you go to Yahoo! and see for yourself.' As she cut the phone off, she did not forget to say, 'Take it easy, you know, please don't take it too seriously, OK?'

Rekha's heart was pounding like a drum when she logged on to the 'River Side Residents' Yahoo! group. Already fifty-four people had reacted to the posting of Suja's from K-306 under the title 'We are all swimming in urine!' Each reaction she read made Rekha retch; tears rolled down her cheeks when she imagined how each one had used her dear little child as a ball to kick around.

'How dirty, oh my gosh! I would never swim in that pool ever again. Recently, I had developed itchy skin, now I know why.'

'I agree with Suja Srinivasan's suggestion, we should never let a kid under five enter the pool. Although this might hurt Rekha's feelings, I know she is broad-minded enough to understand.'

'How on earth do you assume that adults never pee in the pool?'

'I like your sense of humour! Adults . . . peeing . . . in the pool? Ha-Ha-Ha!'

'Let me tell you something that you might not know. I know of some women who go the pool even during those days of the month . . . you know . . . I know who. But I am not going to disclose.'

'Some of us who are just beginners end up swallowing the water while swimming, yuck, knowing what we know, how can we encourage anyone to learn swimming?'

'Definitely no one under five in the pool.'

Each reaction was like a new arrow in her chest; reading them all slowly turned her sorrow into acute anger. She looked at her darling falling asleep on her soft cottony toys and started to feel a boiling rage, thinking of the mean mindset of all those who were thoughtlessly attacking her child. She sat down to prepare a suitable response as her anger crystallized against the entire apartment complex.

'I would like to express my two cents' worth . . . as I write these words, I mean no disrespect for Suja and Srinivasan, a couple who as we all know are probably beyond forty years in age and have no children of their own. I am not interested to know whether it is by choice or due to some other problem, but I can say for sure, they have no idea what having children means. Only those who bear children for nine months inside their womb and deliver them after experiencing excruciating life-and-death pain know the pleasures and pains of having children. Such parents would never be so heartless as to ever resort to restricting entry of children into a swimming pool. I have my sympathy to those issueless parents; however, I cannot condone the vengeful attitude of such people who act this way because of what they don't have. Let such couples who have no right to talk about children stop their arrogance. Rekha Joshi (E-208).'

Having posted the message to the residents' group, she came and picked up her daughter, embraced her and kissed her on the cheeks, saying emotionally, 'Rishi, even if the entire world is up in arms against you, I shall stand here to protect you.'

≈

When the phone rang the first time, Suja was fast asleep. Srinivasan had gone to Jayanagar to exchange the ring. Suja woke up after Akruti called, which was within five minutes of the first call.

'Please visit the Yahoo! group right away, your message is being hotly discussed.'

'What message?'

'Don't be silly . . . mouthwash with pee!'

'Oh . . .'

'Rekha has responded, you know, read it, but take it easy, you know, don't take it too seriously, OK?'

When Suja logged in, there were seventy-eight responses already. Many residents who were on foreign assignments had responded from the USA, UK and other places, giving rise to new issues for further debate. It took Suja a while to even realize what was being discussed or debated. People had used strange logic, and she was amazed and even scared to see how so many people had blown a silly matter to such ridiculous proportions. She was furious with Srinivasan for this nasty exchange.

Rekha's message and her implication that she was childless hurt her the most. Many a parent had supported Rekha, while some unmarried people and a few couples living together had blasted Rekha in their own way. 'Just because, maybe out of lust, some people might produce children, that does not automatically qualify them to understand children, nor is it necessary to beget children to be able to understand them,' so on and so forth.

Suja felt miserable and ran to the kitchen to drink a glass of water. The sight of oil in a pan in which something had been fried earlier disgusted her, and she ran to the bathroom and threw up.

Dirty water oozed out of her nose. The emptiness of her stomach made her feel truly empty. She felt extremely lonely as she sat in the bathroom, sobbing helplessly. She tried to console herself as she washed up. She tried to control the sensation of light-headedness by sitting upright and breathing deeply. When she felt a little better she went to her cupboard. She moved things about and found Jagan's picture, which she had hidden amidst her garments. She wiped it clean with her scarf and kissed it, saying, 'I miss you, I miss you very much,' and broke into sobs again.

≈

Rekha felt she could not focus on anything; she kept refreshing her Yahoo! group page again and again to check if there were any more responses on the group. She read her own messages several times and read a few selected messages again and again, typing out some strong responses but deleting them without sending them, out of some unknown fear. She called Akruti a few times and asked her, 'Please tell me frankly, have I hurt anyone's feelings?' Akruti's words of reassurance gave her no consolation. She got tired of clicking the mouse to see if Suja had responded to her message and saw none. 'I am not going to be afraid, she is the one who started the fight,' she said loudly, as if to console herself.

In the meantime, the doorbell rang. And when she opened the door, there was Suja, right in front of her. As soon as she saw her uncombed hair, her red swollen eyes and her exhausted face, Rekha thought, 'I shouldn't have been so harsh.' Although she was waging a war mentally all this while, when she saw Suja in person she felt scared and unable to even speak. Having raised the sword in a Yahoo! duel, she barely managed to say 'please come in'.

Suja said nothing; she simply gave her the picture of Jagan, which she had carried with her to Rekha's. It showed a three-year-old boy in a pair of fancy jeans, a red T-shirt and a cowboy hat, leaning forward with his hands locked behind his back, as though he was getting ready to shock and scare someone with a peak-a-boo! A pair of shining eyes, slightly elongated face and dimples made the boy in the picture look extremely cute! Rekha, dumbfounded, silently gestured to Suja asking who the boy was.

'Well, this is my boy that I bore in my womb for nine months and delivered after feeling that excruciating life and death pain . . . just as you have written, you know . . .'

'I am sorry.'

'Why are you sorry, he is still alive, he is in tenth standard . . . lives with his dad. No matter how much I appealed he did not agree to allow him to live with me. Even the courts did not support me, do you know why? Because I work day and night . . .'

'. . .'

'You have suffered equally, I know, just like me, but you have succeeded in gaining custody of your child. So . . . congratulations for that.'

Rishika rolled around in her bed of toys, and a rubber toy made a whistling noise on being squished under. Both the women turned and looked at the sleeping girl. Neither wanted to speak any more; Suja took back her son's picture and quietly walked away, leaving Rekha to stand alone to burn in guilt.

Rekha felt the burden of having committed an unpardonable crime; she kept muttering 'sorry, sorry' endlessly. She went to the computer to see if she could delete her message, but found that that was impossible; she felt like kneeling before all the River Side residents and asking for their pardon. She sat down in an attempt to string together some words to express her feelings.

'Just a few minutes ago Suja came to my apartment to show me the picture of her lovely son from her previous marriage. I have called her childless and insulted her in front of all of you; I have hurt her feelings beyond imagination. I am ashamed of myself and I am burning with guilt. I am asking for your pardon knowing

full well that I have committed an unpardonable sin. Rekha Joshi
(E-208).'

~

Suja opened the door and entered her apartment. She realized that
Srinivasan was back simply by noticing his shoes in the corner. 'Sri,'
she called out. She called out again and he did not respond. She was
worried now. She looked for him in the kitchen, in the bathroom,
and finally found him in front of his computer. 'Why aren't you
responding?' she asked. He turned the computer screen towards her
and looked at her silently. His eyes were brimming with tears. It did
not take much time for Suja to realize something must be terribly
wrong. She slowly read the apology message posted by Rekha. In
her eagerness to express remorse, Rekha had, albeit unintentionally,
injected bitterness into Suja and Srini's highly personal domain.

'Sorry, Sri, I had no idea she would write this kind of an
apology.'

'Let it go, this message must have given you a lot of relief; the
entire River Side complex now knows that our problem is not
one of your infertility but one of my sterility. I am sure you too
somehow wanted to share this with the entire world that you are
not the one to blame.'

'For heaven's sake, Sri, please do not blow this out of
proportion. For ten years I have lived with you as your partner and
have never ever looked down upon you. Your love has been more
important than my own child's; in fact, you are my baby . . .'

'All the 500 households would have read this message by
now . . .'

He wept like a baby; she cuddled him and consoled him,
clasping him to her chest and caressing his hair.

~

Neither of them was in a mood to attend the wedding reception, but the groom was such a close friend that they could not skip it. So they got into the car and left quietly. Suja had put the diamond ring back into its box and wrapped it in some gift-wrapping paper that she could find; neither committed the crime of suggesting what the other should wear for the reception.

Srinivasan drove like a maniac even under normal circumstances, and today he was completely agitated and restless. He was driving mostly on the wrong side of the road. He continually yelled and cursed at all the rickshaw drivers who crossed his path. When he cursed at one of them, 'You stupid man, can't you see?', the driver put his head outside the auto and spat at Srinivasan, cursing back. Under normal circumstances, Suja would calm him down, but today she remained silent, afraid of how he might react. Her seeming indifference and awkward silence were more than merely irritating to him.

In order to avoid the traffic on the main road, Srinivasan resorted to a shortcut through an unknown cross-road. As ill-luck would have it, they encountered a guy sitting in his car blocking the way and talking on his cell phone with no consideration whatsoever for the traffic behind him. When many rounds of honking did nothing to move him, Srinivasan tried to drive through the narrow space between the car and the edge of the building. When he reached the side of the car that was blocking the road, he pulled his window down and screamed at the guy, who was still talking on the cell phone nonchalantly. 'You bloody bastard, you son of a bitch, don't you realize this is a public road, or do you think it is your father's personal property, you rascal . . .' The guy in the car took a careful look and stared at Srinivasan yelling at him as he passed him. The big, thick, shiny gold bracelet on the guy's wrist and the brand-new gold chain around his neck shone in the street light.

Srinivasan had hardly moved a few hundred feet ahead when the guy in the car behind drove through the narrow gap, banging

Srini's car as he passed. He then stopped his car across the lane and blocked Srini's way. When Srini realized his car was totally dented on the side, he switched off the engine and got off the car, cursing 'You fucking idiot', he yelled, and and started examining the damage. The guy too got out of his car and started walking slowly towards Srini. Suja got frightened. She could no longer be a silent spectator, and got out of the car too.

The entire episode was unfolding so fast Suja could hardly make sense of what was going on. She could only see the hefty guy with the shining gold chain and thick bracelet walk towards Srini, and the next thing she knew he was holding him up by his neck. Srini collapsed like a rootless banana plant and fell flat on the ground while the guy gathered his entire sputum and spit on him, producing a disgusting sound as he walked back to his car and sped away.

'Srini, Srini, what happened? Are you okay?' Suja ran to him, crying loudly. He looked at her with the most miserable helpless face she had seen and said in a meek voice, 'Sorry.' She took his head into her lap to console him, and suddenly felt a wetness in her lap. Her white Kerala sari was now red from Srini's warm blood that was fast turning cold. She started to scream uncontrollably. The lights from the houses on either side of the lane started coming on one by one.

〜

Akruti Sharma had not anticipated such devastating news. On the contrary, when she got the call from Suja she thought she was calling about the continuing discussion on 'mouthwash with pee'. Suja was crying nonstop as she described how Srini had been murdered by some random rowdy in a dark lane inside the city. When she heard how the murderer had slit Srini's throat in an instant, an indescribable chill went down her spine. Suja begged her to come to her immediately, as she was too scared to be alone in that unknown lane. Akruti assured her that she would get there as quickly as possible; she took the car keys, did not even bother to change, and was ready to leave.

Just as she was about to lock her door, the laptop on her sofa caught her attention. She said to herself, 'no', but could not resist the beckoning call of the computer. She opened the laptop and logged on to Yahoo!. Under the subject title 'Srinivasan Namboodri's barbaric murder', she typed with trembling fingers:

'I am deeply saddened to inform you that Srinivasan Namboodri of K-306 (Suja's husband) was brutally murdered by an unknown assailant on a road inside the city. Suja Srinivasan just called to inform me of this sad news. Akruti Sharma (E-108).'

She checked the spelling, posted the message and ran towards the parking lot. Before she ran down the steps of the basement and got into her car, there were already five responses to her message. All of them had expressed condolences and had requested additional information.

14 September 2006

Copyright Credits

All the stories included in this volume have been originally published in Kannada by Chanda Pustaka, Bengaluru, in the following collections.

In *Hampi Express*, 2008:
    'The Red Parrot' ('*Kempugini*')
    'The Cracked Tumbler' ('*Seelu Lota*')
    'Two Rupees' ('*Eradu Rupaayi*')
    'The Unforgiving City' ('*Kshameyilladurinali*')

In *Mohanaswamy*, 2013:
    'Recession' ('*Durbhikshakaala*')
    'The Final Offering' ('*Poornaahuti*')
    'Rare Blood' ('*Bhagavanta, Bhakta mattu Rakta*')

In *Vishama Bhinna Raashi*, 2017:
    'When the Music Stops' ('*Vishama Bhinna Raashi*')
    'Ambrosia' ('*Amrutha Soppu*')
    'Beyond Rules' ('*Niyamabaahira*')
    'Nimmi' ('*Devil Dog*')
    'The Gift' ('*Vaahini*')

the unforgiving city

and Other Stories